OUTSIDE THE CITIES

OUTSIDE THE CITIES

Book 2

LAUREL SOLORZANO

To my husband, Yader, for helping
me pursue my writing dreams

The door felt cold under Scarlett's hand, as though it hadn't been used for years, even though she had just been shoved into the cell behind it a few hours ago. With a death sentence hanging over her head, however, those hours had passed quickly, too quickly. When you only have a day to live, that day is never long enough.

Scarlett's stomach felt sick; she might vomit on the cement floor. But yes, the door was opening. The door she had heard lock so clearly was opening under her desperate push. Scarlett half expected a dozen Whites to be standing outside, ready to tackle her or maybe haul her up to the light of day and make her face judgment sooner than expected. None of that. The hallway was as still and empty as a mausoleum.

Scarlett whipped her head behind her to go over the cell one last time with her eyes. There was nothing to bring with her, nothing to help her in case she needed to fight her way out. She would have to be prepared for hand-to-hand combat, and while she could take a female her size no problem, she didn't know how well she would be able to handle a male with a gun in the same situation.

"Okay," Scarlett breathed out, the sound barely audible. Her eyes were on the stairs to the right of the doorway, the stairs that she knew would lead right past the Black's office, through the dormitories, and to a door that required a passcode to get out, a door that only allowed individuals out when it was their specified time to leave. Several plans ran through Scarlett's head. She could go upstairs, then down to the main floor and blend in until it was time for her crew to go out. Who knew that she was sentenced to death? Just the Black? Everyone?

As she considered her options, a pang hit her stomach hard. Rhys, her best friend, was gone. Scarlett sucked in her cheeks. Surely, everyone had to know what was going to happen to her because they would have been asking about Rhys's disappearance as well. Had they held some sort of funeral service for him or had it all been a quick burial, an out of sight, out of mind sort of thing?

Scarlett heard a rustle down the hallway toward her left, and as she turned to defend herself against whatever it might be, a hand clapped over her mouth. However, she had enough control not to scream, which might bring more guards. She would take this one out on her own. Throwing an elbow back, Scarlett felt a jarring impact as though her elbow had hit bone, and she doubled over as the pressure released somewhat. The person then gripped her tighter, this time grabbing her arm as well.

"Scarlett," the voice said, lips only a few centimeters from her ear. "Stop fighting." The mere order, from someone she could tell was a White based on the flashes she had seen in their quick scuffle, caused her to pause. "I'm going to get you out," the voice continued. "Stop fighting, and don't talk."

After a few moments, the hand released, and Scarlett whirled quickly around and away from her attacker. It was Phan. "Phan?" Scarlett whispered, half- obeying his order not to talk.

Phan nodded, allowing her a few seconds to adjust to the idea. Then, Phan motioned her down the hallway to the left. Scarlett looked back at the stairs that led upward. If he was going to help her escape, why was he leading her away from the only route out of this dungeon?

Scarlett marched behind Phan for a few minutes, trying to connect the hallway she was taking to the mental map she had of the base. The walk underneath her feet sloped upward, and the walls around her started changing from stone to cement. The place suddenly looked familiar. Scarlett wanted to say something, but Phan's strides were purposeful. She had no choice but to trust him, and honestly, anything would be better than being executed.

"Wait here," Phan said when they reached the doorway where the baby had been held. Scarlett peered into the room as Phan rustled around for a few contents. He came back holding a pouch only slightly larger than his hand with a belt that would easily wrap around her waist. Scarlett put the pouch on her waist without checking what was inside.

"I'm going to guide you outside the City," Phan explained, his voice so low that Scarlett was reading his lips more than hearing the words. "Once you are out, you must get away from this City as quickly as possible. Find the Fringe, and stay with them. They will guide you."

Scarlett nodded, accepting her task as though it was an assignment to be completed during her shift. Then, Phan started moving down a different hallway, and Scarlett followed him on the balls of her feet. At the end of this hallway, Phan scanned a card. A door popped open.

"Hold that open," Phan said, his words so low that Scarlett had to lean forward to catch them. She kept the door open with her foot and turned back to see Phan wiping the machine's memory from the last five minutes. Huh, Phan seemed to be pretty smart.

Scarlett looked out the doorway and saw that they were facing the side of the fence that she had seen when first entering City 6.

Through the fence, she saw the vast expanse of prairie, the wild grasses stilted in their growth and stopping less than a meter high. Phan passed her, taking responsibility for the door, then motioned for her to walk along the fence with him. Less than two minutes later, Phan stopped at a section of fence that looked completely normal.

"Dig here," he said, pointing at the orangeish dirt where the fence was buried. Scarlett looked up at him, confused. Why wouldn't he help her? But he just crossed his arms and waited while she followed orders.

What choice did she have? Even a chance at freedom was better than none at all.

After a few minutes of digging, during which Phan ordered her to go faster, she saw that the fence was loose. Scarlett pulled back at the sharp edge until there was a hole. She wasn't sure she could fit through the tiny hole that was made in the fence, but Phan urged her forward. He kept looking over his shoulder as though expecting someone at any minute.

"Hurry up. Go through," he said, his whisper not nearly as patient as before. Scarlett heard a motor in the distance, but it was getting closer. Who was driving a vehicle? Scarlett hadn't seen a vehicle used since the day she entered the City.

Scarlett got on her stomach and pulled on some of the long stalks of grass. She wiggled forward, feeling the rough dirt on the inside of the fence digging into her like sharp points of rock. Finally, she was on the other side. Scarlett looked down and tried to brush the dirt off the front of her uniform, but Phan stopped her.

"You will need it for camouflage." Phan looked around once more, then leaned forward into the fence as he began covering up the hole with his foot.

"You need to find the Fringe. They will help you survive and learn how to live off the land. You must never, *never* return to this City or one of the others. You must remain away from the Cities, and you will be safe. Now, go toward the forest, and stay low so no one spots you."

Scarlett looked to the forest on her right. The trees rose tall, and she didn't know how she felt about entering the place on her own. She looked back, but Phan was already entering the building again. She was truly on her own.

Scarlett started walking toward the forest, the bright Blue of her uniform standing out against the brown of the grass. She brushed some of the dirt off her stomach despite what Phan had said and saw that there was a small tear in her uniform by her stomach area. Scarlett had thought the sharp pain she felt in her stomach was from a rock, but she hadn't thought that the rock had torn her suit. Scarlett obsessively touched and rubbed the hole as she walked, feeling a hint of sadness about the hole, a sadness that didn't make sense. She was no longer a part of City life. Everything she had always known and worked toward was. . .gone.

That thought brought a thousand more tumbling into her brain. She would never be a White, something she had worked toward her whole life. She would never have the chance to wear the honored medals on her shoulder or command others beneath her. She would never see any of those people again, not even her best friends from the training center, Miya and Jaylin.

As she reached the edge of the forest, Scarlett hesitated. How would she possibly find this Fringe group? Was she just supposed to wander in the vast forest until she happened to stumble upon the group? Were there any guards in the forest to avoid? Scarlett felt unprepared, but as she looked over her shoulder at the strongly-built concrete buildings scattered among the falling-down huts of the Citizens, Scarlett knew she had no choice. She would have to use the little training she had about survival in the wild.

First thing was first: leave some sort of trail so she wouldn't get lost. A few meters into the forest, Scarlett broke off the end of a branch at waist height. She looked at the branch from both ways; hopefully, it would be memorable in case she needed to get back.

Next, she was supposed to search for water. She had no idea how, but she should be on the lookout for it. Last, or at least the only other thing she remembered, was that she was supposed to find a safe place, off the ground, to sleep at night. Scarlett shivered at the idea of climbing a tree and balancing precariously in its branches while trying to sleep. Unless she saw signs of a bigger animal, she might just forgo that piece of advice.

"Okay," Scarlett started talking to herself, her finger going to the hole in the front of her training suit again, touching the dark birthmark through the hole. "You are leaving a trail; now look for signs of water."

Scarlett spent the rest of the day, or the evening, for it had started to get dark a short time after she had entered the forest, walking more or less in a straight line. Darkness started to fall, and Scarlett felt a moment of panic. The temperature was dropping, and while it wasn't cold, she couldn't imagine curling up on the ground and falling asleep. In fact, Scarlett couldn't think of anything else except going back to the City and pleading for forgiveness.

A nasty thought crept through her brain. Maybe if she turned Phan in and exposed him for the traitor he was, they would have mercy on her. She could even throw in the information about the baby, for surely the child was far enough away that they wouldn't be able to locate her. Perhaps, if she told the Black all that she knew about Phan, then he would believe in her again, trusting that she would be an asset that the Government couldn't afford to lose.

A tiny voice in Scarlett's head screamed that they might still kill her. After all, she *had* run away. But surely, the information she had to give would outweigh the negative of her previous actions. Scarlett stopped in her tracks and turned around 180 degrees. She looked back through the broken brush and the twigs, back over the trail she had made. Could she? She didn't have much choice. Wandering around in the forest until she died was no way to live. Even though she felt a nasty turn in her gut, she had to turn Phan over to the Government.

CHAPTER 2

Scarlett marched back through the forest, following the amateur trail she had created that afternoon. As the darkness began to fall more completely, Scarlett had trouble seeing the markings she had made. With the City's electricity highly monitored, it didn't exactly glow brightly through the trees.

Scarlett sat on a fallen tree and took a few moments to rest. There was no time constraint on getting back, but it felt like the more quickly she did it, the more likely it would turn out in her favor. Besides, a corner of her brain was telling her that this was the wrong, wrong decision.

Scarlett heard a sound behind her, and she jumped up and whirled around, expecting to see one of those bears she had heard about standing on its back two legs and roaring in her face. Instead, she saw a male, a male who was dressed neither like a Citizen nor like a guard.

They sized each other up for a moment, and the male reacted before she did, leaping forward and propelling his body's weight against hers so that she was flat on the ground with the air knocked out of her only a few seconds later. It was an easy task for the male to secure her hands behind her as she gasped for her next breath.

By the time she was able to breathe again, he was pulling her to her feet. Scarlett wiggled her body, trying to free herself from his grasp, but the male pulled her arms backward in a swift motion. The awkward an-

7

gle shot pain through her shoulders. Scarlett relaxed, and the male's grip relaxed as well.

He led her purposefully through the trees, away from the path she had been taking. They walked in silence, the quiet only interrupted by the occasional night noises of animals rustling within the forest.

Scarlett decided it couldn't hurt to start a conversation. "Where are you taking me?" she demanded, her voice sounding surprisingly authoritative.

The male, his hand constantly on the rope where her hands were tied, responded after a few moments. "You're not supposed to be out here. I want to know exactly what you were up to."

The male's voice sounded different than Scarlett had expected, less refined. His voice was gruff, and his words stretched out over several syllables.

"Well," Scarlett wasn't sure exactly what she was supposed to say. Explain that she was out there because she was scheduled to be executed? That didn't bode well for anyone giving her a place to stay. Scarlett thought for a little longer before her mind connected all the dots. This male must be part of the group that Phan had mentioned, the . . . what was it? The name had escaped her mind, but maybe this male would know Phan.

"Phan led me out here," Scarlett said. She couldn't see the male's face without twisting to an awkward angle, but she felt his grip tighten.

"That so?" the male responded. Scarlett felt disappointed. She had expected her announcement to bring relief, perhaps even a welcome gesture on the male's part. But he didn't appear to know or care who Phan might be.

"Yes, uh, he sent me out here to find a . . . group. Do you know them? They're called the . . . I don't remember. Do you have that baby, that small female?"

This time the male *did* stop. He came in front of Scarlett, and she felt her body tingling as he released his grip. Now was her chance. She could run. She could run fast, probably faster than this male. But where would she go?

"Who are you?" the male asked, his gaze piercing.

"Scarlett, I am, well, I used to be a guard for the Government."

"And . . . why are you not anymore?"

Scarlett chewed on her answer for a few moments. She couldn't tell him the truth, that she had shot her best friend. Her eyes welled as she thought of Rhys, the corkscrew curls on his head and the way he was so patient with her when they were climbing or training. She didn't seem to remember the reason for their fight.

"There was a skirmish," Scarlett finally answered. "The Black didn't like how I handled it. I was sentenced for execution."

The male's eyes expanded slightly, and he uncrossed his arms. He rounded her and took hold of the rope once more. "Let's get you to the others, then we'll decide what to do with you."

"What others?" Scarlett asked.

"You'll see soon," the male said, his words drawn out once more.

They marched for at least half an hour when Scarlett began to hear human noises, not just the array of animal noises that had been croaking, chirping, and cawing in her ears. They were human voices, then there was a little cry. Scarlett's heart jumped at the cry. Was it the small child? Was she here?

The male led her to one of the circles around a dying fire, the glow hardly reaching a couple of meters. "I need the council to meet in the tent immediately," the male said to the nearest group. Scarlett heard the message being passed to the various groups sitting around dying fires. Her eyes scanned the faces, but she recognized none of them. They all had a woodsy smell, and their clothes were mostly brown, some with fur on them. Were they wearing animal skins? Why?

Scarlett was led into a structure about a quarter of the size of her dormitory. The structure had none of the stones or cement used to build the base and the training camp. Instead, it was made with several long branches tied together to form a point. Strips of animal skins covered the branches, forming a small but warm space.

Scarlett was ushered to a mat that was placed upon the floor. She sat on it awkwardly, her hands still behind her. A group of three males and two females entered the tent, sitting on similar mats. They sat with their backs to the only opening. The opening flapped closed, and one of the females came closer and untied her hands.

"There, that should feel better," she said in a friendly voice. "I'm Laya."

Scarlett nodded, her eyes quickly scanning the other faces. All of them had the tanned skin of many days spent outdoors. Only one female had the light-colored eyes so highly esteemed as beautiful at the training center.

"We would like to know your story," Laya said, once she was sitting comfortably on her mat again.

"Okay, I already told him," Scarlett pointed at the male who had brought her here. "I'm a guard. Well, I *was* a guard in City 6. Phan helped me escape," Scarlett said. Everyone traded looks at his name.

"The strange thing is," one of the males interrupted, "you mention Phan, but he has not communicated anything with us. And he . . ."

The others cut the male off before he could finish. Scarlett waited until she felt all of their eyes on her again. She knew they wanted her to continue, but what else could she say?

"Why did you need to leave the City?" Laya asked.

Scarlett hesitated. "There was an accident involving a gun," she responded.

"If you won't be straightforward with us, then we can't help you," the original male said, his voice no longer drawn out but more irritated.

"One of the other guards and I got into some sort of fight," Scarlett felt her eyes filling up with tears, and she hated herself for it. She pinched the skin between her first finger and thumb in an effort to fight the tears. "I don't remember what happened very well. We were talking, and then somebody moved. I remember hearing the gunshot, but I don't remember shooting anything. Then, my friend was on the ground, and they were arresting me." She took a breath.

Laya stood and approached Scarlett slowly before sitting at her side and wrapping an arm around her, pulling Scarlett's head to her shoulder. "There, there, it's okay. I know that must be so difficult." The motion felt foreign. She didn't know Laya. Why was Laya trying to comfort her? "Sometimes, when something difficult occurs, our brains start blocking out the hard parts."

"Laya!" one of the males scolded. "She just told us that she murdered her friend, and you want to sit there and act like she's the victim!"

Scarlett stiffened as though detecting an enemy. She sat up, clearly separating herself from the female. Laya was already responding to him. "She has clearly gone through something very traumatic, and being raised in a training center, can you blame her if she is confused?"

"Oh, I forgot! Phan gave me this," Scarlett said, taking off the small pack. "You can have it." Laya moved forward and took the pack, opening it and examining its contents right away.

"Time to confer," the other female said, nodding toward the flap of skins.

All five filed out, leaving Scarlett sitting on the mat. She could hear them talking just outside, but her legs suddenly felt weak as though there was no way she could stand. She felt herself nodding forward in the warmth of the tent and the comfort of the mat. Despite her best judgment, Scarlett curled her exhausted body into a ball and fell asleep on the mat.

Chapter 3

Scarlett awoke suddenly, sitting and standing in one fluid movement, her eyes sweeping around the tent as she tried to remember how she had gotten there. The tent was empty, but there was a thin line of light filtering under the edge of the skins. It wasn't night anymore.

Scarlett reached the door of the tent and pushed back the flap of fabric, feeling the skins for the first time. One side was rough while the other was soft and hairy. As soon as she moved the fabric, the male who had brought her to camp blocked her way.

"Good morning," he said, though his movements didn't seem as welcoming as his voice sounded. "Laya would like to speak with you."

Scarlett looked around. "Okay, where is she?"

"I'll take you," the male said. "I'm River, by the way. You must be Scarlett."

Scarlett nodded, trying to remember if she had told him her name the night before. River motioned toward another tent then moved the flap aside so she could enter. It was dark inside, and Scarlett stood still for a moment as her eyes adjusted.

"Come here," Laya's voice sounded from the darkness. Hands in front of her, afraid of stumbling over something, Scarlett took nervous steps forward. Her eyes finally adjusted, and she could make out Laya's form sitting on the other side of the tent, holding something. The something squawked, and Scarlett knew immediately that it was the small child.

"Oh!" she said, falling onto her knees and reaching out for the child. "She's here! She's alive. I didn't know if she was okay."

"We were able to contact Phan, and he confirmed your presence here. I am sorry for the cold welcome you received last night. You have to understand that your presence, if you were to report back to the City, would be detrimental to us. It could put lives like this one in danger."

Scarlett reached for the child, touching the tips of her fingers and running her hand along the child's cheek. "She seems to be a bit fatter than before," Scarlett said. "That's good. You have the right food to feed her?"

The female nodded. "Yes, we will take care of this child as best we can. Would you like to hold her?" Scarlett nodded and took the small bundle. She was stirring, half-asleep, but one of her eyes was trying to open to see what was going on around her. Scarlett smiled.

"She is so beautiful."

"Yes, and . . ." the female paused as though considering if Scarlett should be privy to the information she was considering sharing, "I don't know how much you know about City life, even though you were living there. Her brain was scanned, and they determined that her hippocampus is larger than other children of her size. They believe that this capacity to capture and hold extra memories would make her an excellent guard. Phan, as he always does when he can, arranged for an accident to be faked to keep her from being sent to the training center. She is believed dead in the City, but here she shall have the chance for a happy life."

Scarlett heard a sound behind her and was instantly alert, shielding the small child from harm. A male entered the tent. He was carrying a sack of food which he set on the floor.

"Good morning," he greeted cheerfully, his beard bobbing up and down as he spoke. "I am Ignatius."

"I'm Scarlett," she said, nodding toward him. Ignatius reached down as though to hug Scarlett, and she shied away, eyes wide.

"Ignatius," Laya said. "She's just come from the City not twenty-four hours ago. You must remember."

Ignatius smiled broadly, his beard curving upward. "I'm sorry, Scarlett. It's been a while since a City-folk like yourself has joined our group. I have trouble understanding what it's like growing up in a place with so many rules."

"Where did you grow up?" Scarlett asked as he divided the food from the sack into three equal piles.

"I'm quite an old chap, y'see. If I think hard enough, I can remember the days when there were just a government, no big G. Back when we had a bit more freedom."

"Really? I've never met anyone who remembers that."

"Maybe you do, but they just ain't allowed to talk about it in the Cities, 'least that's what I've heard. Laya and I was farmers. It's the city-folk and those in the suburbs who got roped into this City idea the easiest. We who were used to living off the land, we didn't need the idea of equal sharing. We were against it from the start, and while that didn't stop nothing, it did mean we had time to escape before we was rounded up and put in a City as well."

The information was too much. The idea of people living on their own without rules and regulations- it was something she had grown up learning. But she had never met someone who had lived that way and wanted to keep living that way.

"But weren't you ever hungry? Weren't there some years when the crops didn't come in? That's why the Government was created, so everyone would always have food, no matter if the profession you had was an important one or not."

"That's what they teach you to believe, but the Government, the group of elites, live better than them kings from hundreds of years ago. You and everyone else are working to support them and their families, and they are simply kind enough to keep you fed so you can keep on working. It's been thirty years since the system was put in place, and it doesn't treat the Citizens any better now than it did before."

Scarlett clutched the child closer, feeling sick to her stomach. This male was speaking against everything she had ever believed, and she didn't like what he had to say. The Government was there to protect them. It always had been.

Scarlett looked down at the child in her hands and imagined two different lives in front of her. A life very similar to Scarlett's- daily training, friends, and an important mission- and a life living with these people. She imagined hunger and fear. Even though Scarlett had fallen asleep easily last night, she couldn't imagine feeling safe from the Government's watchful eye. They had to have discovered she was gone by now, and they would begin searching for her in the forest.

"How do you know that she will have a better life here than at the training center?" Scarlett asked.

Ignatius and Laya looked at each other, seeming to have a conversation with their eyes. Scarlett remembered what that had felt like, talking to Rhys only by raising her eyebrows or nodding her head. She looked down at the child and kissed its forehead briefly, trying to distract herself.

"Hand me the child," Ignatius said. "I'll take care of her while Laya shows you around our little village."

Scarlett stood, curious, and ready to see if this life could be better than what the Government offered- stability. "May I come to see the child later?" Scarlett asked.

"Yes," Laya responded immediately. "Of course you may. This child needs as much love as she can get. We can tell that she spent many days alone in those first few weeks. She was so detached when she arrived."

Scarlett looked at the child once more, nestled into the male's arms. It was a strange picture- one so small and perfectly innocent being held by an old male who distrusted everything in the world.

"Come," Laya said, pushing back the flap and reaching for Scarlett's hand. It was a strange gesture. Scarlett didn't even hold her friends' hands, though she knew some females who did. But Laya's hand was warm, and the scene around Scarlett was so strange that she needed something to help her stay balanced.

There were children, so many children. Some of them were barely clothed, only a small piece of cloth around their waists. But they all seemed so full of energy, not like the children who had hidden behind their parents in the City.

A group of males, about the age of Yellows, were running after a ball. A female, clearly much younger, tripped after them trying to keep up. Laya smiled as she pointed to the children. "All of those children, with exception of the dark-haired boy, were rescued from Cities."

"Boy?" Scarlett hadn't heard the word before. Laya tilted her head to the side as though trying to think of a good explanation.

"It's what we call small males. This word was used long before certain changes to the vocabulary were forced upon Citizens by the Government."

The word sounded strange, like a bouncing noise. Scarlett didn't like it. "So, Phan got them all out?" Scarlett asked.

Laya shook her head. "No. Remember, there are seven Cities, and we have contacts in each one."

Scarlett considered the idea of traveling all over the world with so many small humans. It must be hard work. And now, this was the life she would be living. She had no choice.

Laya whistled, and all the children turned to look at her. They smiled and came over, babbling over each other. But what Scarlett heard most was the word "grandma." Wasn't her name Laya or had Scarlett misremembered?

"I want to introduce you to someone," Laya said once the group of six children had all gathered around. "This is Scarlett. Can everybody say hi?"

The males all waved, still bouncing on the balls of their feet. The small female toddled over and wrapped her arms around Scarlett's knees with a vice-like grip. Scarlett patted the female awkwardly on the head before the little one threw her arms up as though about to clap her hands high above her head. Scarlett stared at her, not sure what was going on. The little female bounced, her arms still in the same position.

"She wants you to pick her up," Laya interpreted.

"Oh," Scarlett said, looking at the child who could clearly walk. At the training center, they were only allowed to hold the children who could not yet walk. After that, if they were to carry the children, it might inhibit the growth of their leg muscles. Scarlett felt uncertain.

"Go ahead," Laya encouraged. Scarlett bent down and scooped the little female up, one hand around her waist. The child was much bigger than the infant Scarlett had been holding, and she felt as though she was going to slip free.

"One hand under Stella's bottom," Laya said, grabbing Scarlett's hand and guiding her to support the female. There- at least Scarlett didn't feel like the child would slip to the ground. Now what? She looked at the child's brown face which was framed by curls similar to Rhys's. Her inquisitive eyes looked right back into Scarlett's with no sign of shyness. Scarlett felt her eyes tearing up.

"She's so . . ." Scarlett couldn't find the right word. "Her skin and her hair, they remind me of my friend from City 6. I wish he could be here with me to meet everyone." And suddenly, Scarlett knew that was why she felt so unhappy that morning. All of these things- the people, the food, the environment- were beautiful in a different, strange way. She wanted to experience them *with* someone.

"Perhaps I can go back to the City," Scarlett suggested, "there is someone who-"

But Laya didn't allow her to finish. "No, you may not go back to the City. Our interactions with the Cities are few, and we keep them that way to prevent them from detecting and attacking us."

"You *never* go into the Cities?"

"I personally have never been. We have a team of adults- Ignatius was one of them- that makes the journey when necessary. If you were to do so," Laya said, the warning clearly in her voice, "it would be punishable by banishment from the Fringe."

"What is banishment?" she asked, even though the word sounded foreboding in Laya's mouth.

"It means you would not be welcome to stay here any longer; in other words, you would have to survive on your own in the forest."

Scarlett nodded, understanding now. "Oh, okay." She mentally thought through her list of friends in City 6. Rhys was gone; there was nothing she could do to change that. She wasn't sure if she could count Devon as a friend after he had betrayed her, even though he said he hadn't told anyone about her deception. There was Malak, but he would never leave. He loved the City, the Government, everything they stood for as guards. Scarlett let out a deep breath. To be honest, would she have ever left if she hadn't been forced to do so? Even looking around at the groups of people smiling and laughing, she didn't think so.

The female was beginning to weigh heavy in her arms, so Scarlett bent over and set her on the ground. The child studied Scarlett for a moment before running off in search of the small males.

"So, how do you live if you don't partake in the sustenance the Government provides? And . . ." Scarlett looked around, "how does the Government not find you?"

Laya waited, making sure Scarlett had asked all of her questions. "As I'm sure you found out from your journey here, we are at least half a day's walk from the City. During the day, the City is busy and loud, so our children can be loud. At night, we keep our lights and noises to a minimum. We also don't stay in the same place for very long."

Scarlett looked startled. "What do you mean?"

"We move approximately every two weeks, sometimes sooner if we feel that we are in danger." Scarlett looked around at the expansive camp.

"How can you move everything? Isn't it heavy? I don't see any vehicles or animals."

"We all work together," Laya answered, "and with everyone doing something to help, we can clean up camp in under an hour. You'll see soon. We're leaving in about five days."

"Five days?" Scarlett felt both excited and nervous to leave.

Laya nodded, "Unless something alerts us that we need to leave sooner. You asked another question as well. How do we feed ourselves? We have farms in different areas of the forest, hidden from those who aren't looking for them. We take care of them and let nature take its course. Then, at harvest time, we split up and work hard to take in as much food as we can. You would also be surprised at how much the forest has to offer. I bet one of the hunters would teach you how to hunt."

"Hunt?" Scarlett knew the word, but she couldn't believe that these people killed the animals for their food. She had once seen a video of people skinning a rabbit, and she had nearly vomited.

"Sure, we have a group of males who go hunting daily. We also have some gatherers who need to find edible wild plants to supplement our diets. There are also some of us, such as myself, who stay in the camp to care for the children and prepare the food once it is brought. There is also a group of the most well-trained watchers who guard the camp at all hours and alert us should someone come after us. Ignatius was a hunter, but since he hurt his leg, he doesn't have the quietest step anymore. He supplies the hunters with their arrows and knives and such now."

Scarlett saw another group of males and females, probably Green age, talking and laughing.

"Don't they have professions?"

Laya shook her head. "They help us when we move camps, but right now, their duty is to grow strong and healthy." The group stopped and stared at Scarlett then came closer and began circling her.

"Where'd you get these clothes?" one of the females asked, touching Scarlett's battered, Blue uniform.

"She's from the City," one of the males said in a not-so-subtle voice. "That's probably what everyone wears."

"But no one this old ever comes from the City," another female countered as though Scarlett couldn't hear their conversation.

"This is Scarlett," Laya said. "She has come to live with us due to City life no longer being a possibility for her."

"Did they try to kill you or brainwash you?" one of the males asked. He noticed the empty holster on her hip. "Whoa! Was that for a gun? Did you have a gun?"

Scarlett nodded, feeling the emptiness by her side. She hadn't remembered them taking the gun, but the whole day with Rhys was a blur. She didn't remember much of anything except him falling to the ground, then not moving anymore.

The children continued chattering and asking questions, but Laya seemed to sense that Scarlett was overwhelmed and led her back to her tent. "You will be staying in our tent until we move. Feel free to come here and lay down when you like. You can wander around the camp and explore anything you want. Unlike the Cities, we don't have secrets here."

Scarlett nodded and sat upon a mat next to the sleeping baby. She hadn't even stirred upon their entrance. Even though Scarlett had slept quite a few hours the night before, her body felt exhausted and overwhelmed. Snuggling into the animal fur, Scarlett watched the baby's rising and falling chest until she fell asleep as well.

CHAPTER 4

Scarlett awoke to a rustling noise by her right ear. No morning fogginess crowded her brain. She sat up immediately, alert. The child was waving her arms and making a gurgling noise. Scarlett smiled at the baby and immediately picked her up. The child looked straight into Scarlett's eyes, and she saw the child's eyes clearly for the first time. They were a slate gray color. The baby waved her hands again, bubbles gurgling over her lips. Then, without warning, the child's happy demeanor changed to an angry one.

Her mouth opened wide, and she gave a startlingly loud piercing noise. Laya entered in a rush and saw Scarlett holding her.

"I didn't do anything," Scarlett promised. "I don't know why she's crying like that."

"She's hungry," Laya said. "I'll take her to her wetnurse."

"Wetnurse?"

"This is how she is fed," Laya said. "You are welcome to come with us, but I don't like her to be crying for long. Hurry up if you're coming."

Scarlett leaped to her feet and hurried after Laya. Laya entered a tent only a few meters away, and Scarlett pushed the flap aside to enter with her. A larger female was resting on a long mat. Beside her was another tiny child. This one was bigger than the female Scarlett knew.

"It's time," Laya said, handing over the small female. The large female sat up and stretched before smiling down at the little one.

"Hungry again, are you? I understand. Your poor little stomach can only hold so much." The female pulled her top up, and Scarlett watched in amazement as the child latched on, sucking hungrily.

"What is she doing?" Scarlett asked, unable to take her eyes off the process.

Laya smiled. "They don't teach you much in the Cities," she said. "She is feeding the child. Women are made to create milk when they have a baby. Fortunately, Mara here had a child only two months before this one was born. Because she was still suckling one baby, her body was able to adapt for two. And we greatly appreciate the nutrition she provides for our new child."

Scarlett looked toward the other child. This child was laying on its stomach, its head up and turning this way and that. The child moved its limbs as though trying to swim. It was definitely more alert.

"The child is beautiful," Scarlett said, approaching and reaching out to touch the decidedly chubby hand.

Mara smiled. "His name is Moses, for he is our promise of a better life."

"Hi, Moses," Scarlett said, bending down and waving at him. Something suddenly occurred to her- the small female had no name, at least no name that she knew.

"What's her name?" Scarlett asked, pointing to the child who was still eating greedily.

"She has no name yet," Mara answered.

"Why not?"

Mara frowned as did Laya. They were both quiet for a few moments before Laya answered. "We do not give children names until they celebrate one month of life. So many children die in that first month. While we can produce our own food and create our clothing, medicine is harder to replicate, especially for a small child who cannot drink the herbal teas and concoctions we would prepare for an older one. This little girl will receive a name in a few days' time."

Scarlett understood what was not said: provided she survived. And from that moment, Scarlett accepted it as her purpose to make sure the child survived, to make sure she would receive a name and have a chance at life, no matter that the life might look much different than what Scarlett herself had experienced.

Scarlett played with Moses until the baby was done feeding. Her head was drooping, and Scarlett could tell she was tired. Scarlett reached for the child, but Mara held up a hand. "She should be changed before she sleeps."

Scarlett saw that the female's nappy was much different than what she had before. This nappy was a cloth greenish in color. Mara removed the nappy and placed it on top of another slightly smelly nappy. She quickly wrapped up the child with a clean nappy and handed her to Scarlett.

"Bring her back here when she is hungry. I'm going to try to take a nap meanwhile." Mara leaned over her child. "Right, Moses? Naptime now?"

Moses just stared at the female, not understanding a word. Laya had left the tent to prepare the midday meal, so Scarlett cradled the small female and wandered the camp, interested in every corner and detail she could learn. Scarlett passed by one tent that made her halt in her tracks. The voice inside had a ring of familiarity. Scarlett clutched the child to her chest as she leaned closer to the tent flap.

Her heart jumped. Was Malak inside the tent? But how? Scarlett froze. Should she go in and speak to him or hide from him? Was he there to drag her back to her execution? But then Malak's voice cut off suddenly as though someone had slapped a hand over his mouth. Her worry for him trumped all. Laya had said there were no secrets, right? Scarlett pulled the flap aside and stepped inside the tent.

CHAPTER 5

The tent was empty, not empty of belongings, but certainly empty of people. Scarlett shifted the child to a more comfortable position in one of her arms as she took several steps further into the dark interior. The tent was not large. She could cross it in three long steps, and she was sure there was no one. Her confusion cleared when she heard Malak's voice again from the small box in the middle of the room. Scarlett found a soft mat and placed the child gently on it. The child stirred but did not wake.

Scarlett opened the box and clutched the familiar radio in her hand. She gently touched each of the buttons as though they could bring her back to the reality of being a guard, when she had had so many hopes and aspirations.

She adjusted the volume button, turning it down so the staticky noise wasn't as loud in her ear. Then, she waited. She sat there at least half an hour before she heard anything else. This time, it was definitely Phan. "Malak, Devon, report please." Scarlett held her breath as she waited for the report.

Malak's deep voice rang out, the voice that had been responsible for giving her so much information. "We're in the southeast quadrant. No abnormal activity here." Devon chimed in with his agreement, and longing filled Scarlett, a longing to be with them. She fingered the 'talk' button carefully. She could say something, tell them that she was still alive.

But no. That could put all of these people in danger, and Malak and Devon would not be the only ones to hear her. Anyone with a radio tuned to the right station would be sure to hear what she said. No. Replying would only cause harm.

Scarlett set the radio down and stared at it, occasionally switching the stations to hear other teams communicating.

"... everything's ready for the twenty-five year celebration."

"All Citizens will report to the Obsequium. . ."

"... Citizen needs help."

She didn't know the members of the other teams well, but the familiarity of their communications brought a strange desire to her gut.

She wasn't sure how long she stayed there in total, but the child started fussing softly behind her before Scarlett was shaken from her thoughts.

"It's alright," Scarlett said, scooping the baby up and finding her way back to Mara's tent. She was surprised to see that the sun was already creating evening shadows. She hadn't felt a tinge of hunger the whole time she had been listening to the radio.

Scarlett wanted to bring it up to Laya, but she didn't know how to avoid it being awkward. Besides, Laya had said that all communication with the Cities was prohibited, and if so, then someone in this camp had a forbidden radio. Scarlett wanted to find out who.

After the baby was fed, Scarlett scooped her up again and was surprised to find that her arms were tiring. The child didn't weigh much, but carrying her for a long time worked different muscles than Scarlett expected.

"Come on. Let's go for a walk," Scarlett said. She turned the child so that she faced outward. Scarlett pointed to various things as they walked even though she felt ridiculous talking to the infant.

"That's the tent you sleep in unless someone takes you on an adventure like I have today. Look at those children. One day, you'll be running around like that, fast as they are. And that looks like what will be our dinner, well, *my* dinner. You already had yours." The child's eyes were half-closed, and Scarlett hugged her just a little tighter. She didn't understand the feeling of care rising in her for this child who she didn't know very well. She felt . . . happy that the female would have a chance to grow up with these other children. "Maybe you'll be good friends with Moses," Scarlett said, but when she looked at the female again, her eyes were almost completely closed. "Am I boring you?" Scarlett asked.

She had arrived by the side of a fire. It wasn't dark yet, but they appeared to have the evening meal almost ready. Scarlett sat on a convenient, fallen log and laid the child on her legs, stretching her arms out to the side and up and down.

"We have a childpack," Laya said, appearing by Scarlett's side and making her jump slightly. "That way, your arms aren't so tired."

"What is a childpack?" Scarlett asked.

"It's like a backpack, but for a child. You wrap it around you, and it keeps the baby snug. It can be a bit much in the hot weather, but on days like these, it is a great help."

"Yeah, sure," Scarlett said. She paused as she tried to think about how to bring up the radio situation. "I'm just curious. How do you communicate with Phan if you are half a day's journey from the City? How did you know he would bring this female?"

Laya was thoughtful, and Scarlett studied her carefully to make sure she wouldn't be telling a lie. "We have our ways. Sometimes, our guards are in certain locations at certain times of the night. If there is a message to be passed to us, then someone will pass us one then. It's best you don't know everything about how we work."

Because you don't trust me, Scarlett thought. She nodded instead and waited for her portion of food to be served. The food was delicious, and it had more flavor than Scarlett had tasted in her life. Most of the time, she simply ate to have strength. But this food made her want to eat more, even though she was full. She was surprised to see people filling their bowls again.

One of the little children, a female the age of a Yellow, came over and sat beside Scarlett. She reached out and touched the baby's cheek. "Is this your child?" she asked Scarlett.

Scarlett shook her head. "I'm a guard," she responded. "I can't have children." But the line was one she had been taught at the training center. Guards don't have children; they have a higher mission in life. But she wasn't a guard anymore. Did that mean she could have children now? Scarlett wasn't quite sure it worked that way.

"My name is Ariel," the female said. "What's yours?"

"Scarlett," she said.

"Oh." Ariel licked her bowl clean then offered to take Scarlett's. "I'll clean your bowl if you want since you're a Mam." Scarlett didn't know what that meant, but let the female take her bowl. A few minutes later, Ariel was back. "You're so young to be a Mam."

"What's that?" Scarlett asked.

"What? A Mam? It's when you have a baby. Well, you said you didn't have that baby, but she's from the City and you are too. So it's kind of like you're her Mam. I want to be a Mam one day too, but you have to be a wife first."

"Oh," Scarlett nodded as though Ariel, a child, didn't know more about all this than she did.

"What's it like living in the City?" Ariel asked.

"Well, it's very different depending on whether you're a guard or a Citizen," Scarlett said, rubbing the baby's stomach gently as she talked. The soft curve of it fit into her hand perfectly. "I was a guard, and I loved living in the City. Yes, I had to work hard, and there were times when things didn't always make sense, but all of my friends are there."

"So, why did you leave if you loved it so much?"

Scarlett turned the question back to Ariel. "Would you ever leave this place?"

"We leave every two weeks," Ariel responded, missing the point of Scarlett's question. "I think it would be boring to live in the same place your whole life. I mean, you wake up and see the same thing and do the same thing every day. What's the fun in that?"

Scarlett twisted her lips into a thoughtful knot. "But what about these people? Would you leave them for any reason?"

Ariel shook her head hard. "No way. I mean, there are a few rules, and if you break those rules, then you get banished. But I would never break one, so I never have to leave."

"What are the rules?"

Ariel ticked them off on her fingers one by one. "No communicating with anyone in the City. No going close to the City. No talking to strangers. You're kind of a stranger, but the elders said you're a good stranger, so it's okay."

Scarlett nodded, wanting to dig further. "What if you accidentally did one of those things and you got in trouble, even though you didn't want to break the rules?"

"How can you accidentally go into a City?" Ariel asked, her face confused. "They're far away, so it'd be hard to go all that way just by accident." It was starting to get dark, and Ariel said she had to find her sleeping tent. "But, I want to talk to you tomorrow. I can braid your hair and make you look so pretty."

Scarlett nodded, not knowing what a braid was but tired of asking for explanations for everything. She took the child once more to Mara's tent. She wasn't sure if the child was hungry, but Scarlett was tired of caring for her. She left the child there and returned to the tent where Laya slept.

As she lay there, sleep didn't come easily. Scarlett wondered if she could somehow use the radios to communicate with Malak and Devon. She wanted them to know that she hadn't shot Rhys on purpose. She felt as though she had to clear her name. She had no way of knowing what story they had been told by the others about her disappearance. Were they searching for her?

CHAPTER 6

The next day, Scarlett slipped into the communications tent when she knew her friends would be on duty. She was surprised to see someone sitting in there, listening to the radio. The female, her hair streaked with gray, looked back at Scarlett with equal surprise.

The female's eyes scanned Scarlett, and she motioned to a mat on the other side of the box. Scarlett sat down, feeling out of place. Clearly, they weren't trying to hide the radio. And the fact that Scarlett had just burst in like she belonged there declared that she had been there before. Scarlett sat in silence as the radio crackled. She could hear a voice, but she couldn't make out who it was or what it was saying.

"Perhaps you can help us," the female said. "I'm Verona. I know you must be Scarlett."

Scarlett nodded. She seemed to be well-known in this camp. Everyone knew her name and at least a little bit about her story. The radio let out a piercing squeal, and the female adjusted the volume.

"I think you could help us," Verona said. "We've been hearing the same codeword over and over again, but haven't yet determined what it means. I want to finish hearing what I can from this conversation, then I'll tell you about it." Scarlett nodded and leaned forward to get as much as she could. There was silence for a moment, and the female adjusted the tuning slightly. That seemed to make a difference as the voices were suddenly clear.

Devon's voice was panicked. "Reinforcements immediately! Phan, Phan, do you hear me?" A pause then the crackle again. "Malak is down. He's hurt!" Scarlett stood, energy coursing through her. Who had hurt Malak and why?

"Can anyone hear me?" Devon shouted into the radio, his voice panicked. Scarlett shifted back and forth on her feet as Verona motioned for her to sit down. Scarlett ignored the female's suggestion and continued to rock back and forth on her feet. She wanted to press the 'talk' button, but she knew she couldn't.

"Code yellow," a deep voice came through. Verona made eye contact with Scarlett as though to identify that was the phrase she didn't understand. But all Scarlett could focus on was the voice. It had sounded just like Rhys. But that was impossible. Rhys was dead. Right?

A female's voice came over the radio. "We're on our way. Devon, what's your exact location?" The voice sounded familiar, but Scarlett couldn't pinpoint it for sure.

"We're by House 30," Devon responded. "Hurry up, Gayla."

Scarlett heard an inhumane screech before Devon let up from the 'talk' button. Her heart was racing as Verona turned the volume of the radio down and made eye contact with Scarlett once again.

"Do you know anything about that situation, specifically the 'code yellow' terminology?"

Scarlett shook her head. "I've never heard Devon so panicked either. He's usually calm and cool. And Malak, he's been my friend. He's hurt."

Verona ignored the pain in Scarlett's voice. "So you don't know what they meant by 'code yellow'?"

"I've never heard that phrase before in my life," Scarlett said, holding up a hand as if to swear it was true. "Turn up the volume again. I want to hear more." She had to know if Malak was going to be okay.

The female frowned at the notebook that had a group of tiny symbols written in it. They were written so small that Scarlett couldn't tell if they were letters or pictures. She adjusted the volume herself and continued to rock back and forth as she switched channels, trying to hear, then switching back, afraid she was going to miss something important.

Verona finally stood. "Feel free to listen as much as you like," she said, "but don't get any ideas about going back to the City. We here at the Fringe are serious about banishment for that sort of infraction."

Verona left the tent, and Scarlett leaped for the radio. Before she knew what she was doing, she pressed the 'talk' button. "Devon, is Malak okay?" She let up and listened, waiting for some sort of confirmation. Had he not heard her? Had something happened to Devon? "Rhys?" Scarlett said, already distrusting what her ears might or might not have heard several minutes ago. "Are you there?" Nothing.

Then, Devon cut in as though he hadn't heard her. "Phan, we need more backup. Gayla is here, but all of the Citizens are out of order."

Phan responded. "We are two minutes away. Hold fire."

"Devon?" Scarlett responded then jumped at a laugh behind her. Verona was back and was laughing. At her?

"The radio has been disabled from responding," Verona said. "You see, we had a situation just like yours a couple of years ago. Did you know that guard's response on the radio cost us eighteen lives? Eighteen men and women died protecting the rest of us, covering up for that mistake. Looks like you would have just killed another eighteen of us for the pleasure of speaking with your friends."

Verona's face showed no mirth now. "I suggest you give up the idea of Cities and City life. If you care for the children out there at all, then don't bring an early death to them or their mothers and fathers."

Scarlett nodded as though she understood. She did in a way, but she also knew that Verona couldn't understand the tugging inside her, the tugging to speak with her friends. Laya came into the tent then, holding the small female. But the small female's normally calm face was scrunched into the picture of anger as she waved her miniature fists around and squawked unhappily.

"I can't feed her," Scarlett said, feeling like everyone was expecting too much of her.

Laya shook her head. "She's already been fed, but she won't calm down."

Scarlett shrugged. She didn't know very much about babies at all, just that they ate and slept a lot. How could they expect her to know how to calm a baby?

"Just take her for a few minutes," Laya said, holding the squealing child out. "If she doesn't calm, I'll take her back." Scarlett sighed and reluctantly took the child. She wiped the tears from her cheeks and supported the head covered with small tufts of dark hair in her hand.

"Time to calm down and go to sleep," Scarlett said, turning the child to see her angry face. "No need to be angry. There, that's it," Scarlett said. And surprisingly, the child's angry thrusts with her fists slowed. The coughing, squawking sound stopped as well. The child's fist grabbed hold of a strand of Scarlett's long hair and pulled. Scarlett winced and claimed her hair once again.

"There, see," Laya said. "She feels more comfortable with you. There is sometimes a connection between people, I believe, a connection that cannot be forced, where two humans know that they are meant to experience life together." Scarlett gazed down at the baby with a little smile, surprised that she had been able to do something seemingly without trying. "I'll bring you the childpack, and you'll see how easy it is to do things with her strapped to you." Laya gazed around the tent. "Are you being trained to work with the communications team?"

Verona laughed from the corner where she was fidgeting with a radio that didn't appear to work. "More like causing trouble. She tried to communicate with the guards as soon as I stepped out." Scarlett felt her cheeks flush. She had, but she had certainly not been trying to hurt anyone. She simply hadn't been thinking. Laya looked alarmed.

"I'm sure Verona filled you in on the dangers of any communication. We take it very seriously here."

"I told her about the last time it happened," Verona said. "Still, I wouldn't trust this one." Scarlett frowned and stepped out of the tent. She didn't trust Verona either. There was something about the angry look in her eyes, and Scarlett wondered if any of the eighteen had been Verona's friends.

CHAPTER 7

Ariel caught up with Scarlett early afternoon the next day. "I didn't see you yesterday. Where were you? Where are your blue clothes?"

Scarlett paused, turning slowly as she was still getting used to the childpack. "Oh! Hi, Ariel. Laya gave me this to wear. She said the Blue color of my uniform made me stick out a bit too much in the forest."

Laya had given Scarlett a garment similar to theirs that morning. The garments were double-sided so that short animal hair was both on the inside and the outside. The pants were loose and flowy, not like the typical clingy material she was used to wearing.

"Yeah, we have to wear brown and green, because it helps us camouflage. Did you know that people used to wear the colors of the field? My mam showed me a picture of her grandma wearing pink!" Scarlett smiled. She too had seen pictures of those from olden times. Their clothing looked strange, though, and Scarlett couldn't imagine being comfortable wearing so little.

"Where are you going?" Ariel asked.

"I'm just . . ." Scarlett had been on her way to the communications tent to listen to the radio some more. She knew it wasn't time yet for the typical shift where Devon and Malak would be working, but she wanted to see if she could hear anything about what had happened. She wondered if Malak was okay. "I was going for a little walk," Scarlett finally concluded.

"I'll come with you. I can show you this super pretty place I found the second day we were here. It's got flowers of all colors. But Mam said we can't pick them because then they'll die. Come on."

Even though Scarlett wanted to hear what she could from the City, part of her was pulled toward Ariel as well. Scarlett wasn't quite ready to embrace the idea that she would essentially have to live with this group of people forever, but a short walk with the nine-year-old couldn't hurt anything.

The two moseyed further into the forest, Ariel bouncing ahead then back to check on Scarlett's more solid pace. "It's not too far," Ariel said. "And not a lot of the children come here, just me. They always want to play soccer, but I like doing art."

"You don't like to exercise?" Scarlett asked, remembering days when she had played soccer during exercise time as a Yellow.

Ariel tilted her head. "I exercise like right now. Walking is exercising. But I think playing soccer every day is so boring. I like to do different things."

"Like what?" Scarlett asked, looking back at the cluster of tents which was no longer visible through the trees even though they had only been walking about fifteen minutes. She could still hear some noises from the children, however.

"I like making patterns and jewelry for everyone. Sometimes, when we stay somewhere closer to the water, I paint pictures with the water." Ariel smiled. "But I have to work fast, so it doesn't dry."

"I'd like to see that," Scarlett responded genuinely.

"And I can make art with hair too," Ariel said. She shook her dark brown hair around. It was free and wild. "Not on myself, because that's super hard when I can't see. But I always do my sister, Stella's, hair, and sometimes Mam lets me do her. I can do you," Ariel said. "You can't see it, but other people can, and they can tell you it looks good."

Scarlett smiled, but her smile froze when she saw the hundreds of flowers in an undisturbed carpet before them. Ariel stopped reverently before it. "This is the fairy garden."

"Fairy garden?" Scarlett asked.

Ariel laughed. "No fairies actually live here. I don't even know if fairies are real. But I imagine little fairies living in each flower, hiding when it's raining or something." The flowers were all of the same type, a wide head with petals in a single layer around it, but the colors varied-yellow, white, pink, purple.

"I didn't know flowers could be such colors," Scarlett bent down and fingered a petal carefully. She held a hand protectively around the child in case the childpack should dump its contents. "Beautiful. Thank you for sharing it with me, Ariel."

Ariel smiled and patted a piece of ground covered with moss. "You and baby can sit here. I'll do your hair." Scarlett sat down.

"But how will you . . ?" She stopped as Ariel produced a small comb from her pocket. Scarlett had learned that a few products were precious in the group, and among those were anything that had to do with beauty.

"This is mine," Ariel said. "My mam gave it to me for my birthday. I don't know how she got it, but I love that I can make hair art so much neater now." Ariel began working the comb gently through Scarlett's hair.

Scarlett stroked the baby's fuzzy hair, wincing a few times as Ariel's comb found a stubborn tangle. "I love having new hair to do," Ariel said. "Sometimes, the other girls get tired of me doing their hair, and they say no when I ask. And my Stella is so movey that I can't."

"How old is she?" Scarlett asked.

"She's two. And her hair is kind of short, but it's still fun to do. I can show you my sister when we get back."

"How many people live here?" Scarlett asked. She hadn't counted the tents, but there had to be more than thirty.

"I don't know," Ariel asked. "You can ask Grandma. She knows everything about that stuff."

"Who's Grandma?"

"Well, her real name is Laya, but we call her Grandma, 'cause she's kind of old."

"Oh," Scarlett responded, her thoughts whirling. Scarlett was surprised that Ariel's hands in her hair actually felt good once she had gotten through all the tangles. Scarlett felt her hair drawn up on the top of her head, twisted and turned until she was sure it was going to be impossible to untangle later.

"Sorry," Ariel kept saying. "I try not to pull hard, but I don't want it to fall out later."

"Oops," Ariel said later. "Did it again. Sorry." Scarlett tentatively patted her hair, which was all balanced on top of her head somehow.

"I wish I could see how it looks; it feels so different."

"Kind of like this," Ariel said, grabbing a chunk of the hair on the right side of her head, crossing it over to the left, then grabbing the hair at the back of her head and dividing it in two. "I still need to practice more, but I think it looks good," Ariel said.

"Thanks," Scarlett said, as the small child began waking. "We should start walking back, so this little female can eat."

"Okay," Ariel agreed happily and led Scarlett back into the camp.

As soon as Scarlett dropped the baby with Mara, she went to the communications tent. She peeked her head in cautiously, but neither Verona nor anyone else was there. Scarlett hurried over to the radio, which was off, and turned it on. She switched channels, listening briefly to one before continuing.

Nobody seemed to be talking, so Scarlett sat in anticipation. Phan had always wanted them on channel four, so she switched to that channel. It wasn't quite time for the start of her shift, but she couldn't help waiting impatiently. The thought dawned on Scarlett. Had Phan always insisted they remain on the same channel so that those in this tent knew where to hear him? Had he ever sent secret messages using the radio that they all took for normal communications? Scarlett had misjudged Phan from the beginning.

She finally heard the sound of her shift checking in and first shift checking out. "We're headed west," Malak's voice said a few minutes after 16:00. Scarlett's heart leaped. He was okay. Whatever had happened the day before had not been fatal, and it obviously hadn't been bad enough to knock him out for a couple of days.

She listened for the next two hours until the evening meal was ready. But no one said much of anything. The two words from the day before, code yellow, still rang through her ears. It had sounded so much like Rhys. And she couldn't be confusing his voice so soon after she had last heard him. It had to be him! But if he was alive, why had she been sentenced to an execution?

Scarlett clenched her teeth, wishing she could communicate with them. Then another thought hit her. Depending on how strong their security was she might be able to take a walk in the forest and end up in the City. She knew what Laya had told her, but she hadn't seen much security for herself. She would just have to be careful to leave in the early evening and get back by morning time. She had to find out if Rhys was alive, and if he was, well then, she might just convince him to come with her to the Fringe.

As Scarlett sat listening to the static, she planned how she would make her getaway. She would need to make sure she didn't run into one of the watchers that Laya had mentioned were stationed around the camp. The only way to do that would be to find out exactly where they patrolled and base her plan off that.

Scarlett hurried out of the tent and started into the forest in the general direction of City 6. She picked a flower that she knew Ariel would like, and she thought carrying the flower helped with the pretense that she was merely taking a walk.

Scarlett saw some movement through the trees to her left, but when she turned to search for who it might be, she didn't see anything. Scarlett paused for a few moments then continued. Once more, she saw movement, so Scarlett hurried toward the location of the movement. Another quick movement to her left again, causing her to turn a complete 180 in order to chase after it.

This time, she saw a male arm moving behind a tree.

"Who is it?" Scarlett asked. Her heart was beating soundly. Was this how they did things here? Hide and follow you instead of just stopping you and making you go back? Scarlett ran, deftly jumping over roots and other objects that might trip her, even though she wasn't familiar with the forest atmosphere. She rounded the tree and found a male standing there. It was River.

"What are you doing?" Scarlett asked.

"My work," the male responded. He didn't look happy about it.

"You are supposed to follow me?" Scarlett asked, crossing her arms, which caused her to crumple the flower she had been holding.

River shook his head. "No, I am supposed to keep everyone in the camp safe, and people wandering outside this boundary area is unsafe."

"So, why didn't you just say, 'Yoohoo! Hey, you've gone too far now'?" Scarlett was desperately trying to think about how this could affect her night escape. Would this male tell Laya or someone else? Would they keep her in their sight 100% of the time now? She had to stay casual, angry at being followed but casual.

"Well, to be honest, you're the first person who has come out this way. Everyone in the camp knows that they should keep their walks and such in that direction," the male pointed back toward the camp and through it, the direction Ariel had taken her that afternoon.

"I was going for a walk," Scarlett said, uncrossing her arms and trying to remain casual. "I'm sorry if you don't like that, but no one informed me that walks have to be in that direction," Scarlett said, motioning over her shoulder. "So, you know, next time, helping me out instead of acting like you are hunting me would be a lot more helpful."

Scarlett whirled on her heel and marched back to the camp. At least she had more of an idea about the lay of the land. She and Ariel hadn't run into anyone on their walk. Potentially, she could exit the backside of the camp and go around the camp, making sure to circle wide enough that she wouldn't run into anyone.

Scarlett counted her steps under her breath as she made her way back to camp. She wanted to know about how far that watcher had been from camp, then make sure to go doubly that far around. She had a long night ahead of her.

When Scarlett got back to camp, she went in search of two things: some food and the small child. Somehow, caring for the child helped give her purpose even when she felt as though all of the goals and ambitions she had previously reached for had been taken from her.

She found the child, dressed for the first time, in a small brown garment. It was strange to see her in something other than a nappy and a blanket.

"What's the special occasion?" Scarlett asked, scooping up the little female, who was awake for once.

"Tonight will be her naming ceremony," Ignatius said. "Laya ain't told you?"

"I haven't really seen Laya all day," Scarlett responded. "How does a naming ceremony work?" Her real question was how long it would take. She had been hoping to set out as soon as it was dark. It was hard for her to calculate exactly how much time it would take her to reach the City since her arrival to the camp had been a bit of a scattered walk. Besides, if she was going to spy on Malak and Devon, and maybe Rhys (her heart started beating faster at the thought that he might be alive), then she would need to arrive in the City before midnight, when their shift ended.

"After the evening meal, a few of the children will perform artistic pieces they have been preparing since they met the baby. Then, you, as her adopted mam, will tell us about what she will accomplish in her life, and you will present us with her name."

"I, uh, me? I don't know how to do that. I've never even been to a naming ceremony, and you want me to be part of one? Maybe Mara would do it better."

"She already Moses' mam, so she can't be no mam for another baby so quick. Besides, everyone has seen how bonded the two of you are, unless, of course, you rejecting that bond and don't want to take the place as the child's mam."

"Maybe Laya would be better? I think I'm not the best one for this."

Ignatius cocked his head to the side as though thinking about her proposal. "I reckon that Laya would take the child if you reject her, but with all that she do around the camp, having someone else dedicated to the child's care would be best."

Scarlett was stuck on the phrase he had said about 'rejecting' the child. Besides, what could one night change? She would still have a chance to go to City 6 and spy on her friends before they left. First, she only had to get through the awkwardness of participating in this ceremony. And a name? Scarlett had never chosen a name for anything, not even the scorpion that had made its home in the females' bathroom for the longest time at the training center.

"Um, so, what's her name going to be?" Scarlett asked.

Ignatius shrugged with a little smile curling up the corners of his lips. "I don't know no names. I'm not the mam. The name must come from you. You will know the right one before tonight; I guarantee it."

Scarlett nodded uncertainly and left the tent with the child. She felt nervous. The only names she could think of were ones of females from her dormitory. Scarlett looked down into the miniature face, the eyes so gray. She imagined putting one of her friends' names on her. Jaylin? Miya? No, it didn't fit her. She was her own person, not a copy of one of Scarlett's friends. Scarlett tried to imagine the real mam of this child. She remembered her large figure, but couldn't remember her face very well, much less her name. Maybe Phan knew, but it's not as though Scarlett could ask him between now and the naming ceremony.

Scarlett sighed and took her time settling the female child in the childpack. Scarlett looked at her carefully and tried the other female names that came to her mind- Gayla, Amirah, Nadia. "You don't look like any of those names," Scarlett said. "You remind me of hope, hope that we can have a better future."

Suddenly, a little song that she had learned as a Red popped into her head, a song about the qualities they should always exhibit and in one of the ancient languages- "Yo tengo amor, amor, amor, gozo, esperanza, y paz." Scarlett bobbed her head silently to the tune that she had sung often when she was younger.

"You look like a little esperanza," Scarlett said. She wasn't sure if the name quite fit, but it was better than anything she had come up with so far. And with only a couple of hours to prepare, she thought it was a good solution. "Whew, that's done," Scarlett said, smiling at the young female who was bobbing her head sleepily. Scarlett whispered the name a few more times to herself. "Esperanza, Esperanza, Esperanza." With each repetition, it seemed more like a fit.

She arrived at the edge of the fire where several females were cooking and settled onto the log where she ate every evening, the child curled on her lap. Laya came over and gave the little female a pat on the head before sitting next to Scarlett.

"Are you ready for the ceremony?"

"Not really," Scarlett admitted. "I don't know what I'm supposed to do exactly."

"The most important part is the name. Do you have a suitable name for the child?"

"Yes, I decided-"

"No!" Laya held up her hands. "You mustn't tell anyone until the naming ceremony." Scarlett looked back over the way she had come to the fire, whispering the name at different volumes. "I will indicate when you are to come up and introduce the child to us. We will all send our good wishes and prayers for her direction and promise to care for her and support both of you as best we can. Then, the ceremony is over. We sometimes have a special treat to eat, but the berries haven't been plentiful in this part of the forest this time of year. It looks as though the birds got them before us."

Laya stood as the bowls began to be served and brought Scarlett a serving. "Here you go, and I can take the little one for you while you are eating." Scarlett shook her head. The child, Esperanza, Scarlett whispered the name inside her mind, seemed comfortable as she was, and it wasn't as though Scarlett couldn't eat around her.

Scarlett took the first few sips of beef stew, blowing off each spoonful before she ate. When she looked up, Laya had been replaced by Ariel. Ariel's hair was on her head in a series of knots. Scarlett wanted to reach up and pat her head, wondering if she looked the same. The lack of mirrors sometimes made her forget how she looked, and she wasn't sure if that was a good thing or a bad thing.

"How's the soup?" Ariel asked, looking down at her untouched bowl.

"It's delicious, and yours?"

"It's the same soup," Ariel laughed. "If yours is delicious, then mine is too." Scarlett smiled at her logic and drained the soup bowl. She knew she could get seconds here, but after staying at the base and living on a restricted diet, it felt wrong. Scarlett wondered what Rhys would have thought of the soup. He loved anything with meat in it, so he would most certainly rave about the soup.

A low drumming noise was heard, and the groups of people talking around the fire hushed. It was that strange time between day and night when the air was an orangish color. Those who were outside of the firelight came closer. Scarlett realized that this must be nearly everyone from the Fringe gathered together, and she felt more nervous about standing in front of them and announcing the baby's name.

Ariel stood and hurried away, saying something about having to get ready.

"Tonight, we are celebrating life," Laya shouted from the other side of the dwindling campfire. "Tonight, we have a small one in our midst who was born in the City, born to a mother who would have loved her very much. She was ripped away from that mother at only a few days old and set for a training center. But now, she has been given the chance to understand and experience real freedom." General cheering and clapping echoed around the fire. Scarlett glanced in the direction of the City. She knew that they were far away, but it still felt like they could be heard at any moment.

"But before presenting this beautiful gift from above, we have some dancers who have prepared a work of art in celebration." Laya stepped away, and Scarlett turned to a group of three who began beating time on drums and shaking maracas. The people seemed to know the tune and took up singing a song, one that Scarlett had never heard before. The song woke little Esperanza, and Scarlett smiled down at her, rubbing her arms as a comfort in the ruckus.

Ariel and three other females, the age of Yellows, danced around the fire. The smile on Ariel's face told Scarlett that she was enjoying this night to the fullest. There were two more artistic interpretations before Laya announced that they would meet the child. Scarlett hurriedly took Esperanza out of the childpack and turned her to face the groups of people. Sounds of admiration flooded Scarlett's ears as she stood beside Laya. Laya drew away, and Scarlett was left alone with hundreds of eyes on her.

"Hi," Scarlett said, her voice sounding low. A few people leaned in, and Scarlett cleared her throat to start again. "Hi, and thank you everyone for welcoming me into your group. I appreciate the second chance." Scarlett smoothed the garment the child was wearing, her eyes staying on the fragile structure of the baby. "This beautiful baby is not mine, but it seems that we have a special connection."

There were a couple of short cheers for that. "The name I have chosen for this baby is Esperanza. She is giving me hope that we will have a better future, and I hope that she will give you that same feeling as well." Scarlett tugged at her tunic, then gave another nod and headed back to the log where she had been sitting. There, she was done. Now, her thoughts turned toward the City and how she could get in to learn if Rhys was dead after all.

CHAPTER 8

Scarlett left the baby with Mara after the ceremony, saying that her stomach wasn't feeling well. It really wasn't. The thought of going to the City now, after the unity she had felt during the ceremony, twisted her stomach into nervous knots. Scarlett didn't know if they would miss her, or if they did, what they would think. Would they know right away she was going into the City? Scarlett had thought she would wait until they were closer to leaving the area, but then a fear had gripped her. What if they left early? Laya had said that if something startled them, they would pick up and leave without notice. Scarlett couldn't take that chance.

She began walking deeper into the forest, *away* from the City and to the series of holes that were used as toilets. After all, if she wasn't feeling well, a long stint in the toilet wouldn't be suspicious.

Once Scarlett figured she was at least a kilometer outside of the edge of camp, she turned right and planned to walk at least two kilometers. She had to make sure she was giving the camp a wide enough berth that no one would see her. Once she felt confident that she wouldn't be seen by a watcher, she could begin jogging toward the City. Scarlett didn't have a timepiece of her own anymore. Hers had been taken when she was thrown in the cell, and timepieces were not common in the Fringe. However, based on the time of darkness, she had approximately four

45

hours to reach the City before her old shift would go back inside the compound. It had to be possible.

Such thoughts of uncertainty kept her mind busy as she turned right again. She would have to walk at least another two kilometers before she could be sure that she had passed the watchers. Then, she had no idea how many kilometers to the City. She knew the forest backed up to the fence on the west side, the side she had patrolled far from the hole in the fence where she had escaped. She had walked past the fence with tendrils creeping up from the forest. She knew that her shift would be sure to walk by that area at least every quarter hour. The real challenge would be making sure she wasn't seen by the wrong person.

Scarlett began jogging toward the City, and she felt encouraged when she saw the harsh lights that surrounded the base peeking through the trees. She was making progress. Scarlett had no way of telling the time, but her panicked brain kept telling her she was too late, too late, too late as she approached the fence.

Scarlett squatted under the natural covering of tangled bushes, about two meters from the fence. It felt so close after not seeing City 6 for days. She regulated her breathing then waited to see something. Whether it was her shift or the third shift, someone would have to pass by soon.

Then, she saw movement. Scarlett held her breath, her eyes the only piece of her not covered. If they shone a light directly at her, they would know a human was in the forest. Scarlett couldn't give them reason to discover her.

". . . after everything that happened last night," a voice was saying. And Scarlett knew the voice! Her heart jumped, then sank, because it wasn't Rhys's voice. While seeing Malak's tall form come almost within touching distance was exciting, she knew she couldn't allow herself to be seen. He was nothing if not loyal to the Government. Scarlett reached for her hip, but there was nothing in the holster. There was nothing she would be able to do to protect herself. They had guns, and she didn't. She exhaled slowly and took another long, deep breath.

"This is why I'm glad you're my partner," Devon said. "Could you imagine Rhys being there? I mean, he's good in action, but he's boring when it comes to walking around for hours at night."

Malak kind of chuckled, but Scarlett only focused on one thing. Devon was talking about Rhys like he was still alive! That meant if she stayed there another fifteen minutes, Rhys should come walking past with . . . well, she didn't know who his new partner would be. That might be a problem, but surely, either Rhys or she could convince the new partner to keep his or her mouth hushed about a conversation with Scarlett.

Scarlett mentally made a list of possible people who could be Rhys's partner. Who would be most likely to accept her and not report their conversation? Scarlett was hoping it would be more than a conversation, however. She was hoping that Rhys would come with her. And there would be no hiding that. Unless he hated her for what had happened. Scarlett swallowed. He couldn't. She wouldn't allow it.

Scarlett waited what felt like a long time. Then, she saw two figures again. She held her breath, wondering if she should jump out or figure out who was with Rhys first. Scarlett's heart pumped hard as the figures drew closer. Her legs were in the position to spring, twitching with anticipation. But she froze when the light of the torch fell on their faces. Neither was Rhys. The female was Gayla, but she didn't know the male.

Where was Rhys? She asked herself as she drew back into the covering of the forest. There was no use waiting there any longer. She would only see the same pairs pass by again, and she couldn't see anything positive coming from surprising either of them.

What should she do? Scarlett's eyes roamed the fence. She couldn't scale it. There was barbed wire at the top, and being up that high would make her an easy target. They might think she was a Citizen trying to escape. The fact was, even if they knew who she was, they would probably shoot to kill. Two Citizens crossed the walkway and entered another house, and that was when Scarlett realized how early it was. Her walk through the forest had felt like hours and hours of walking, but in reality, she had gotten to the City before curfew. Scarlett breathed a sigh of relief. She had a plan.

Scarlett hurried around the corner and through the field back to the hole through which she had escaped a few days ago. She dug it out and scurried under the fence. She didn't want to take the time to cover it up, especially if she needed a quick escape. She didn't know any other way out of the fence except by the main gate, which wasn't an option for obvious reasons.

Scarlett jogged behind houses, at first in unfamiliar territory but quickly reaching the streets she knew. Her stomach furled and unfurled, in constant motion of queasiness. Finally, she reached the house where Kendrick lived. She had no way of knowing if he was inside or how many minutes until curfew was enacted. She knew he lived with his mom and dad, and she had no idea if he had ever told them about his conversation with a Blue one day. But right now, he felt like the only person she could talk to who wouldn't turn her in.

"Kendrick," she said in a voice barely over a whisper. "Hey, Kendrick," she said. She was beside his house, pressed against the wall. She didn't dare go to the door where she would be in plain sight of anyone on the walkway. Scarlett heard some shuffling, then the front door opened. Scarlett once again looked around for a weapon before settling on her fists. She should have grabbed a branch from the forest at least.

"Hello?" Kendrick's familiar voice called softly out the open doorway.

Someone further down the street answered him. "Looking for someone?"

Kendrick shouted back a "no." Scarlett saw the light from the house begin to fade as the squeaking hinges indicated he was closing the door.

"Kendrick!" Scarlett said again, a little louder. The door froze in its closing, and Kendrick clumped down the three front stairs. He stood in front of them for a moment then turned into the alley between the two houses. He saw Scarlett standing in a strange combination of ready to fight and utter relief at having found him.

Kendrick smiled. "Didn't expect to see you," he said. "Why don't you come in the house and we can talk?"

"And your parents?" Scarlett asked.

"They are both working an extra shift in production," he frowned. "Everyone has to work one extra shift this week." Kendrick clumped back up the stairs and held the door open. Scarlett peered both ways down the street and saw it was clear before darting inside. Kendrick closed the door behind her in an unhurried manner. Scarlett quickly surveyed the shack. It was very similar to the one in which she had helped the female give birth, except that this one had a mattress of sorts set up on the floor beside the door to the toilet.

"So," Kendrick said, sitting on the edge of the big bed and propping his foot on the chair that was already settled at the perfect angle for him. Scarlett remembered the flash of gunfire from the skirmish when Phan had accidentally shot Kendrick's leg. "What brings you here?"

"What do you know already?" Scarlett asked, hungry for news from the City as she sat on the other wooden chair in the place.

"I know that you shot one of your friends apparently," Kendrick cracked a smile.

Scarlett frowned, feeling anger for him boiling up inside. "It's not funny actually. Rhys was my best friend. And I didn't shoot him. Well, I kind of did, but it was an accident. I don't even remember exactly how it happened."

Kendrick studied her face, waiting for her to finish. "What they told us was that you were executed for your crimes."

"You thought I was dead? They told everyone I was dead?"

"Sure they did, but we all know they are liars. It's not surprising to find out different. Now the real question is, if you're not dead and you really did shoot your friend, what are you doing here?"

Scarlett weighed how much to tell Kendrick. She knew he wouldn't go tell any of the Whites where she was, even for extra rations, but at the same time, it could be dangerous to spread around too much information about the Fringe.

"I escaped," Scarlett said, without elaborating.

Kendrick pointed to her clothing and raised an eyebrow. "And?"

"And, I found some people who helped me in the forest."

Kendrick leaned forward, his eyes firmly on hers. "You found the Fringe?"

Scarlett swallowed. How did he know about them? "I . . .how . . ."

Kendrick shrugged and leaned back like the whole thing didn't matter to him. "I mean, you don't have to tell me anything. I get it. Knowledge is dangerous. I mean, I didn't even know if they were real or if it was just a story our parents told us to give us hope."

Scarlett swallowed, a lump in her throat refusing to go away. Why couldn't she tell Kendrick about the Fringe? He had told her that his life here was as good as ruined anyway. She could at least give him the opportunity for the kind of freedom she was going to experience. How could she count herself more worthy than him? She revealed the next pieces of information carefully.

"Yes, they are real," Scarlett said. "I don't think it's a safe idea to tell you very much about them unless you agree to come with me."

A couple of emotions flashed across Kendrick's face- disbelief, amusement, confusion. "Why did you come here?" he finally asked.

"Here? To the City? I, well, I came because I thought Rhys, the one I shot, might still be alive. I don't know. I couldn't believe he was dead, then I was spying, and it sounded like he was alive. Like Devon was talking about him in the here and now."

"Oh yeah, your buddy is alive," Kendrick said, nodding as though he was merely commenting on the possibility of rain.

Scarlett stood up immediately, her muscles racing to do something, to tell Rhys that she was here, alive as well. Did he believe she was dead too, that they had executed her quietly? But then, if he wasn't dead, why had they lied to her? Scarlett turned back to Kendrick who had stopped speaking to stare at her strangely.

"I wouldn't exactly go storming the doors of the base to go talk to him," Kendrick said. "Sit down."

Scarlett didn't like his order as though she were a Red standing during quiet time. She crossed her arms. "If you thought I was dead, then he probably did too. I need to get to him. I need to tell him that he can come with me, with us if you want, and we can have the chance at freedom."

Kendrick shook his head and motioned for her to sit again, which only irritated her further. "What?" she said, a bit louder than she should for a private conversation. They both froze for a full minute, waiting to see if someone had heard them. Nothing.

"Rhys, your friend, is different," Kendrick said. "I don't know. I mean, being shot changes you," he said pointing to his leg with an unenthusiastic guffaw.

"What do you mean? Where was he shot? Is he incapacitated in some way?"

Kendrick shook his head. "No, his limbs all appear to be working normally, but he's different now. He's like. . .the harshest guard you've ever seen."

Rhys? Scarlett wouldn't believe it. "Maybe it's because he thinks they killed me for shooting him, and he's mad about that or something. So I just need to figure out how to talk to him, but I didn't see him working the same quadrant, and. . ."

They were interrupted by a loud voice shouting outside that curfew was now in place, and everyone needed to turn out their lights. Kendrick obediently stood and shuffled around Scarlett to do so. They were in complete darkness. Then, Scarlett's eyes adjusted, and she could see the general shapes of objects from the strip of moonlight that filtered in under the door. Her stomach quaked as she thought about leaving the City again. Without the occasional Citizen in the walkways, she would stick out even more. But she couldn't worry about that yet. She had to contact Rhys.

"Where does he normally patrol?" she asked. "Is he in a different quadrant?"

"He's on third shift," Kendrick said. "At least, he was working this morning when I went to get our well water for the day."

Scarlett calculated backward. She knew it had been his voice on the radio that day, unless it hadn't. Maybe it had been the male with Gayla who said "code yellow." Her brain was confused over the events, and it didn't matter what shift he had been working when she was listening to the radio. What mattered was when he would come out now.

"Do you know who his partner is?" Scarlett asked. "Maybe you don't know his or her name, but I could figure it out from a description."

"Oh, I know who it is," Kendrick responded with a shake of his head, settling onto the edge of the bed again. "It's Irin. He's with a White." Scarlett's stomach clenched. It would be so much harder to reach him. Unlike Phan, Scarlett didn't think there was any possibility that Irin was apt to aid her in escaping. Why had they paired Rhys with a White? Did they not trust him very much anymore?

"I'm going to try to talk to him," Scarlett said, firm in her decision. With that settled in her mind, knowing she would need to wait at least another two hours before seeing him, she sank into the chair again. Then, she seemed to remember the invitation she had first extended when she entered the little abode.

"You should come," she said. "I can show you how to get out of the City, and you can wait a little ways into the forest. When I come with Rhys, we can all-"

"No," Kendrick was shaking his head. "I would only hold you up." He pointed at his bad leg. "This thing is not easy to deal with. I can walk, but there's always the pain. And the pain only worsens with distance. I don't know where their camp is, but I know it can't be very close."

"It doesn't matter," Scarlett said. "We can take our time getting back to the camp. Maybe you can lean on me or on Rhys."

Kendrick was already shaking his head again.

"What?" Scarlett asked in an exasperated tone.

"You take for granted that Rhys will agree. Let me present you with a probable scenario. You help me out. I wait for you. You talk to Rhys. Rhys and his partner arrest you, and you are executed. I die waiting for you in the forest."

Scarlett rolled her eyes, though Kendrick couldn't see in the darkness. "Yeah, but I try not to think worst case scenario. I mean, what do you lose if you try? If I were to never return," Scarlett continued in a very sarcastic voice as though what she was saying couldn't possibly happen, "you can always just find them yourself. Just keep walking into the forest, and you should come to them before too long. You could explain what happened. They are kind, and you would be safe." Scarlett looked around at the hut and the dry array of food that was included in the rations. "Besides, the food is amazing. Better than anything I've ever tasted. It's so fresh."

Kendrick smiled, the light from the moon glinting on his teeth. "Thanks, Scarlett. I wish I could, but, I can't. And I think you should leave behind the idea of talking to Rhys. He's different; I'm telling you."

"Different how? That's what you're not telling me."

"More serious, more strict, like all he cares about is serving the Government. It happens to all of them, so it's not surprising." Kendrick ran a hand through his hair, smoothing the tangles of the slightly-longish mess. "Blues come here, excited to be fulfilling their goal. They get to know us, ask us questions, and then, it's like they realize that they are here to kill us, not be our friends."

"We're not-"

But Kendrick talked right over her. "From that moment on, usually a couple of months into being here, we know exactly how they are going to treat us. The only point of difference is the level of cruelty." Scarlett felt as though Kendrick were personally attacking her, even though that wasn't true. She wasn't a guard anymore, but it was strange embracing the role of forest-dweller when her whole life had been in preparation for something she only did for a few weeks.

"Fine," Scarlett said. "Then if you're not coming with me, and you think Rhys is a lost cause, then I have no reason to stay here any longer. Thanks." She stood and peeked out the crack between the two window shutters.

The street appeared empty, but she was scared. She never knew when a pair of guards might walk by. She should wait until a couple passed. That would be the only way to assure safe passage from the door to the alleyway. And even then, she still had the streets to cross and the fence to get under before she would feel free again.

Funny how the City had felt so much like home while she hid in the forest. Now, it felt as much like a prison as the cell she had occupied in waiting for her execution. As Scarlett left the City, she wondered with every footstep if she was making the right decision.

CHAPTER 9

Scarlett felt exhausted as she took the long way around the campsite. She accidently stumbled onto the field of flowers that Ariel had shown her, and she lay down beside it. She already had a plan to explain her long absence. Mara had heard her story about her sick stomach. She would claim to have fallen asleep on the edge of the forest nearest the toilets in the case that she had more stomach issues. Scarlett hoped it sounded realistic. After all, they had no reason to disbelieve her.

Scarlett didn't know if it was possible to "fall asleep" on the forest floor, but Scarlett crushed a group of flowers as she laid down and found it was actually quite comfortable. Even though her mind worried over the problem of finding Rhys, she was asleep before the sun began rising.

Scarlett woke up with a shake. Ariel was shaking her shoulder, but in the eagerness of her efforts to wake Scarlett up, she was shaking her whole body. "Everyone will be so glad you're here," Ariel said. "Everyone was so worried, and somebody said you left and went back to live in the City again. But I said no, because that would make you a liar about what you said about us. And so, we started looking for you. Come on! You have to tell everybody you're okay."

Scarlett stumbled after Ariel. The sun didn't look high in the sky, so she had probably only slept three or four hours. She felt exhausted. Ariel skipped ahead of Scarlett and announced to anyone who would listen. "I found her. I found her. She's right here."

Laya heard her announcements and hurried over. "Where were you?" she asked. "You never came into the tent last night!"

Scarlett couldn't tell if Laya was generally worried about her or if she was suspicious about what Scarlett had been doing. Scarlett held her stomach and pasted on her best nauseous look.

"My stomach has been hurting," she said. "I was going to the toilet frequently, and I lay down by the flowers Ariel showed me. I guess I fell asleep. I certainly didn't mean to spend the whole night outside like that." Scarlett cracked her neck.

Laya nodded. "It can take some adjusting to get used to our diet. We have seen the same with other older Citizens who have joined us. We do have a special tea we can make that should help you with your stomach issues. Ariel, go ask your Mam to make that tea, will you?" Ariel hurried off, and Scarlett was left alone with Laya. She wouldn't meet her eyes, but pretended to be searching for Esperanza.

"Where is Esperanza?" she finally said when she didn't see the tiny baby nearby in anyone's arms.

"Mara has her," Laya said. "And I think it would be a great help to her if you took both Esperanza and Moses for the morning. Do you feel up to doing that? Mara didn't sleep much as Esperanza was having a bottomless night."

"What do you mean 'bottomless night'?"

"It means that no matter how much she ate, she was still hungry and wanting more. It indicates that she is growing, which is excellent, however, I'm sure you can imagine how tiring that would be for Mara."

"Oh yes, of course," Scarlett said, turning toward Mara's tent. She almost felt resentful toward the small child as she scooped her up and wrapped her in the childpack, this time on her back. If it wasn't for this little thing, then it would be much easier for Scarlett to slip in and out. Why did she have to be responsible for her? Scarlett scooped Moses up, and balancing the two babies, she walked toward the tent she shared with Ignatius and Laya. It was empty when she entered, for which Scarlett was glad. She was too tired for any more falsely cheerful conversations.

Scarlett set Moses on the mat and undid Esperanza from the child-pack. She laid Esperanza down beside Moses. Esperanza suddenly appeared frighteningly tiny. Sure, Moses had two months on her, but his chubby form exuded a healthy glow, while Esperanza's frame was more bony than bulky. Scarlett wondered if there was anything else she could do to help Esperanza gain strength. And meanwhile, she felt guilty for the momentary dislike of the child. It wasn't the child's fault. And Scarlett wouldn't wish a worse fate on her.

Scarlett entertained the children by rubbing some of the fallen red and yellow leaves from outside above them. Moses tried to grab the leaves, even though they were too far for him to reach. Scarlett tickled his face with the edge of one, and his eyes opened wide as though surprised by the touch. Scarlett smiled and touched his cheek with the leaves again. Esperanza had fallen asleep.

"Don't you want to sleep, too?" Scarlett asked Moses. "Come on, curl up with me, and let's take a nap." Scarlett lay down on the sleeping mat beside them and clutched Moses close to her. He resisted a little, but Scarlett stroked the ends of his fine, black hair which seemed to settle him. They both drifted off to sleep.

When Scarlett awoke, she felt a momentary panic to see that neither child was there. She sat up and looked around the tent as though they had simply rolled off to the side. But neither of the babies was capable of such movement. Scarlett hurried outside the tent and was surprised to see that it was midday. Many were gathered around the fire for their midday meal, but a sense of panic still settled in her stomach. She knew she wouldn't be able to feel calm until she had located the babies. She checked Mara's tent, but Mara was snoozing alone.

Next, Scarlett hurried to the fire to see if Laya was there. She quickly spotted both babies. Moses was on his bottom, holding his wiggly head up and looking around. A group of children laughed. Esperanza was in an older female's arms. Scarlett didn't know who they were, but she didn't feel comfortable with the fact that they had come to get the children out from under her nose while she was sleeping. She settled at the edge of the group, not sure how to voice her discomfort.

Finally, Stella, the small female whom Scarlett had held the first day, pointed toward Scarlett and made a babbling noise that sounded like it could be words. The older female brought Esperanza to her, and as she got closer, Scarlett recognized that it was Verona, the female from the communications tent.

"I'm glad you were able to rest," Verona said as Scarlett took Esperanza from her arms. "Seems like you were very tired after a night of sleeping."

Scarlett wasn't sure what Verona was trying to say. Had she heard something over the radios that indicated Scarlett had been in the City? Surely not. No one other than Kendrick had seen her while she was there. She had made sure to make a careful exit. Still, Verona's reproachful eye said that she knew something.

Scarlett couldn't ask right there. She would have to visit Verona later, when just the two of them could talk. But as Scarlett tried to figure out how to arrange that, she remembered what she had been told, not once, but twice. Associating with the City was punishable by banishment. Would they banish her? And how would she explain Rhys's appearance if he came back with her? Surely they wouldn't turn them both away? She would have no reason to return to the City if Rhys was with her. Scarlett shook her head as she finished the conversation in her head. It was a risk she would have to take. She couldn't leave the area without speaking to Rhys.

As the afternoon approached, Scarlett took Esperanza into the communications tent. Esperanza seemed content and quiet as long as she was fed, so Scarlett absentmindedly patted the baby's tiny back while she listened to the static on the radio. She wasn't sure of the exact time, but it had to be nearly time for Rhys's shift to start, unless he really had moved to third shift. Scarlett wanted confirmation before she spent another night chasing after him. It wasn't that she didn't trust Kendrick, but there were some things you just had to see with your own eyes.

She heard nothing other than unfamiliar voices stating their locations. No signs of riots or disturbances, which jogged Scarlett's memory. She hadn't asked Kendrick if he knew anything about the other night, or code yellow. She wondered if anyone she knew had gotten hurt. Devon and Malak appeared to be fine, but she still hadn't seen Phan. Despite her readiness to betray him a few days ago, she wanted to make sure he was okay after risking his life and position to save her.

Some more crackling, but nothing of substance. Scarlett sighed and gave up. Oh well, there was always after the evening meal. She was sure to hear something then.

But when she came out of the communications tent, Scarlett found Verona standing right in front of the flap. Scarlett wondered how long Verona had been standing there. Had she been waiting for Scarlett or someone else?

"Hear anything interesting?" Verona asked.

Scarlett shook her head. "No, not much happening this afternoon." She stopped herself as she looked across the campground. There was quite a bit of movement, and everyone seemed busy completing a chore. As Scarlett's eyes took in the whole situation, she realized what was happening. They were packing up.

"Oh, we're leaving?" she tried to ask casually, even while she panicked inside.

Verona nodded. "Yes, it's time for us to go on, to let this section of the forest heal from our stay." Scarlett looked around at the trampled bit of forest and tried to imagine it empty. The picture saddened her.

"So, when?" Scarlett asked, trying to get as much information as she could. Surely they wouldn't plan to pack up and leave at nighttime.

"Tomorrow morning," Verona confirmed.

"It seems like things happen all of a sudden here," Scarlett said, nodding to the motions of those getting ready. "Esperanza's naming ceremony, leaving the camp, everything."

"You will understand better what to expect once you've been around for a few months or a year, if you last that long," Verona said the last part quietly, but it dug into Scarlett. What did Verona mean? Did she think

Scarlett wasn't cut out for the tough life of living in the wild? Or did she suspect what Scarlett had done?

Scarlett just smiled as though she hadn't heard the statement at all. "Well, I look forward to understanding your way of life better." But even that sounded wrong, as though Scarlett were still on the outside looking inward. But the truth was that with all of the security this life offered, she still couldn't leave Rhys behind. No matter what the consequences might be, Scarlett had to make one more attempt to speak with him, even if she were out all night.

CHAPTER 10

That evening, Scarlett slurped down her evening meal as quickly as possible. She had thought about skipping it altogether in favor of an early start, but she knew she would need strength for the journey, especially since she hadn't slept much the night before. Ariel plopped down next to Scarlett, just as Scarlett was finishing.

"Where's Esperanza?" Ariel asked.

Scarlett nodded toward Laya who was holding the sleeping child. "She's taking care of her right now."

"Oh, so do you want me to braid your hair?" Ariel asked, reaching up and fingering some of the strands. The braids Ariel had made before had started to come out early that morning, and Scarlett had undone them the rest of the way on her walk back to the camp. She was sure her hair looked frighteningly tangled, and a tiny part of her cared. However, she knew it was more important to disappear quickly.

"Thanks, Ariel, but I think tomorrow would be better. I need to bathe tonight, and I wouldn't want you to go to all that work for me to take it out an hour later."

Ariel agreed. "Okay, I can braid your hair tomorrow when we stop for the midday meal." Ariel didn't move though, and neither did Scarlett. She glanced at Laya who was talking with some of the other older females. Laya smiled at the two of them as she gently rubbed Esperanza's back.

Ariel waved back enthusiastically and popped up to say hi to the little baby who was awake for once. "I'm going to bathe!" Scarlett called out to Ariel. At least if people started looking for her, she had some sort of an alibi, however rudimentary. Scarlett gathered up one of the dried towels that was spread across a rock. As she went through the motions of going off to the river to bathe, she realized how badly she did need to bathe. But she couldn't risk taking the time. Who knew how long it would take everything to dry? Besides, she didn't need squeaky shoes.

Scarlett headed toward the river, planning to leave the towel by the bank. She worried that two nights in a row of disappearances would cause suspicion, but they would know that she had gone to the City anyway in the morning, when she came back with Rhys. She was sure these people would be more apt to forgive than the Government. Scarlett wondered if she should take a set of clothes like she had for Rhys to wear, to help him blend in with the forest more. But at the last moment, she decided that it wasn't worth the half hour trip back to the camp.

The journey to the City was uneventful. Scarlett hadn't run into any watchers, and she had arrived earlier than the night before. It was dark already, but there was much more movement in the walkways. Scarlett was confident that she would be able to blend in more easily.

She had considered her plan all the way to the City, how she would catch Rhys and talk to him on his own, and she had decided that a series of hints would do. She would indicate a certain spot in the City where they could talk, and she would wait there in the hope that he would understand. She would wait until at least two hours into the changeover of shifts. That had to be enough for him to see the signs several times on his shift and contemplate what they meant.

Scarlett gathered a few pebbles from the forest then headed for the hole under the fence. She had to do a crouching run so that the grass in the field would cover her movements. It was painful after a half hour, but once she reached the fence and saw that the hole was still there, she felt a small spark of victory within her. Step one- complete.

Next, she had to lay the signs then wait for Rhys.

Scarlett scattered a few pebbles by the post where their shift always stopped to divide into pairs. She hoped that the pebbles, slightly whiter than those around them, would get his attention. Scarlett heard a noise and ducked into the space between two of the houses. The footsteps of a pair of guards passed by her, and neither glanced down the passageway. Scarlett forced herself to breathe normally as she considered her next sign. The only place outside of the base that they could meet and Rhys would remember being significant would be where the baby had been born. While Rhys hadn't been there during the actual birth, he had heard her colorful rendition of the story and seen the blood on her from the incident.

Scarlett clutched the pebbles she still had. The next sign would be a bit obvious if you were looking for it, but Scarlett hoped that only Rhys would be on the lookout. Scarlett laid the pebbles in the pattern of a 3 and 7. The house number where the child had been born. Scarlett then took the back way to wait beside that house. If she heard someone coming, she could always take the other way to get away from them. Anxious, Scarlett reevaluated the wisdom of her signs, but she couldn't think of any other way of communicating with him. As Scarlett crouched behind the house, her thoughts turned to the house a few doors down- Kendrick's house.

He had made it pretty clear the night before that he wasn't interested. Scarlett didn't know if he didn't trust her, or if he really thought his leg would hold them up. Scarlett traced the uneven edge of her tunic as she listened to the noises around her. It had to be almost time for curfew. If Kendrick was going to leave, he had only a little bit of time before his presence on the streets would be impossible. And if what Kendrick had said was true, then Rhys wouldn't be out for at least another two hours.

Scarlett sighed and scurried behind the houses until she was pretty sure she was behind the one that was Kendrick's. She pressed against its side, contemplating her next move. Should she go up the stairs? Would the other members of his family be home? They probably would not welcome her presence in that case. She would listen for a few minutes.

If she didn't hear anything, then she would call for him like she had the night before.

Scarlett heard movement from inside, but she couldn't tell who might be making the noise. Then, she heard voices. "What are you doing going out right now?" a female voice asked.

Kendrick's voice was clearly the one that answered. "I'm just going to take a short walk before curfew."

"Are you looking for trouble? Curfew is in only a few minutes, and you want to go for a walk, as though you are one of the Elite." Scarlett was surprised at the anger in the female's voice.

Kendrick didn't respond, but Scarlett saw a patch of light on the ground where the door must be opening.

"Fine, go on your walk. Enjoy yourself for five minutes, but don't expect me to open the door after curfew. I'm not condoning that. Worthless son," she muttered.

Scarlett heard the clump step of Kendrick on the stairs, slow and steady. He passed the alley, and Scarlett heard the door shut with a strong thump behind him. Where was he going? But before Scarlett had a chance to answer, Kendrick was there in the alley, next to her.

"I knew you were here," he said. Scarlett had to read his lips more than listen to his words. "I'm leaving with you," he mouthed.

Scarlett's eyebrows rose into her hairline. She opened her mouth to speak, but Kendrick covered his mouth in a 'be quiet' motion. Scarlett nodded and pointed down the alley toward where she was going to wait for Rhys. Once they were a few houses away, Kendrick motioned for them to stop. She saw a drop of sweat forming on his forehead and dripping down even though the hot sun had already gone down.

"This house is empty," he said, motioning to the house shielding them from the walkway's view.

Scarlett, all too eager to explain her plan, told Kendrick about how she was signaling Rhys. She told him where the hole in the fence was and that he could wait outside the hole or in the forest for her. She expected to be there in a few hours, but she *would* be there. Scarlett calculated the journey from the City to the camp. By herself, it took three hours, and that was with the occasional jog. She had to calculate that Kendrick would take longer. And no matter what, they had to reach the camp before daylight. She didn't know what time the Fringe would leave their spot, but she couldn't risk missing them.

Kendrick shook his head. "Don't wait for him," Kendrick said. "He's not worth it. Let's go."

Scarlett scowled. She didn't like what Kendrick was saying. It felt just like when Rhys had tried to control her about visiting the baby. Scarlett still felt like she had made the right decision when it came to the baby, Esperanza, and she felt like she was making the right decision now.

"I have to give him the chance," Scarlett said. "I won't wait long after the shift changeover, but I have to give him the opportunity." Kendrick frowned before finally nodding.

"Okay, I'll wait for you in the forest." He hesitated as though he was about to say something else. But then, he shook his head, turned, and left. Scarlett was alone again. As she watched him shuffle down the alley, she hoped he would be able to make it out by himself okay. Scarlett wanted to shout after him to wait, to let her help him. But she couldn't shout. She couldn't do anything except hope.

Scarlett crouched into position between the houses, waiting and hoping for the next two hours. She heard the changeover of shifts a few streets over. A moment later, she heard Rhys's voice. Scarlett froze as she tried to catch a glimpse of him without being seen herself. While she didn't see the face, Rhys was clearly with a White. Kendrick's assessment of it being Irin was probably correct.

She only caught a couple words from Rhys, before both of them were silent. ". . . strange . . . possible . . . truder." Neither of them spoke again while within earshot. Scarlett didn't know if Rhys had even seen her signs. It wasn't as though she could sneak out and leave better signs. She didn't know what else to do, and if she *did* leave this spot and Rhys came to find her, it would all be for nothing. No, she had to stay as long as she could.

She heard Irin and Rhys pass two more times, and she knew that she didn't have much time. She had to get out of the City and start walking with Kendrick to the camp. It's not as though they wouldn't know where she had been with Kendrick in tow, but she couldn't risk being left behind.

Scarlett began fingering in the dirt, remembering the secret messages she and Rhys used to send each other. When one of them arrived at their designated meeting spot for the day and the other one wasn't there, they would leave messages to help find each other.

Sometimes, Scarlett would arrive at the shooting pod to find a message that Rhys was somewhere else. And now, she didn't care if someone knew she had been there, she had to let Rhys know that he had the decision to leave. She couldn't tell him about Phan; that was too risky. But she could tell him that she was alive and in the forest.

Scarlett wrote only a few words: SACBACRDLEEFTGTH AILJIKVLE MINN OFPOQRRESSTT.

There, that was something that would be clear only to Rhys. And if he didn't find it, he didn't find it. But Scarlett had to hope he would. Scarlett sneaked behind the rest of the houses in that row and waited at the edge until a pair of Whites she didn't know passed.

Then, she darted to the fence and around the fence's edge to the hole. She could see how badly the hole was dug out, and no attempt had been made to cover it. Scarlett had to hope that meant Kendrick had gotten through okay. She made a half-hurried attempt at covering the hole up before running in a crouch toward the edge of the forest. She reached the tree line and immediately began searching for Kendrick, still expecting a shout behind her at any moment. But no, she had entered and exited the City twice now with no one noticing.

"Kendrick," Scarlett called in a soft voice, her eyes searching the forest floor for clues. She found a stick that had been broken off at ankle height and knew that Kendrick's bad leg had probably done it. She continued on, calling his name softly. Something suddenly moved to her right, and Scarlett crouched into fight mode. But it was just Kendrick.

"Hey," he said, smiling as he got to his feet. "I think I fell asleep waiting for you."

"Sh!" Scarlett said, looking over her shoulder. But the lights from City 6 were already little pinpricks through the trees. They had no need to be quiet. As Scarlett turned away from those pinpricks of light, she realized that it would be the last time she saw City 6. She wouldn't be going back.

"Let's go," Scarlett said, facing forward. "We have to . . ." She wondered if the extra kilometers were worth it to enter the camp from the back. They would find out where she had been sooner or later. They might as well let a watcher guide them back. "We're probably going to meet one of the watchers, guards, on our way back," Scarlett said instead. "And they might not be too happy about me having left the camp, but they're going to be fine with it."

"You're not supposed to leave the camp?" Kendrick asked. "I'm not trading one prison for another."

"You can leave the camp," Scarlett amended. "You just can't go to the City."

"Oh, I wouldn't go there anyway," Kendrick said. They walked on in silence. The weariness of two nights with little to no sleep was wearing on Scarlett, and she found herself yawning often.

"So, are there a lot of people in the Fringe?" Kendrick asked.

Scarlett nodded. "I don't know them all yet, but it feels like a lot to me. It's . . . a different type of community than what I'm used to."

"Why?"

"I don't know," Scarlett couldn't quite explain why she felt so welcomed at the Fringe. "It's like everyone looks out for one another, not a competition like it sometimes was at the training center."

"Like a family is supposed to be," Kendrick responded.

Scarlett shrugged. It didn't seem like Kendrick's family was that pleasant of a group of people. "I'm so tired," she yawned again for emphasis, "and I don't want you to worry, but they are planning on moving in the morning. Apparently, they move spots every couple of weeks. They are moving tomorrow, or today, this morning. I don't know what time, but I want us to get back there as soon as possible."

Kendrick grunted, and Scarlett looked over at him. He hadn't said anything, but as she watched him out of the corner of her eye, she saw the pained look when he stepped on his bad leg. No matter how long this night felt to her, it had to feel infinitely longer to Kendrick. Scarlett hoped that they would reach the camp before morning. If not, they would be on their own.

CHAPTER 11

"I have to stop," Kendrick said and immediately collapsed down onto the nearest rock. Scarlett took a deep breath and tried to remain patient. This was the third time they had stopped, and she couldn't help being frustrated. Stopping wouldn't make his leg magically better, and based on her endurance training, continuing to move, even if at a slower pace, was better than stopping all together.

"Okay," Scarlett said in what she hoped was a cheerful voice. "Sure, let's stop for five minutes," but she kept her feet moving, marching in place.

"You can go on," Kendrick said. "I'll catch up when I can. Let them know I'm coming, and they'll wait for me."

Scarlett pressed her lips in a tight-lipped grin. The martyred "leave me and I'll catch up" phrase. She hadn't gone to the City for Kendrick only to leave him in the middle of the forest. Well, she hadn't gone to the City for Kendrick at all. She had just happened to pick him up along the way. Scarlett licked her lips and wished she had brought some water. But any supplies would have given a clear indication about what she was doing.

Scarlett counted off seconds in her head, waiting for the seconds to stretch into five minutes. When the time had passed, she motioned toward Kendrick. "Let's get going," she said, keeping her voice even, but

69

looking in the direction she knew the sun would rise. Was it her imagination or was the sky starting to tint a bit pink?

"I don't think it's that much farther," Scarlett said to encourage Kendrick. Kendrick nodded and pushed himself off the rock. He wobbled for a moment, then took a step forward.

"Yes, let's go," he agreed. Scarlett took a few steps forward before she realized he wasn't following. She turned and saw him leaning against a tree. He was shaking his head. He closed his eyes briefly, then took a few more steps, arriving even with Scarlett.

He nodded at her and continued to take small steps in the right direction. Scarlett turned and matched his slow pace. "Maybe you can lean on me?" she asked, uneasy about the suggestion, but not sure how else she could help him.

Kendrick shook his head. "I don't want to break your shoulder," he half-joked.

Scarlett heard a rustling up ahead, and she knew it must be the watcher. Nervous, but knowing he was going to find out anyway, Scarlett called out.

"Hey, it's just us."

The movements stopped, and no one emerged from the darkness in front of them. "Who are you talking to?" Kendrick asked.

"It's one of the watchers," Scarlett responded. "That means we're pretty close to the camp, less than half an hour."

The watcher suddenly appeared in front of them, causing Scarlett to jump back at the surprise. "Oh, hi," she said.

The watcher studied Scarlett with a frown then turned his gaze upon Kendrick, who was dressed in the thin, gray-colored cloth of those from the City.

"Come with me," the watcher said, grabbing Kendrick's arm as though to keep him from running. He started to pull Kendrick forward, and Kendrick winced.

"Sorry, male, I've got a bad leg here," he said. "No worries about me going anywhere." The watcher studied them both suspiciously as

Kendrick continued limping forward and Scarlett walked patiently by his side.

"What time is it?" Scarlett asked. The watcher studied the sky for a few minutes.

"I reckon we have about an hour until dawn." Scarlett nodded, feeling relieved. Kendrick would have some time to rest before they began their journey for the day. The trio walked in silence for a good quarter hour, Kendrick's labored breathing the only human sound. They reached the edge of camp before Scarlett expected. With the fires out and the tents only lumps among the shadows, it was nearly impossible to see.

"I'll wake the elders," the watcher said as Kendrick sank onto the log where Scarlett had eaten her evening meal so many hours ago. He took a few deep breaths and reached down to gingerly press his ankle.

"Don't wake anyone," Scarlett said. "Let them sleep until dawn. We could use the rest as well, and then, well, in the morning, we can get everything sorted out."

The watcher appeared undecided as he looked over his shoulder into the forest. "No one is coming after you?"

Scarlett thought about Rhys. His shift would be over shortly after dawn. Had he seen her signs? Would he follow them? Or would he miss their meaning completely? Scarlett finally shook her head. "I snuck in and out easily. No one knows I was there."

The watcher eyed Kendrick again.

"Fine, sleep here, by the fire pit," he said, motioning to the circle of rocks with the burned out logs inside. There was still a small measure of warmth coming from the logs that had blazed so high the evening before. Scarlett patted down the forest floor by the fire pit and indicated that Kendrick could lay there. She spread some pine needles over another flat spot and lay by him, her feet by his head.

Scarlett could feel the watcher's eyes on them as they lay there. She wanted to tell Kendrick it would be okay, that the Fringe was actually a friendly group, but she wasn't sure if he would believe her. Scarlett couldn't fall asleep, but laying still, knowing that she was safe, at least for the time being, was enough to lull her into a kind of half-dream state.

A short time later, tent flaps began opening as if on cue. Scarlett rolled onto her back and saw the sun lighting up the sky to the left. It was just a tinge of orange, but she knew that meant the day was beginning, a day that could change her future.

Laya approached Scarlett a few minutes later, and the look on her face was grim.

"Scarlett," she said, and her voice transferred all of the disappointment and deception she felt onto Scarlett's shoulders. Scarlett sat up immediately, already protesting the accusations she felt.

She pointed at Kendrick. "He didn't have a chance in the City," she said. Kendrick pushed himself into a sitting position as well, clearly listening to their conversation. "I had to go back for him," she didn't mention her failed goal of getting Rhys to join them.

She looked in the direction of the City, almost expecting Rhys to come around the side of one of the trees and wave at her. She grit her teeth. She had been so close to him, but there was nothing she could have done. If she had stepped out of the alley, Irin would have captured her. Even if she and Rhys had been able to fight their way out of that (and she didn't know how hurt he was), Irin would have called for backup.

"I'm not the one who needs your explanation," Laya sighed, sitting on the fallen log. "It's the elders you will need to speak to." Laya turned her gaze away from Scarlett to Kendrick. "What's your name?"

"Kendrick," he said, offering his hand. Laya smiled and shook his hand. Scarlett watched their strange exchange.

"I'm Laya," she said. "A few of us females will be preparing the morning meal in just a moment, and we will make sure to fill you up. But you must first talk with the elders. We have only a few rules here, and they are in place for everyone's safety. One of those rules is that no one here may have contact with anyone in the Cities apart from a few trusted individuals who we help out in a mutual exchange. You must understand why we have that rule," she said.

Kendrick nodded. "Yeah, the Government is dangerous, and it feels like they are always watching. If you're already free, why go back?"

Laya smiled as though Kendrick was saying exactly what she had hoped to hear. "Yes, and we have so many little ones here to protect. I'm interested to hear about your life in the City. Were you in school or did you have a profession already?"

Kendrick shook his head and picked at a piece of pine straw, tearing the brown strips into tiny dots. "I finished school already. I was a chopper, so I'm a bit familiar with the forest."

"And now?" Laya prompted.

Kendrick nodded toward his leg. "Now, I have been forced to give up my profession. I feel useless." Kendrick gnawed on his bottom lip. "Last night, when I left, they didn't know where I was going, of course. They just thought I was going out in the streets, visiting friends or something. But they made it seem like they didn't want me back. Well, they got their wish. The house is all theirs."

Laya suddenly motioned for Scarlett to follow her into one of the tents. The group of elders was gathered there. The older male sat down last, then motioned for her to begin.

"You have broken a rule that calls for banishment from our community," the male said. "However, we would like to give you the chance to explain yourself."

Scarlett swallowed and looked to Laya for encouragement. She had just heard Kendrick's story. Didn't she understand now? Scarlett cleared her throat after a heavy silence. "When I left City 6 a week ago," Scarlett said, thinking on her feet as she spoke, "I was unaware of the rule in the Fringe about not being able to revisit the City. In fact, I didn't know if this group even really existed, or if it was a mere story told to children.

"Kendrick, my friend," Scarlett pointed through the wall of the tent, "as you can see, his leg isn't the best. Walking from the City last night took a long time. While I could survive on my own outside the City if I had to, I didn't think it would be fair to him to take away his guaranteed food for something that might not be real. So," Scarlett looked at each elder, making eye contact, "I left the City to scout it out, knowing

I wouldn't be able to return to serve the Government, but planning to return to get Kendrick if you were here. And you were so welcoming to me, I thought that you wouldn't mind one more." The rest of Scarlett's breath came out in a whoosh, and she waited to see what they would say.

She heard a few murmurs of "we can't say no to the lame boy" and "Communication is key." Finally, the male shushed their murmurings.

"If what you say is true, why did you not come to us or at least one of us and explain your plan to retrieve Kendrick? Did you or did you not shoot your fellow guard while you were in the City?"

Scarlett studied the edge of her mat as she tried to think of an appropriate answer. "I did hurt Rhys, but it was accidental. Perhaps I should have told you, but I was afraid you would say no, and Kendrick was waiting for me to come back to the City. And even if you said no, I had to go back anyway. I guess it was better going back not knowing what was going to happen than going back knowing I would be giving up everything here."

"Think hard," Laya said, her voice firm. "Are there any clues that anyone might find that would indicate who we are or where we are going?"

Scarlett thought about the note she had scribbled in the alley near house 37. Only Rhys would understand it. And it was just as likely that someone else would step on it and smear it first. She shook her head. "No. We were very careful."

"We will return in a moment," the male said, standing. The others followed him outside of the tent in an orderly fashion. Scarlett stared at the wall of the tent. She knew that Kendrick was on the other side. Would he say something about Rhys? Would he give away the fact that he wasn't the reason at all that Scarlett had returned?

Scarlett counted the seconds, ticking her finger on the edge of the mat. They were gone nearly five minutes when the flap moved and they all came back through. They settled onto their mats, and Laya spoke.

"You broke one of our rules, and there must be consequences. First, you must understand that you are never to break this rule again. If you do, you will be banished immediately without the chance to explain yourself. Second, you will not be allowed the freedom of moving out of the camp perimeter for a fortnight. You must always remain within sight of one of the elders or one of our designated trusted individuals."

Scarlett frowned, but didn't respond.

"You may go," the old male said. Scarlett rose and moved past them to the tent flap. She hurried over to where Kendrick was still reclining. The rest of the camp was already in motion. Tents were being rolled into compact packs that were strapped onto each person.

The morning meal was well on its way to being fully cooked based on the smell in the air. Scarlett sat next to Kendrick and forced a smile onto her face. "Well, I wasn't kicked out, so that's good."

Kendrick nodded then patted Scarlett's knee. She flinched away from him and found a reason to stand up and cross the cooking area to where Ariel was sitting on the other side of the firepit.

"Esperanza's been crying for you," she said, tugging at Scarlett's tunic. "Mara said she wants her mam. Where'd you go and who's that?"

Scarlett looked over her shoulder. Ariel was pointing at Kendrick. "Why don't you go talk to him?" Scarlett suggested. She was too tired to be very patient with Ariel's chatter. "I'll go get Esperanza."

"No," Ariel protested. "I don't want to go talk to him."

"Okay, then don't," Scarlett suggested, making her way to the place where Mara's tent had been. But it was gone, in its place a folded package of material with an x-shaped set of poles.

"Oh," Ariel said, "Mara is by the river."

"By the river? With two babies?" A picture of Esperanza rolling down the bank and splashing into the water made her break into a jog. She reached the edge of the water in less than ten minutes and found Mara bathing with Moses on her chest. Esperanza was bundled up by the edge of the river. Scarlett scooped her up a bit angrily, shooting Mara a disapproving look before turning back to the camp.

Laya was waiting at the edge of the camp, her arms crossed.

"Ariel, I need to speak with Scarlett for a moment. Why don't you go ahead and get your morning meal?"

Ariel looked back and forth between the two older females then hurried off to retrieve some food. "Don't test the boundaries," Laya said. "When the elders decided you should stay in the camp at all times, they meant within the camp. If you are going somewhere, you need to go with someone, not go by yourself."

"But Ariel . . . and Esperanza-"

Laya shook her head. "No, with an adult. I would respect their decision, Scarlett, as they are being generous. Others have been banished for visiting a City, and they have given you a second chance." Scarlett suddenly remembered the ancient male she had come across with Rhys on the Mound. Had he been banished? Was he hobbling around in the forest waiting to die?

"Okay," Scarlett accepted, but she was irritated inside. Wasn't the Fringe supposed to represent freedom? This didn't feel like freedom at all. Ariel was coming back with a bowl for Scarlett as well. Scarlett motioned toward the log near where Kendrick had been laying, but he wasn't lying down anymore. In fact, she didn't know where he was. Scarlett whipped her head around, scanning the group of people for the gray clothing, which would make him stand out. She tried not to feel panicked as she sat down and ate hurriedly. Why did she have to worry all the time?

CHAPTER 12

Rhys studied the markings on the ground, and he knew exactly what they meant. Irin's eyes were gazing steadily at him. "Do you understand them?" he asked.

Rhys nodded. "The end is smeared, but if that first letter is an 's' and the other letters are 'stt,' then it's simple."

"So, what does it mean?" Irin prodded.

"It means that Scarlett was here," Rhys nodded. "I thought so, but now I know for sure. It says, 'Scarlett alive in forest'."

Irin pursed his lips. "Anything else?"

"That might be an arrow," Rhys said, touching the tip of a faint marking with the toe of his shoe. "If it is, then the direction of that arrow might point to where she is."

"Good work," Irin said. "My guess is that this mark has been here less than a day. Would you agree?"

Rhys tilted his head back and forth as he considered the possibility. "For sure, no more than two. But I'm no expert in tracking. I just know Scarlett."

"Of course," Irin said. "We'll need you if we put together a team to track her down. If she is with a group of people, it could very well be the same group who has been targeting different Cities, stealing supplies, and stealing children."

77

Rhys's eyebrows went up just slightly. "Stealing children, Sir?"

Irin nodded. "You weren't trusted with the information before. Now, you know as much as I do that you are completely trustworthy."

A smile spread across Rhys's brown skin. "Of course, Sir. I would never do anything to betray the Government, you, or anyone working for the Government."

"For some time now, babies have been disappearing from the Cities. These are babies who have been approved to be sent to the training center, babies who would be promising members of the society. Having searched all of the City, it is impossible that someone is hiding the children inside the fence. I'm sure you can understand how this must look to the higher ups. We can't have children disappearing from right under our noses."

Rhys nodded in agreement. "If finding Scarlett helps solve the mystery of the missing children, then of course, it is what we must do."

"Excellent." Irin pointed at the ground again. "Is there anything else from this message? Anything you might have missed before?"

Rhys shook his head. "Nothing else. I think we have gotten all the information out of it that we could."

"Why do you think she decided to place the message here, beside this house?"

Rhys looked at the houses around them then back at Irin. Something lit up behind his eyes. "Do you remember that child?"

Irin shook his head. "I'm not sure I know who you mean? There are many children."

Rhys pressed his lips together, trying to remember. But sometimes, his memories were foggy. Ever since he had woken up from the procedure that had saved his life, occasionally he had trouble recalling the specifics of a memory. The image of the child had just been clear in his head; now, the details were gone. Rhys shook his head, gritting his teeth as he tried to remember.

"I'm sorry, Sir," Rhys finally said. "I don't remember any more. I know a baby was here, but . . . I can't remember why that was important." Rhys looked further down the street and started walking in that direction, the memory feeling closer as his feet moved. He stopped in front of one of the houses, looked back and the other house, then at the house in front of him again. "I still don't remember."

"If you think there could be something here, I say we go in." Irin climbed the two steps to the house. The morning light was just beginning to show over the horizon. The individuals should be just waking up for their day's duties.

Irin gave a perfunctory knock before pushing the door open. Two individuals were lying in bed. The female sat up immediately and pushed her gray hair out of her face. The male gave a few mighty coughs as he sat up.

Rhys's eyes fell on the empty cot on the floor. Seeing the male's face as he sat up jogged Rhys's memory. He could see a younger face with longer hair before him. Scarlett had said his name, but Rhys couldn't remember it. He felt Irin staring at him intently.

"Who slept there?" Rhys asked.

"That's our son's," the male said, coughing again. He pulled out a small cloth and coughed into it.

"Is something wrong?" the female asked.

"Where is your son?" Irin said, his form imposing with his feet apart and his shoulders wide.

"Oh, uh, he must have already gotten up," the female said. She glanced at the empty cot as though noticing it for the first time. Rhys studied her face closely. He saw confusion and perhaps worry there. He stored the information away for later when he and Irin were alone.

"Does he often get up early?" Irin continued his line of questioning.

The female shrugged. "He can't work anymore, due to his leg, so his movements are unpredictable." Irin and the female stood staring at each other for several moments, neither ready to either continue or end the conversation.

"Go about your day," Irin finally said, three fingers over his heart in a sign of respect to the Government. The female mirrored the motion. Irin exited the small house, and Rhys followed him.

"Did anything seem strange to you?" Irin asked. Rhys quickly explained how the female's face had seemed like she was hiding something, like she didn't want them to know how confused she was.

"Let me summarize what I am thinking," Irin said. "We know that Scarlett was near this house and felt safe enough to take the time to carve out that message. There was someone who is normally in that house who was not today. Does it sound like she took a Citizen with her?"

Rhys nodded. It was probable.

"Perhaps Scarlett was facilitating the children leaving the City," Rhys suggested.

Irin shook his head. "She may have been involved and may have helped, but this has been going on longer than the month she was here. It's been going on for years. Come on, let's talk to first shift about the male. Give the best description you can, and we will see if anyone spots him today."

CHAPTER 13

The dawn's light was strong now, and even without sleeping at all the night before, Scarlett felt antsy and ready to get moving. She had strapped Esperanza into the childpack and had taken a roll of mats on her back. Even the children were all responsible for carrying their own mats, except for the youngest. They were just responsible for themselves.

Kendrick reappeared, and Scarlett felt her anxiety level drop just a little. "Where did you go?" she asked.

Kendrick surveyed her new gear. "I was just talking to one of the older males, elders I think they are called. Why are you carrying a child? You're a Blue. Blues can't have children."

Scarlett smiled down at the little female. "This is Esperanza, and she's not mine. She's actually from the City. Anyway," Scarlett looked around before she remembered that she didn't always have to hold in these details like they were secrets. "She was slated to be a student in the training center. She was taken from her mother, and then, I think she was killed, the mother. So, Phan and I helped get her out of the City. And we kind of bonded. It was like she knew that I needed someone, and she, of course, did too."

Kendrick smiled at the two of them. "Cute." Scarlett frowned. 'Cute' was a word used for Reds, not for Blues like her. But then she

81

looked down at the brownish outfit she was wearing. She wasn't exactly a Blue anymore, and she had to stop thinking in colors.

A whistle sounded to the left. Scarlett turned her head in that direction, but she was surprised to see everyone start moving. It must be a universal signal. She hefted Esperanza up once more and began following the crowd. The wind pushed her hair forward, causing it to flap in her face.

Scarlett angrily brushed it behind her ears. "How's your leg feeling?" she asked.

Kendrick nodded, his lips pressed together. "It's fine. I think I've gotten used to it hurting after all that walking." He used his lips to point to the people in front of them. "How long do you think we're going to be walking today?"

Scarlett shrugged. "I am not the right person to ask. I would think a while, but-" She was cut off by some of her hair blowing into her mouth. Kendrick laughed a little as she fished it out. "Anyway, I would think we're going to be walking for most of the day. I don't know where they're going, but my guess is close to another City."

Kendrick's eyes lit up. "I've never seen another City before. I mean, it's probably the same, but I don't know. There's something about traveling the world that makes this journey just a little less painful."

Scarlett nodded. "I was excited to see City 6 for the first time." It felt like so long ago that she had peered around the other Blues as they were patted down and their vehicles searched.

"I wish I could see the training center," Kendrick said.

Scarlett smiled at the thought of the place. She wondered what it would feel like to return. Rhys wouldn't be there. She wondered if Jaylin or Miya had been promoted to Blue. A sudden spark of excitement ran through her at the thought of them joining her in City 6. But then again, she wasn't in City 6 anymore. She would never be again.

"The people in your life are what make it enjoyable," Scarlett finally said after a long silence. She looked up to find Kendrick's gaze elsewhere. Oh well, maybe she needed to voice her statement more than he needed to hear it.

"It's hard to say. I haven't experienced many enjoyable people in my life," Kendrick finally responded. Scarlett had moved on from their conversation in her head, but she backtracked.

"I heard your mother," she said truthfully. "She doesn't seem like the nicest female."

Kendrick did an odd mixture of a shrug, chuckle, and cough. Esperanza startled at the noise, and Scarlett laid a comforting hand on the back of her head. "That is true," he finally responded.

"I didn't mean to cause any sadness," Scarlett began, "but my understanding of families is that there is a great measure of love and . . . togetherness." Scarlett continued to rub the back of Esperanza's head, feeling warmth within her.

Kendrick nodded. "And in most, there is. But some families, everyone actually has so much stress on them. We don't have enough to eat; we have too much work to do. And we have no way of bettering our situation. The only hope one has is to have a baby that is considered worthy of the training center."

Scarlett pointed to Esperanza. "Like her? Is that a good thing?"

"You are given extra rations for a year's time, and occasionally, the chance at a better profession."

Scarlett bit her lip, confused. "So, if the female is given extra privileges, wouldn't she feel proud to have her child serving the Government?"

"Many accept the food gratefully, but it's difficult. I had a brother," Kendrick finally said.

"Brother," Scarlett turned the word over, knowing she had heard it before.

"A male child born before me," Kendrick explained. "He was born approximately two years before me. As soon as he was born, he was tested and deemed worthy of the training centers. My mother, she was given the rewards I talked about. Then, she had another child- me. She was hoping that they would take me too, that she would get a chance at better employment, at more food. But, for whatever reason, they didn't. She's hated me ever since."

"Oh, wow," Scarlett responded. She couldn't imagine living in a place with someone who hated you. "But then, why was this one hidden?"

"People have done all sorts of things to keep their children safe. That one you were carrying with the bent hand? Remember her?" Scarlett nodded. "Her parents poured scalding hot water on her when she was just born. They gave her that defect to make sure she was never chosen." Kendrick shook his head. "You can't win. You keep your child, but what sort of profession can she have now? On the other hand, you lose your child, which is hard after you've birth and everything."

"Well," Scarlett said, looking for something hopeful to say. "Those days are over. Out here, we are free."

The wind whipped her face again, and Scarlett twisted her hair into a horsetail behind her head. There, it was out of the way. They continued for a while longer, walking without talking. Scarlett glanced over at Kendrick occasionally to see the twisted look on his face indicating pain.

"Maybe we should stop for a few minutes," Scarlett suggested.

"While they leave us behind?" Kendrick pointed to the majority of the group, which was in front of them. "No, thanks. I'm like a sheep without an owner out here on my own."

"I mean, we have to stop at some point," Scarlett finally responded. A few of the smaller children were riding on their mother's or father's back. But many of the others were skipping ahead and to the side, always staying within sight of the group.

"Was there anything you liked about growing up in the training center?" Kendrick asked.

"Well, of course." Scarlett looked thoughtfully ahead. "I loved the predictability of everything. I mean, it's not like living here or even in the City where I never seemed able to figure out what was going on. There, I had friends; we had fun. I liked being able to choose what I did with my afternoons. I enjoyed playing games and learning how to fight. There wasn't anything *not* to like."

"Wow, I didn't realize it was a nice place," Kendrick responded. "I mean, I thought to be turning out people like the guards, it must be a torture chamber, basically turning you into robots."

Scarlett gave him a funny look. "No . . . nothing like that. Honestly, I think the training center is way better than these families. I mean, I really enjoyed it. And sometimes, well, I wish I could go back to that time before I realized how many secrets there were. Before I was sentenced to death for something that wasn't even my fault."

"See?" Kendrick said. "That's what I mean. They hand out death orders like sweets. And it's to their own people. I mean, when you were-what's that lowest color again?"

"Reds? Or the Tinies. They wear brown, but they aren't really Browns."

"Yeah, Reds or whatever. You were probably a Red when all of these leaders were Blues in your training center. And they probably had to help out with you on occasion. And they saw you being an innocent baby. Then, they're like, 'Let's kill you!'"

"What does seeing me as a baby have to do with anything?" Scarlett asked.

"Because it's like her. What's her name?"

"Esperanza," Scarlett said, putting a hand protectively over her like Kendrick might try to take her out of the childpack to illustrate. "You wouldn't do anything to hurt her. Ever. Right?"

Scarlett shrugged. "Not now. But what if she grows up and is doing something evil? I mean, the Government-" But Scarlett stopped herself. Everything she had grown up learning didn't matter anymore. Because the truth was that the Government wouldn't protect her anymore. She had no cushion of rules and expectations to care for her.

"Yeah, everything comes back to them," Kendrick mumbled. Ariel pushed through the groups of people and aligned herself with Scarlett's steps. She took Scarlett's hand, and Scarlett smiled down at her, even though holding her hand was inconvenient as they were walking.

"You're from the City?" Ariel asked, peering around Scarlett to look at Kendrick. Scarlett tried to see Kendrick as Ariel must. His dark hair, longish, touched the fringes of his eyebrows and covered his ears. He had a wide, strong body. Scarlett's eyes trailed down to his leg. The way he brought it forward in a stiff attempt at walking made her cringe. She felt sorry for him, even though she was not responsible for his leg.

"Yes, City 6," Kendrick responded.

"How come you left?" Ariel asked.

"Because in the Cities, you have no freedom. You do exactly what you're told when you're told, and if you don't, then you can be killed." Ariel squeezed Scarlett's hand tighter.

"You're scaring her," Scarlett tried to tell Kendrick quietly.

"I'm not scared," Ariel said, letting go of Scarlett's hand and flouncing away. Kendrick shrugged.

"It's the truth. Do you want me to lie about it? Besides, it's better for her not to be curious. Could you imagine if she decided to go explore a City and was caught by your kind? She-"

"My kind?" Scarlett frowned at him. "What's that supposed to mean?"

Kendrick shrugged again, not meeting her eyes.

"My kind?" Scarlett asked again, hating that he was ignoring her question. Esperanza seemed to sense her anger and started moving her head and making bubbling noises. "I don't know what you meant by that, Kendrick, but there aren't 'kinds' of people out here. You and me, we are both newbies to the whole living with the Fringe thing. We are the same."

Kendrick shook his head but didn't say anything, which only made Scarlett angrier. She took the grumbling Esperanza toward Mara, knowing that it was probably time for her to eat. How long had they been walking? Was Mara expected to feed Esperanza and keep walking at the same time?

After a short while more, one of the elders called for a meal break. The word passed among the people, and everyone found a place to sit and stretch their legs while food was distributed. Scarlett took the cold slab of meat and started picking at it. She looked around. Some were diving into their meat, and others were eating more slowly. But what struck Scarlett was the similarity of it all.

Here she was, on the outside of that fence, but was life here any different? Everyone was given food, food that the elders selected and distributed. The elders had the last decision as did the Government, and while the elders weren't executing people, they didn't seem to be very forgiving either. Worry whirled in her stomach. Was this place any better than living in a City?

CHAPTER 14

Once the group had settled for the night, Scarlett's body felt exhausted. Everyone was gathering around a small cooking fire for their evening meal, but Scarlett didn't have the energy. She crawled into the tent, which had been set up in less than five minutes, and lay on her mat, her eyes blinking shut in exhaustion. Esperanza was with Laya. She could get some rest.

But as soon as her eyes closed, a particularly cold gust of wind flapped the tent door open and closed. Scarlett's eyes were wide open, staring at the door and through to the groups of people beyond. The wind came again, whipping it with a ferocious indignation. Scarlett turned over so that her back was to the door. It didn't help. The wind howled and howled, flapping the door and shoving its cold fingers up Scarlett's back.

Scarlett sat up and, rubbing her exhausted eyes, stepped outside the tent, since she obviously wouldn't be able to sleep. She was surprised to find almost everyone still gathered around the fire, which was dancing in a frenzied manner.

Scarlett heard the low conversation between Laya and the other elders.

"Based on those clouds, this storm might be as bad as that one ten years ago." Their faces were serious.

"We need to send a hunting party out now, and it may be too late already," River chimed in. "If we don't get some meat before tomorrow, then we'll be out of luck."

Scarlett frowned. They didn't have enough food for everyone. She glanced toward the empty pot from the evening meal. Maybe she shouldn't have been so quick to give up her portion after all.

The elders seemed to notice her hovering nearby, and Laya motioned for her to come over. Scarlett stepped uncertainly into the circle. This group of people who had just the day before denounced her for being a terrible person were inviting her to chat with them casually?

The wind grabbed the ends of her horsetail and pushed them into her mouth as she tried to speak. She pulled them back and looked up at the sky. The trees around her were swaying, not the casual sway of gently rocking a child, but the rapid sway of someone about to jump from a swing.

"Did you have something you wanted to say?" one of the males asked.

Scarlett shook her head. "The wind woke me up, so I came outside to see what was going on."

"It looks like a hurricane," Laya said. The worry on her face was clear.

"What's a hurricane?" Scarlett asked. The word had an edge of familiarity to it, but she couldn't place the meaning.

"This," one of the elders said, pointing up at the sky. "Heavy winds, rain. They are destructive."

"So what are you going to do about it?"

"It looks like we're in front of it," Ignatius said. "We can keep going, but there ain't no way we gonna outrun it. The best thing we can do is find higher ground in case it floods. It'd be best if there wwas a place away from the trees to avoid lightning."

Scarlett bunched her lips in a knot. Shouldn't they know the forest? Sure, it was big, but they had been out here all their lives. "So, how far are we walking tomorrow?"

"Scouts're out right now trying to find a better place for us to hunker down and wait. We take things hour by hour in situations like this. Ain't no knowing what the sky'll look like in an hour."

"So, what should I do right now?"

An elder spoke up. "We'll be assigning groups shortly. Groups should stay together at all times, and we'll be checking in frequently to make sure everyone is accounted for."

Scarlett nodded and looked around. Even though it was completely dark already, it seemed as though the excitement riding on the wind was keeping everyone awake. Scarlett realized she didn't know where any of "her" people were. She was about to ask Laya, but Laya was already speaking with another elder about something. Scarlett decided to leave them to their discussion while she found Esperanza and Kendrick on her own.

The tents were in different positions, and even though they all looked slightly different, she couldn't recognize which one was Mara's. She didn't want to just start poking her head in random tents. Scarlett found Verona who was sitting by herself outside one of the tents.

"Is this the communications tent?" Scarlett asked, pointing to it and lighting up with the idea of hearing Rhys's voice.

Verona frowned at Scarlett. "We're too far out of range to hear anything from the Cities. This is my and my daughter's tent."

"Oh," Scarlett stopped. "Do you know where Mara is? I'm trying to find Esperanza."

Verona shook her head. "No, I don't."

Scarlett frowned, but continued walking up to random groups of people. She didn't have any luck, so she finally went back to the tent and laid down, a wave of weariness coming over her. She could always find them tomorrow.

CHAPTER 15

Rhys stood beside Irin in the Black's office. Irin was recounting what they had discovered during their shift. Rhys was yawning. He felt ready to shut down after his long shift.

"Do you have anything to add?" the Black asked, staring directly at Rhys.

Rhys straightened up. "No, Sir."

"Irin," the Black said, turning to him. "Put together a team to go after this female and anyone who might be with her. If she is brazen enough to enter a City that knows she should be dead, then who knows what she will do if she reaches other Cities? I don't want the other Cities to know about this."

Irin nodded. "Sir, I'll bring you the list of guards by this evening."

The two were dismissed from the Black's office, and Rhys made for the stairs. He clomped down them methodically, his whole body feeling exhausted. His eyes barely staying open, Rhys pushed into the males' dormitory. His bed had been moved since he had woken after the surgery. He was now right by the dormitory door.

Rhys collapsed onto the bottom bunk. As soon as he stopped moving, his eyes closed, and he was asleep.

When Rhys awoke, he felt full of energy. He automatically got up and went to the exercise room. He hadn't exercised much since he had arrived in the City, but now, it was necessary to keep his body in the best condition possible. Even though the doctor had told him he might feel weak after the surgery, the only word to describe how he felt was neutral. Sure, he felt tired after a long shift, but he felt far from weak.

Rhys counted to twenty in his head before putting the barbell down and turning to the leg machine. He pushed with his legs in and out thirty times before moving on to the next machine in his routine. By the time he had finished, he was covered with sweat. His stomach was ready to eat.

Irin interrupted Rhys's walk to the cafeteria.

"We need to talk."

Rhys pointed to the machine where he would input his number in exchange for food. "Is it alright if I eat while we do?"

Irin nodded. "Sure, go ahead. Find me once you have your food." Rhys followed Irin's orders, getting his food and meeting Irin at a small table at the back of the dining hall. He mindlessly began shoveling the food into his mouth.

"I'm considering the list of guards to present to the Black. I want your opinion on them as you know Scarlett best. Right now, I'm thinking a team of six of us. You and I, of course, Gayla, Marse, Phan, and perhaps, Malak."

Rhys took another bite of food. Something about Phan's name rang a bell in his head, as though the idea of Phan and this mission didn't match, but Rhys couldn't quite pinpoint why. "I think Phan shouldn't come," Rhys responded.

Irin nodded and waited for Rhys to suggest a replacement.

"We need more than six people, too," Rhys said. "If there is a group of people in the forest, then six people, even if we have guns and they don't, won't be enough. We should have at least twenty."

"That would leave us bare here in the City," Irin pointed out. "Besides, being subtle with twenty people unused to the forest would be difficult."

"That's my suggestion," Rhys responded, focusing more on his food than the conversation. He knew they would consider his opinion then do what they wanted to do anyway. He had little or no knowledge of what he was doing, but sometimes, the answers just seemed to come to him.

"Who would you suggest to replace Phan?" Irin asked.

Once again, something in Rhys jerked at Phan's name. He shook his head.

"He may be an idiot sometimes, but Devon is a loyal idiot," Rhys said.

Irin nodded. "Noted. We will set out tonight."

Rhys's eyebrows went up. He knew it was urgent, but the change in routine needed a moment to process. "What time?"

"Once the Black has approved our team, we will grab our supplies and go."

Rhys decided to make his daily report to the doctor right then so he would be ready when they needed to leave. He marched to the doctor's office and rang the bell when he got inside. Rhys stood by the mirror, staring at himself.

The mark stood out on his forehead, a triangular dip in his skin from falling on a sharp rock when everything had happened the week before. His dilated pupils stared back at him in the mirror, dwarfing the brown color of his irises. He saw himself, but he didn't feel like himself. Something since the surgery was different, and different was the only word he could put on it.

The doctor entered, pulling out a screen and marking a couple of observations before asking the customary questions.

"How are you feeling today?"

"Fine, as always," Rhys responded, sitting on the paper-covered table. The paper crinkled underneath him.

"Any strange thoughts or feelings?" the doctor asked.

Rhys shook his head.

"Any pain in the last twenty-four hours?"

Rhys shook his head again, paused, then continued shaking it.

"Any symptoms of fatigue, dizziness, or nausea?"

"I guess fatigue, but isn't that normal?"

"On a level of 1 to 10, how fatigued?"

Rhys cocked his head to the side. "I guess it depends on the time of day. When I finished my shift early this morning, I was nearly a nine. When I woke up after sleeping, a one or a two."

The doctor made some notes. "Any extreme fatigue?"

"No, not really."

"Any other unusual side effects or symptoms that you want to report?"

Rhys thought for a few moments. He had felt this strange, out-of-body experience ever since he had woken up, as though he wasn't himself, but watching everything from the outside. "I'm not sure if this is normal," Rhys said. "But I keep feeling . . . not like myself. I'm not sure how to explain it."

The doctor typed out something on the screen before looking up. "Do you want to act on that feeling?"

Rhys frowned. "I'm not sure what you mean?"

"Does it make you want to do something to make you feel more like yourself?"

"I don't think there's anything I can do, is there?"

The doctor made another note. "What are you working toward today?"

Rhys frowned. That question was new. "Well, Irin and I are heading up a team to go after Scarlett." He cocked his head, waiting to see if the doctor was looking for something else.

"Who is Scarlett?" the doctor asked.

"Another guard," Rhys corrected himself. "Former guard."

"What is your relationship with her?"

These questions were getting a lot deeper than they normally did. Rhys tried to think carefully on how to best describe the relationship they had. At that moment, it was nonexistent. They had no communication. Rhys remembered climbing the Mound with her before they were shipped out to City 6. Something in him stirred, but he immediately started feeling a knocking on the right side of his head, like a migraine starting to bore through his skull. Rhys rubbed his head and shrugged.

"I think we used to be pretty good friends. But now, I mean, I don't see her, so I don't think we have any sort of relationship."

The doctor took a good many notes about that statement. In fact, he was tapping away for so long that whatever he typed had to be double what Rhys had said.

"I'm starting to get a migraine," Rhys said. "Can you give me something for that? I don't want to start this mission not feeling well."

The doctor fished out a white pill. "Here, you can take this for your head. I'll entrust Irin with some as well. If you ever aren't feeling well, talk to him about it, and he can give you whatever you need."

Rhys took the pill, drinking from a tiny plastic cup of water. He closed his eyes and squinted against the pain. But as he thought about the mission before him, his migraine slowly began to subside into a dull throb.

Irin found Rhys in the exercise room. "We're leaving," he said. Rhys set the barbell on the support and followed Irin out of the door. His heart was pumping quickly, speeding up as if pumping his blood more quickly would give him more energy.

"What do I need?" Rhys asked.

Irin pulled him through the doorway that led to the doctor's room. He then opened the door to the interview room, the one that had metal loops on the table for stringing handcuffs through. Rhys met the eyes of each person in the room- Marse, Devon, Malak, and Gayla.

"Our team is complete," Irin said. He handed each of them a walkie-talkie and a pistol, their normal equipment for patrolling the City. "I have some information to share before we begin our journey." Malak's ears perked up, but Devon looked confused.

"We found a break in the fence behind this compound. Clearly, someone was using it to escape. Have any of you seen someone using the back door, or someone behind the compound who shouldn't have been?"

Everyone shook their heads.

"I didn't even know that there was a back door," Devon responded. Rhys hadn't either, but now he did. Collecting information was better than announcing you didn't have any.

"Our mission is to collect Scarlett and bring her back here, alive if possible."

Gayla's eyes widened slightly, but she stayed quiet.

"We will be tracking her down, and from what we learned, it's possible that she is with a group. It's possible that another Citizen, a large male with an injured leg, is with her."

Gayla raised her hand timidly, and Irin stared at her as if daring her to speak. "Sir, who is this group of people? Have many Citizens fled the City?"

Irin studied her for another moment as though deciding if her question deserved an answer. "There are a few people who are living outside the Cities, unauthorized, of course. They don't receive the benefits of the Citizens, and so far, they have not bothered us. We have not wasted resources trying to find them. However, their presence is now too much of a taunt to tolerate. If we do find them, we will get backup and eliminate the group."

Everyone nodded their understanding.

"Let's move out," Irin said, motioning toward the door. He led them out the front of the compound and around to the side where a few vehicles were stored in a garage. They were hardly ever used, except when making a long journey outside of the City. Irin hopped into the driver's seat, and Rhys climbed into the back. Being in the back of the truck felt familiar, as though he was reliving the day he had arrived in City 6. But this time, he was leaving.

Gayla climbed in next to him. They sat facing Devon and Malak. It felt almost like their original crew, except for the obvious difference. The Jeep started up, and they drove toward the front gate where they were searched. Rhys obliged, his gaze on the forest to their far left. He wondered how long it would take to walk versus go in the Jeep. Surely, they would catch up with Scarlett quickly, especially if she were traveling with a handicapped male.

Once everyone was in the Jeep again, Gayla leaned over so that her lips were almost touching Rhys's ear. He felt something stir within him as she whispered, "Isn't Scarlett your best friend?"

Rhys looked back at her, confused by her words. Scarlett- the one who had shot him? Why would someone shoot their best friend? The answer was simple- he wasn't her best friend. Rhys shook his head, his brows creased in an angry wrinkle.

Gayla's eyebrows went up, but then she shrugged, mumbling something about none of her business. Devon seemed all too happy to engage in conversation, however.

"Yeah, they were close, but now, Rhys is all like, 'Whatever. That's in the past.'"

Rhys stared at Devon. He didn't like being talked about as though he weren't there. However, he didn't say anything. The migraine in his head began to pound again as the Jeep bounced through a field, cutting through the grass, which only sprang back halfway, as though unsure if it should try to continue growing upward.

"So, what happened? She shot you, right?" Gayla asked, trying to piece together the story.

Rhys didn't answer; he just kept staring at Devon. Devon continued talking as though Rhys's death stare meant nothing to him. Rhys's eyes turned to the sky behind Devon's head. It was turning a grayish color, and the clouds did not look inviting. Would one of those rainstorms be coming, the rainstorms he had always heard about but never seen while living at the training center?

"Yeah, she shot him, and she was all like, 'Somebody shot him. I don't know how it happened. Get him a doctor.' And when I arrived on the scene, they were collecting his body. I thought he was a goner, but I guess the doctor here is super good or something. Because when I next saw him, he was all pieced together and back to normal." Devon motioned to Rhys who was still staring a hole through him. "Although, I think your brush with death made you lose your sense of humor."

Gayla looked at Rhys out of the side of her eyes. "I suppose it could do that to anyone," she said. Rhys finally turned his gaze away from Devon and looked through the front seat at the forest in front of them. They had to find Scarlett and anyone with her. Rhys wouldn't allow anything less to happen.

CHAPTER 16

When Scarlett woke up, the sky was still dark outside. But despite the darkness, the Fringe was alive with movement. The wind whipped at the tents, and when Scarlett emerged from her tent, trying not to be loud, she saw that at least two tents had blown over during the night. They were laying in a sad pile of poles and fabric.

Scarlett went over to examine one. She was not the only person awake. At least a dozen others were walking around the camp, examining wind damage. Scarlett saw Kendrick, resting with his back against a tree, watching the movement. She jogged over to him.

"Hey! Where were you last night?"

Kendrick nodded toward one of the fallen tents. "I *was* asleep in there before it collapsed on us. Where's the baby?"

"Esperanza? She's with Mara, I think. She should be anyway." Scarlett's eyes scanned the tents. A huge gust of wind blew her hair into her face. Instead of letting up, it blew stronger, as a few droplets started to fall. Verona and another female were going to each tent and waking the occupants. Scarlett knew something was about to happen.

Scarlett watched as everyone poured from their tents and dismantled them in less than five minutes. Ten minutes later, everyone was gathered in the center of the camp. Laya began splitting the people into groups, two to three families per group.

99

"Stay with your group at all times," she said. "If you get separated, remember that we are heading west. Always stay west." She came to where Scarlett was sitting with Kendrick. "You'll be with Mara and her family. You are group eleven."

Scarlett stood and scanned the faces until she saw Mara holding both babies. Scarlett hurried toward them before Kendrick's voice drew her back.

"Hey, a little help here."

He was trying to get up from his position at the tree, but he seemed to be stuck. Scarlett swallowed her look of amusement and reached her hand down to him. Kendrick grabbed her hand and pulled hard. She almost lost her balance, but Kendrick was on his feet.

He smiled. "Thanks. The tilt of that hill . . ."

Scarlett nodded, but she was examining her hand as though she had touched something forbidden and was trying to make sure no remnants of her misdeed remained. "Hi," Scarlett said to Mara before reaching for her baby.

Esperanza smiled and waved her arms up and down. Scarlett kissed the child on the forehead before arranging her in the childpack. The droplets of rain became more insistent, and Scarlett looked around for a nearby shelter as she had the first time it had rained in the City. But of course, there were only trees and dismantled tents.

Kendrick took one of the tents on his back, and Scarlett took another. Mara and the male with her, which Scarlett soon learned was called a husband, had grim faces.

"You won't find any shelter from the rain while we're walking," the husband told her as he saw her looking around. "Best to just keep the baby dry." Scarlett saw how Moses was wrapped in some animal skins, and Mara handed her a similar covering. Scarlett fumbled with it awkwardly.

"How do you . . . it's not quite . . ."

"Here," Mara said, stepping forward. She wrapped the skin so that it covered Esperanza completely, but Scarlett could still pull back a flap and see the child.

"Thanks, I've never done that before."

Mara smiled, her face weary. Her husband took the pack on her back so that Mara was only carrying Moses. "I don't think I introduced myself," her husband said, once their belongings were situated comfortably. "I'm Derrico."

"Nice to meet you. Scarlett."

"Kendrick," Kendrick stuck his hand out, and Scarlett watched as they shook hands. Derrico offered his hand to Scarlett, but she shied away. This idea of touching between the genders still needed some time. Derrico smiled before turning his attention to Laya who was offering some last-minute information. The wind grabbed her words as soon as they left her mouth and carried them away to a different part of the forest.

It was only once they started marching that Scarlett realized they hadn't been given any breakfast. She looked around at the different groups to make sure she hadn't missed anything. No one seemed to be eating.

"Did they give out breakfast, and I missed it?" Scarlett asked Mara, who had a permanent look of exhaustion on her face.

"No, not this morning. We need to get to a safer spot to weather the storm. We're too low. We will eat once we reach the spot."

Scarlett frowned, and she remembered her thought from the night before about not having enough supplies. Was the Fringe that much different from the Government?

Kendrick marched in silence, but whenever Scarlett looked over at him, she saw the pained look pass over his face. She soon noticed a slight incline as they were walking. The rain started coming down harder, and it became difficult for Scarlett to see. She squinted into the needles of water that fell on her face. Esperanza became restless under her covering and started fussing.

"Trust me," Scarlett said, "it's not any better out here." But, of course, young Esperanza did not understand her words, so Scarlett tried to soothe her as best she could with pats on the back. They had been walking for a few hours at least, but the sky didn't seem to get any lighter. It was as though the sun had not risen. And among all of these worries, Scarlett was thinking in the back of her mind about Rhys and what Verona had said. She would have no way of contacting him. She had no idea how much time would have passed by the time they camped close to City 6 again.

"Where are we going?" Scarlett asked Mara, but Derrico answered.

"We're going to camp near the Government City."

Scarlett's eyes widened, and she felt excitement rising up in her. She had always wanted to see the Government City. She had heard stories about what it looked like, but only the most respected Whites had even a chance of seeing it with their own eyes.

Kendrick was shaking his head, the ends of his dark hair flinging drops of water on Scarlett. "I'm not sure I want to see what kind of luxury they are living in at our expense."

Scarlett couldn't accept his negativity. She just smiled, suddenly eager to move forward and thinking less about what was behind her. Derrico looked at the two. "You won't be going into the City. Only the most trusted will go to the very edge to meet our contact. We would never risk going inside."

Scarlett accepted what he was saying, but despite the fact that the elders had already warned her once, she found herself preparing to break another order. She *had* to know what this City looked like. The rain was by then coming so hard that anytime Scarlett opened her mouth to speak, it filled with water. All conversation ceased as they focused on staying within view of the group in front of them. Finally, Kendrick broke the silence.

"I *have* to sit down. I can't keep going," Kendrick said, plopping down on a fallen tree. Derrico, Scarlett, and Mara surrounded him. Derrico pointed at the group in front of them that continued to move forward. Group twelve passed them.

"I'm sure we'll rest soon," Derrico said, "But we can't lose our group in this weather."

Kendrick pulled up his pants leg, and for the first time, Scarlett saw where he had been shot. An angry red line framed a circle beneath his knee. Inside the circle, the skin was almost black. In fact, it didn't look like skin at all anymore. Scarlett felt her stomach turn over as she covered her mouth.

Kendrick lowered his eyes, seeing her disgust. Derrico nodded, knowing exactly what it was. "Fine, stay here. I'll alert two of the other groups that we're taking a short rest. I'll be right back." Derrico jogged off. Kendrick dropped his pants leg. Mara took the time to shift Moses's position and begin feeding him. Esperanza seemed to sense that there was feeding going on and she wasn't a part of it. Her fussing became stronger.

"Hold on," Mara cooed. "You'll get a turn in just a minute."

Mara switched babies with Scarlett, and she took the pudgy Moses. He was only two months older than Esperanza, but his rolls of skin were quite a bit heavier. Scarlett shifted back and forth on her feet, watching different groups pass them, some just looking at them, others asking if they needed help. Kendrick kept his eyes averted.

Scarlett finally sat beside him on the log, her whole body wet and starting to shiver. "How are you feeling?" she asked.

Her question seemed to touch a nerve. "I'm fine!" Kendrick practically shouted. "I know I'm holding everyone up. You all can just keep on going. I'll catch up when I can." Scarlett looked to Mara, her eyes asking for help. She didn't know how to deal with this.

"We don't leave people behind," Mara said. "We know where they are going, and we can rest as long as you need."

Kendrick didn't respond, but Scarlett watched as he gently touched the wound through the fabric of his pants. She looked at his hands, the one she had grabbed that morning to help him stand. They were so rough, and she imagined him working long days as a chopper. Her eyes traveled upward to his arms. The muscles bulged underneath his shirt as he scratched the back of his head. Scarlett wanted to touch the muscles on his arm. She wanted to feel them in comparison to hers, tiny rocks underneath her shirt sleeves. Kendrick looked at her, his face a mask of annoyance. Scarlett turned away, pulling back the flap over Moses to check on him. He smiled up at her and reached one of his arms out of the warm cocoon, trying to finger her face. Scarlett smiled before shoving his arm back down.

"You're going to get all wet," she said.

Derrico came back and let them know that groups twelve and thirteen knew where they were. Scarlett suddenly realized that no other groups were passing them. They were officially the last ones, only making her more anxious to get moving. She stood and started shifting back and forth again, and Kendrick finally got the hint, standing and hobbling after the groups.

Scarlett matched his pace, walking beside him.

"Are you okay?" she asked. Mara and Derrico were walking a couple of meters in front of them.

Kendrick shook his head. "I'm not sure if I'm cut out for living with the Fringe. I wasn't fit for the City either. I just thought this would be different."

Scarlett could hear the sadness in his voice. She started to reach out, then drew her hand back, fighting within herself. If this was Jaylin or Miya struggling with their feeling of purpose, she would have hugged them without a second thought. Even if it was Rhys, she might give him a squeeze on the shoulder. But with Kendrick, she felt so out of place. Scarlett hesitated, lifted her hand, then placed it on top of Esperanza.

"This isn't normal," Scarlett said instead. "When I was here, it was mostly just taking care of Esperanza and exploring the forest. Not a lot of walking. I'm sure once we get somewhere, you'll find where you fit in."

Scarlett saw Kendrick nod out of the corner of her eye. "I hope so. If not, I don't know."

"You don't know what?"

"If I'll stay."

Scarlett reached out then and grabbed Kendrick's arm before she thought about it. "You have to stay! Where else could you go?"

Kendrick's movement slowed, and he looked at where she was gripping his arm. He smiled at her. "I thought you weren't supposed to touch males?" Scarlett rolled her eyes and pulled her hand away, but

Kendrick reached down and plucked at the edge of her hand again. Scarlett looked down at where his fingers, so much wider and longer than hers, were touching her hand.

Scarlett grunted, but Kendrick didn't look her in the eyes. Instead, he intertwined his fingers through hers, like he knew where they were supposed to go. Scarlett hated the restricted feeling as his fingers closed around her hand, like a handcuff keeping her in place. Scarlett shook her head and tried to pull her hand from his grip. He let go, and their hands slid away, the rain making them slick.

Scarlett looked up and saw that Derrico and Mara were at least six meters in front of them. "We need to walk a bit faster if you can," she said, pointing to the two of them. Kendrick grimaced and started moving a little more quickly.

By the time they stopped for the midday meal, Scarlett was starting to shiver. The wind was still blowing, but her hair was plastered to her head with the rain. She felt jealous of little Esperanza in her cocoon of warmth. Mara gave each of them a large spoonful of cold porridge in their bowl, and Scarlett turned her nose up at the stuff. She took a few bites to soothe the hunger, but couldn't eat more.

"Not going to eat that?" Kendrick asked, pointing to her mostly full bowl.

Scarlett happily handed it over to him, taking his empty bowl in her hands.

"Wow! I haven't had this in a long time," Kendrick said, shoveling in a few more spoonfuls. Scarlett watched him enjoy it with fascination. "There's something in here to give it that taste," he said, smacking his lips.

"I think it's just oatmeal and ginger," Scarlett said. "And water."

"Ginger," Kendrick nodded at the word. "That's it."

"So, what do you normally eat?" Scarlett asked.

"A lot of pasta, a lot of grain, crackers. The only protein is beans. A lot of rice. Fruit or vegetables are rare. Meat rarer." Scarlett thought back on the meat she had had regularly at the training center. She was surprised that Kendrick viewed it as a delicacy. "The same thing over and over again, until you're eating just to stay alive, not because you enjoy it."

Scarlett reached to take his bowl, allowing some rain to clean it out before using her hands to scrape the last bits clean. She secured their bowls in her bag again and stood. Everyone was doing the same. One of the male elders was coming through with an update for each group, checking that everyone was there.

"We've got about two more hours of walking, then we'll be on high enough ground," he said. "We'll stop there for the night and try to put up our tents if the wind will let us."

Scarlett shivered involuntarily. The cold rain felt like it was seeping through her skin into her bones. Suddenly, as if in opposition to their plans, the raindrops increased in size. They pelted down like tiny bullets from the sky. Scarlett covered her face as she doubled over. The rain began stinging her back. She wrapped her arms around Esperanza and crouched there, waiting for the rain to let up, even if only slightly. She peeked up to see everyone in similar postures of self-preservation.

Esperanza started crying, and Scarlett didn't know if the rain was soaking through her covering or if she was just upset at the sudden change in position. "Shh!" Scarlett tried to soothe, but the rain bounced off her lips causing her to gargle the sound. Scarlett coughed and coughed and coughed, choking on the rain. She kept her head down and eyes closed.

Suddenly, a gust of wind blew at them so hard that she felt as if a human hand were pushing her over. She fell on her side, the mud soaking into her immediately. Half of Esperanza's covering was soaked in the mixture of mud and water that stood at least two centimeters over the top of the grass. Scarlett heard a cry, but this time it was coming from her own throat.

"We have to keep going," Kendrick's voice said in her ear. His hand was on her arm, and he pulled her into a standing position. Scarlett felt as though her legs were blocks of cement as she stood. She shivered again and looked to Kendrick. He nodded at the group of people in front of him. They were moving upward, upward, always upward, trying to get out of the standing water.

Kendrick didn't remove his hand from Scarlett's arm, supporting her as they moved forward, even though he was the one with the injured leg. Scarlett couldn't feel her feet. Even when she lifted them to take another step, she couldn't feel them. It was as though she were walking along on legs without feet.

"A few more steps. You've got this," Kendrick said. Scarlett took a few more steps. She looked up. The rain entering her eyes was too painful. She looked back at the ground, watching her feet lift out of the water then set back down.

"Where are Mara and Derrico?" Scarlett asked, almost shouting her words so that Kendrick could hear.

"Right behind us!" Kendrick shouted back. Esperanza wasn't stopping her tears now. She continued screaming and screaming. Scarlett wanted to tell her to shut up, but she knew that she wouldn't understand. She just gritted her teeth and took a few more steps.

Scarlett felt Kendrick's grip on her arm tighten. She tried to turn as she felt him pulling her backward, but Kendrick's weight on her arm was too strong. She heard a thump of some sort then felt herself pulled down to the ground. Scarlett would have hit hard, but the water supported her somewhat. The mud sucked her legs and arms. Scarlett tried to orient herself.

She heard a gurgling sound and realized that Esperanza was submerged. Scarlett scrambled to stand, to get the baby's head out of the water. She was on her knees, and she pulled back the covering. Esperanza wasn't moving, wasn't screaming. Nothing. Scarlett patted the child's back, desperately looking around for help.

Kendrick had slid several meters down the hill. He wasn't moving. Derrico was hurrying down the hill to check on him. Mara bent over Scarlett, fumbling to pull Esperanza out of the childpack. The baby was getting soaked, but she didn't move. Scarlett panicked and tried to get to her feet as Mara turned the child on her stomach and pounded her back hard.

Esperanza's mouth opened, and a tiny stream of water fell out. She startled and began crying. The poor child was soaked, and her pack was now too. Scarlett wanted to give up. She wanted to curl into a ball and cry. But she couldn't. She didn't have the luxury of giving up.

CHAPTER 17

24 hours earlier

Once they reached the edge of the forest, Irin hopped out of the Jeep. Everyone else stayed put, waiting for orders. The trees were close together. The Jeep could pass, but it would be close. Rhys studied the clouds whirling in the sky. He felt a droplet of water on his face and reached up to wipe it away. He waited for more, but they didn't come.

Irin returned to the Jeep and patted the side of it affectionately. "We're going to take it on foot from here. We've already made several hours progress over them, and the Jeep will be too loud." He gave an order to the extra White who had ridden along with him, and that White turned the Jeep around to head back to the City.

Rhys focused on following Irin through the forest. The sounds in the forest were different from the ones in the City. He heard some animals trampling the fallen leaves nearby. Each step seemed to make some leaf crackle or a branch crack. To him, they sounded like elephants. No way they would be able to sneak up on anyone.

Gayla pointed to something a meter off the path they were taking. "Someone was here. Look at how the plant is bent." Everyone crowded around the plant, and Rhys nodded. Gayla had good eyes. Someone had bent part of the plant's stalk when they were walking through.

"Fan out," Irin ordered. "A meter between each person. Look for more signs. We need to follow this path." A huge gust of wind blew through the group, and Rhys took his place, a meter from Irin. Malak was on his other side.

It became clear soon after that the path, while heading mostly straight away from the City, had a decided tilt to the left. The group followed it, eyes constantly on the ground. Rhys stopped after they had been walking a few hours. He felt something in the wind. He closed his eyes for a moment, feeling the urgency of the wind slapping his face. The hum of some nighttime insect began, and Rhys opened his eyes again. The team had moved forward, forging through the forest without a worry for him. Rhys lengthened his strides and caught up with them. A bush had been crushed by something bigger than the typical footstep.

"Looks like they stopped here to rest," Malak said, examining the spot closely. The darkness of heavy clouds was fading into the real dark of night.

"You may turn on your torches," Irin advised. "We'll do one torch per two people. We don't know how long we may be out here and want to conserve the batteries."

Malak and Rhys gravitated toward each other while Gayla and Devon paired up. Malak and Rhys walked forward in silence. Finally, Malak pointed the torch directly at a group of ferns that had been crushed.

"I believe if we were unsure about the injured male's presence, we can be sure of it now. This looks like something was dragged through the fern, which would make sense if he was nursing his leg."

Rhys nodded in agreement, his eyes constantly flicking from the pool of light to the darkness that lay ahead. Rhys's stomach grumbled in a way that didn't mean hunger. Rhys looked toward Irin. Irin had his medicine. He was supposed to report if he felt differently, but he hated anything that made him look weak. He was not a weak guard.

All six of them stopped at what was clearly the remnants of a camp. Rhys kicked a rock that was at the burnt edge of where a fire had been.

He placed a hand on the coals, but they were cold. "They were here, but they've been gone a while."

"Look, over here!" Devon shouted. "Another fire! How many people do you think there were?" The group walked the circumference of the camp, then everyone turned to Malak who was furiously calculating figures in his head.

"Bascd on the space trampled and the number of campfires, we are looking at a group of perhaps a hundred."

Rhys's eyebrows went up. "Do we have any guarantee Scarlett is with them?" he asked no one in particular.

"Let's find out which direction they went when they left camp," Irin decided. Everyone began searching the perimeter of the camp. A path was found but was followed to a river. Nothing else was found from the river, so they tramped back to the camp to try again.

"We're losing time!" Irin shouted in frustration. "Every minute you spend acting like clueless Reds, they get ahead of us!"

Rhys ignored Irin's anger and forced himself to think about it logically. They wouldn't want to go toward the City. There was nothing else toward the east, except the ocean a few hours away. Rhys marched to the west side of the camp instead and began inspecting the underbrush a few meters outside of camp. It looked less and less trampled the farther they moved out, then he found something that could only be identified as a path.

"They went this way," Rhys announced. He didn't wait for everyone to discuss the possibility of his statement. He began marching down the blazed trail. He had to find Scarlett, and he had to bring her back to the City. That was his mission, and he would complete it.

They walked for another five hours according to Rhys's timepiece before Marse insisted they take a break. "We don't want to stumble upon them and not be ready for it," Marse insisted.

Irin finally conceded. "Fine, take out one package of rations. We'll rest for half an hour then keep going." Rhys plopped onto the ground and pulled out the rations from his backpack. He wondered how long Irin thought they would be out there, what with the rations and being careful with the torch batteries. If Scarlett and her group were moving forward at a similar pace, it could be awhile before they outpaced them. But Rhys didn't think this group of rebels would be able to move as quickly.

He ate his rations as Devon tried to start a conversation. "Do you think we'll be able to find her?"

Rhys pointed to the clearly crushed underbrush in front of them. "They left an obvious trail," he stated matter-of-factly. Devon cocked his head back and forth.

"I know, but I mean, if there really are a hundred people . . . what if they have guns?"

"Those are questions for Irin, not for me," Rhys responded.

Devon rolled his eyes at Rhys. "Male, you are no fun anymore. It's like you don't care about life, which is strange because if I had almost lost my life, then I would be, I think, crazier and even more excited to still have it."

Rhys didn't respond, and Devon finally moved over to sit with Gayla who would engage him in conversation. Exactly thirty minutes later, Irin was urging them to stand and continue. Rhys felt strangely energized by the food, and even though it had to be nearing midnight, he didn't feel tired. Malak, however, continuously stifled yawns.

The march was boring, but a necessary step to complete the mission. Rhys's joints began to feel sore, but he continued moving forward.

Irin finally called for a rest. "We will sleep four hours and four hours only," he said. Rhys lay down on the pine floor, closing his eyes obediently, but he didn't feel tired. His body was exhausted, but his mind continued turning over and over. Irin came over and handed him the pill he had been taking every day. Rhys didn't feel any pain.

"I think I don't need it today," Rhys said, "I'm not hurting."

"Then the pills are working," Irin said, extending his hand further. Rhys took the pill and swallowed it. He closed his eyes, but couldn't detach himself from the rough wind blowing against the side of his face. It beat the left side of his face until it began to feel chilled. Rhys watched the sun begin to rise, then slowly drifted off to sleep.

When he awoke, the world was different. The clouds above were covering the sun. The pink hope he had seen just before drifting off to sleep was gone. The world was covered in a gray shawl, as if trying to hide something from them. The rain began falling almost as soon as Rhys opened his eyes. He immediately located Irin who was looking up at the sky with a worried expression.

"Orders, Sir?" Rhys asked, standing straight and making the sign of the Government over his heart, three fingers pressed to his left breast.

"Pack up. We'll eat while we move." They consumed one packet of food each, and as they started moving, the rain fell. This rain was not the warm summer rain that Rhys had laughed at the first time he felt it fall. This rain was hard and driving, as though punishing them for interrupting the space between the cloud and the ground. Irin pushed them forward, always motioning toward the west.

Three hours after they started moving, they came across a larger area that had been disturbed. But unlike the first camp, this one was not as clean. They found a wooden bowl, carved out of the bark of a tree. It had been cast aside. Irin stuffed the bowl into his bag. There was a broken tent pole. A firepit, but this one was not as carefully constructed. It was created in a hurry. Irin called them to a meeting around the firepit.

"We are on the right path. This weather must be affecting them the same way it is affecting us. It's sure to slow them up. We want to stay close, but not too close. We can't be our stealthiest in this weather. Let's keep moving, but no faster than they would."

Rhys squinted against the rain and nodded. He felt the pistol at his waistband, the metal sliding easily under his wet fingers. This mission would not take long.

CHAPTER 18

Scarlett felt Kendrick taking something from the pack on her back. She didn't protest. She could only hope that he wouldn't require her to move. Esperanza's screams filled the air as another gust of wind blew Scarlett into the mud. She felt like a tuft of dust, too weak to fight the wind.

Kendrick pulled her to a fallen tree and sat her there. Then, she felt something dripping being pulled over her head. Scarlett protested. She didn't want this wet monster of a thing attacking her ability to breathe. But Kendrick insisted. Then, he was under it with her. She saw him tying it to the log. Scarlett felt a cold drip falling from the covering onto the back of her neck like a snake worming its way into her skin. The sound of the rain on the covering became monotonous.

That was when Scarlett realized she wasn't being soaked through anymore. Even though the covering itself was wet, it wasn't letting new water through. She became aware of all the details she hadn't noticed before. The tip of the covering was flapping against the log as though protesting its captivity. Esperanza had lulled herself to sleep with her crying. And Kendrick, Kendrick was huddled under the covering, only a few centimeters away from her, examining his leg.

"Thanks," Scarlett said.

Kendrick looked up and smiled. "I don't want you to worry or anything. Mara and Derrico decided we needed to stop. We'll catch up with the group when we can, but there's no way we can keep moving in this weather."

Scarlett looked at Kendrick's leg. His leg was a patchwork of blues and purples, but in no way was it a work of art to be admired. Scarlett felt herself drawing in her breath. "That's from when you fell?" Kendrick nodded, running his hand over the bruises then gently pressing them and wincing.

"Yes. I don't want to try walking again right now."

Scarlett still felt wet, and she shivered, the weight of the wet covering pressing into her back. "How long do you think we'll stay here?" she asked

Kendrick shrugged. "Until the storm stops, I guess." As if in defiance, a particularly large gust blew through their tiny tent. Scarlett grit her teeth together and wrapped both of her arms around Esperanza. Her feet, which were dangling on either side of the log, started to feel numb. Scarlett looked down, and under the cover of the tent, she could see that her feet were completely covered in water. Something at the back of her brain told her she should pick her feet up, get them out of the water. But when she first tried, the task seemed so difficult that she gave up immediately.

Kendrick rolled his head back on his shoulders, his feet next to him on the log. Scarlett studied him, her eyes half-closing. She suddenly felt so tired; the exhaustion from trying to push through the weather all morning was catching up to her. Scarlett pulled back the covering on Esperanza's childpack. She checked her, and she seemed warm enough, though still wet. Scarlett leaned against the side of the tent, waiting until the tension was just right before letting go of her body weight. Her eyes closed, and she drifted off to sleep.

Kendrick awoke Scarlett a short time later. He seemed to be yelling for no reason. Esperanza started crying, and Scarlett heard her cry echoed. She rubbed her ears, then realized it was Moses. ". . . fine in here!" Kendrick yelled.

Scarlett couldn't hear what was being shouted from the other tent very well, but she picked up a few words. ". . . out of the water."

Kendrick looked at Scarlett's feet. "You should keep your feet out of the water," he said. Scarlett looked at her feet. The water had to be at least ten centimeters deep by now. If she were to stand, it would come halfway up to her knees. The way the log was situated, it would cover where she was sitting if it rose another ten centimeters.

"You have to get your feet up," Kendrick said again as though Scarlett hadn't heard him the first time. Scarlett tried, she really did, but she had no strength left in her body. Scarlett groaned as though she were attempting to lift bulks of concrete.

Kendrick leaned down and pulled her leg up, breathing heavily. It thunked onto the log. He did the same with her other leg. Scarlett felt something like pain in her knees, but she couldn't be sure. Kendrick looked at her, his eyes wide as he brushed his wet, dark hair out of his face again.

"We're going to get through this," Kendrick said.

Scarlett nodded, checking on Esperanza again. "Yeah, we'll get through it." But it was hard to keep her mind positive when the world around them was flooding. "What will happen if the water gets as high as we are?" Kendrick had lived in the Cities longer than she had. Surely this had happened before.

Kendrick pressed his lips together. "I only remember one of these hurricanes when I was a kid. I think I was eight or nine, and it rose so high that it got in the house. We sat on the bed, and when the bed started getting wet, we hunched on the kitchen counter. That's when it stopped." Kendrick licked his lips, looking anywhere but at Scarlett. "One of my friends died in that storm. The supports under his house broke, and the whole house collapsed. He drowned. He was stuck under the wood, and he couldn't breathe."

Scarlett covered her ears as if she could keep the story at bay. She didn't want to hear anything else painful. She needed hope.

"The worst part was that his parents didn't have any sort of funeral or register his death. They didn't want to lose his food rations which they continued eating. So, people didn't know for weeks until his body was found. I would go and ask if he could play after he missed school, and his mom would say he wasn't feeling well. The liar!" Kendrick's voice was loud and angry.

Scarlett waited as his anger simmered. Kendrick picked at the hem of his pants which was around the knee of his colorful leg. "What was something good you remember about your childhood?" she asked.

"Childhood," Kendrick repeated. He looked up at her, sadness still crowding the corner of his eyes. "No, I like this, right here, more."

Scarlett looked at him like he had lost his mind. "You like almost dying in a rainstorm?"

"No, I like the unity in this group, the way they look out for each other. There are groups of people who look out for each other in the City, but it's mostly everyone for himself. Don't worry about the people you hurt in the process. It's like the older I got, the more I hated the Cities. But here, maybe I could live here."

"I wish I could go back," Scarlett admitted. Kendrick looked confused. "I mean, here, it's pretty much the same as in the Cities. You have a group of people making decisions for you. They say there are no secrets, but I still feel them in the air. And at least there, we wouldn't be stuck on a log with a wet blanket over our heads trying not to die."

"Correction. *You* wouldn't be. My situation would be about the same, because of the holes in the roof."

"Why don't you get them fixed?"

"Where would I get the material? If I take wood or even bark from my profession as a chopper from the edge of the forest, I would be called a thief. I could be punished for stealing something that no one is going to use. And it's not as if the Government cares about the holes in our ceiling."

"I'm sorry," Scarlett said, She wiggled her toes, or at least she tried. Her shoes still felt heavily waterlogged, but she was encouraged by feeling some movement. She scooted closer to Kendrick, so that their legs were touching, her fabric-covered one against his bruised one. "It seems like life is never quite what you were hoping for."

"But you're dumb enough to hope anyway," Kendrick said. "I mean, not you, you're not dumb. Just people in general who hope it's going to get better."

Scarlett laughed a little bit. "Don't worry. I'm not easily offended." She thought about Devon and how she had acted when she thought he had turned her in. "Unless you betray me. Then, we are done."

Kendrick plopped his hand onto her knee. Scarlett looked at it as though one of the scorpions that had frequently run through the open area outside the training center had approached her. Should she smash it or just let it pass on its merry way?

"I kind of like you," Kendrick said, looking at where his hand rested on her knee.

Scarlett smiled. "Good, I like you too!" she responded cheerfully.

"You do?" Kendrick looked surprised. "I mean, you always act so . . . serious. And, I couldn't tell what you were thinking."

"If I didn't like you, then why would I have helped you get out of the City?" Scarlett asked as though she were talking to a Red.

"I don't know. Maybe you just thought of me as a friend or you felt sorry for me or . . ."

"Duh, I think of you as a friend," Scarlett responded, raising one eyebrow. "Do enemies usually put up with you like I have?" She tried to smile to show him she was joking.

"Well, uh, I thought you, I was . . ."

"What?"

"Nothing, never mind. I'm . . . glad we're friends." Kendrick finally finished his garbled speech. Scarlett nodded, feeling her eyes start to droop shut again. If they weren't walking, she might as well be sleeping, right?

"I'm going to try to sleep while I can," Scarlett said. "Wake me up if anything happens." A particularly ferocious gust of wind pushed at the tent just then, and they both chuckled.

"Good luck," Kendrick said, leaning against the covering. Scarlett leaned against the other side, and it stretched. Her eyes closed fairly quickly, and despite the dangerous weather outside, she felt herself drifting into dreamland.

CHAPTER 19

Rhys trudged through the forest, but the mud was sucking at his boots. The clouds seemed unable to make up their minds. Would they throw rain down on them or would they not? Malak was leading the pack now, his eyes tirelessly finding more signs.

The wind picked up and started burning Rhys's eyes as he walked forward. He squinted and tried to turn just slightly, but the wind continued to find ways to bother him. Then, the clouds made up their minds, and the rain began to pour.

Devon complained behind Rhys. "Great. Now we're going to die out here. Can't you die from overexposure or something?"

Rhys ignored his attempt at talking and forged ahead, following Marse's boots. Devon persisted. "Don't you think we should stop and put on the rainproof gear?"

Rhys looked up at Irin and saw that Irin already had on his clear plastic cover. Rhys hurried to get his out, wondering how long he had been wearing it without Rhys noticing. He slipped the cover over himself and his pack, pulling it tightly underneath his chin. There was a harder piece of plastic jutting out over his face. Rhys knew it was supposed to keep the rain from getting in his face, but he felt like it limited his vision.

He marched onward. Well, he wasn't needed as the lookout at that moment, so his limited vision shouldn't matter. Their fate depended on Malak. Malak pulled up. Rhys nearly bumped into Marse. Instead of waiting around, he hurried up to the front to see what had stopped Malak. The rain still found a way to spray his face on its way down. The mud was thick, and as Rhys hurried up beside Malak, he felt his foot sink a good four centimeters into a puddle of water. His shoe was submerged and his foot soaked. Rhys shook his head and saw what Malak saw- another wooden bowl. This bowl had landed right side up. Interestingly enough, it wasn't yet filled with water. Rhys took in all of these details at once, understanding what they meant. They had almost caught up to the group.

Irin held up two hands as if everyone was going to come running forward at once. He surveyed the bowl and determined that there was no way it was leaking. "Let's pause here a quarter hour," Irin decided. Everyone gathered around the bowl as if it was the most interesting thing they had seen in ages.

Irin motioned for them to back up. Rhys started pacing back and forth, his mind turning over his mission. He felt fatigued, but he didn't want to stop moving. Everyone spread out, eyes half-open but mostly looking for some relief from the weather. After a quarter hour, Irin motioned them all over. Malak made his speech.

"Based on the rate the bowl is filling, we would expect it to be completely full in less than two hours. That means that they are probably only an hour and a half ahead of us."

Something clicked in Rhys, something like determination. He was close to completing his mission. He nodded and started walking in the direction they had been going. Depending on how quickly they walked, they might be able to catch up before the end of the day. Might? Probably.

"Hold on!" Irin called back at Rhys. Rhys turned, but maintained his position.

"We don't want to confront them in this weather. It would be hard for them to run, but harder for us to get a clear picture of the camp. We need the storm to pass before we do anything."

Devon complained. "So we just sit in the mud and let them get farther ahead? That doesn't seem . . ."

Marse cut him off. "That's exactly what we're going to do. They're probably moving more slowly. They may have children with them and could stop if they haven't already. We don't want to accidentally stumble upon them in this rain and send them scattering."

Irin grunted. "Lucky for you, I have a waterproof tent. We need to stake it to the ground and some of the nearby trees, but we will rest inside until the weather calms down." Irin pulled the tent out, and Devon and Rhys scrambled to set it up quickly. It wasn't meant for six people, but they squeezed in anyway, leaving their muddied boots right by the zipper. Rhys massaged his toes, making sure they were all still there.

"Sir," Malak said after a while. Gayla and Devon were asleep. Rhys was leaning comfortably on his jacket, listening to the rain pound on the roof of the tent. For some reason, he couldn't sleep.

"Yes?" Irin asked.

"I have a proposal. I think it could be more beneficial in the end than simply storming the group of people. As you said, we are only six, and we don't know how many of them there may be."

Irin grunted to let Malak know that he was still listening.

"Maybe it would be better if Rhys were to go in alone."

Rhys sat up when he heard his name. Malak smiled at him. "Sorry, male. I was going to let you know what I was thinking, but I thought you were asleep there."

Rhys shrugged like it didn't matter to him, but it did. How was he supposed to accomplish his mission of capturing Scarlett if she had a hundred others backing her up against only him?

"If I am understanding the situation correctly, Scarlett invited Rhys to follow her. Maybe she even dropped those things on purpose to make it easier to find her. She will be expecting Rhys to come. Rhys can go in, meet her, learn more about the Fringe, then bring her back here to us. Once we know more about the group, we can plan an appropriate attack."

For the first time since Rhys had arrived in the City, he saw Irin smile. "Malak, this is why you will soon become a White. Your maneuvering and strategizing are above your level." Irin turned to Marse who was also nodding.

"I agree, Malak. Well done. I think your plan stands a good chance of being successful."

CHAPTER 20

Esperanza stirred on Scarlett's chest and yawned, the cutest yawn ever, her tiny lips stretching wide in an oval. Scarlett patted her, but Esperanza was not to be soothed. She started fussing, quietly at first then louder. "Shh!" Scarlett said, sitting up and groaning a bit with the pain in her neck. She wasn't used to sleeping in such a strange position. Kendrick stirred and opened his eyes.

"I think she's hungry," Scarlett said. "Maybe I should find Mara."

Kendrick nodded, slowly stretching as well. Scarlett looked down to the patch of ground she could see under their covering. Except, it wasn't a patch of ground. It was more like a river. The water was rushing downhill as though called somewhere important. Scarlett wasn't sure how deep it was.

Scarlett pulled the covering off her head, blinking in the brightness of the day. The sun was still covered by clouds, and there was a steady wind. But at least the rain had stopped. Kendrick brushed the covering away as well and squinted up at the sky.

"Is it over?" he asked.

Scarlett didn't respond as she looked around, taking note of how empty the forest suddenly felt. She could see the tent where Mara, Moses, and Derrico must be. But other than that, they were alone. Scarlett shivered. Would it be hard to find the group?

"Mara," Scarlett said. Her voice was scratchy, so she cleared her throat and tried again. "Mara, I think Esperanza is hungry." There was some movement under the tent as though Mara was struggling to get out. Scarlett looked down at the river of water under her feet. She was scared to step into it, but Esperanza had to get to Mara somehow. Scarlett didn't want Kendrick getting swept away again.

"I'll be right back," she said, plunging her feet into the water. She was surprised at the warmness of the water. It was as though it had come straight from the training center showers. She smiled. "This isn't so bad." She took a few more steps to where the covering was moving and just reached the edge of it when Mara's head popped out.

"Moses just ate, so I figured Esperanza would be ready any minute," she said. She held her arms out, and Scarlett handed Esperanza over. Derrico cradled Moses. Scarlett watched as Esperanza hungrily began drinking, and Scarlett placed a hand on her own stomach.

"I'm pretty hungry, too," she said.

Derrico glanced up the hill where their group had gone. "I think once the babies are settled we should start up that way to meet up with everyone else. This water might not go down for a couple of days, so there's no use waiting for that."

Scarlett dipped her hand into the water, then yanked it back. Something had hit her hand. Her eyes widened as she saw an animal floating just under the surface. Her stomach turned over in disgust. She couldn't tell what kind of animal it was because its fur was mangled. Kendrick seemed to catch sight of it just after Scarlett's grunt alerted him that something had happened.

"That's a muskrat," he said. "Grab it!" Scarlett looked at him as though he had grown another head.

Kendrick laughed at her look. "Aw, it's gone now. Next time, we can cook that thing up and eat it." Scarlett curled her lip, but she saw Mara and Derrico nodding at his statement. She pressed her lips together to keep her stomach from feeling sick. The idea of that mass of mutilated animal entering her mouth made her want to vomit.

Finally, Esperanza was satiated, and Scarlett settled her back in the damp childpack. "I don't know if I'm dry now, or if I've just gotten so used to being wet that I can't feel the difference."

Kendrick moved his legs over to the water, hesitating before standing up. The water pulled at his leg. "Do you think you can do it?" Scarlett asked, wading over to him.

Kendrick nodded. "I'm fine. Just, might be a little slower. I don't want to fall." He looked at the direction the water was rushing and shook his head.

"I've got you," Derrico said, packing their covering and everything else into his pack. Scarlett watched as he helped Mara to her feet. He then leaned in and kissed her lips. Mara smiled at him before Derrico hurried over to be there in case Kendrick felt unsteady. But that kiss stayed in Scarlett's mind. It wasn't like the kiss she gave to Esperanza on her forehead or cheek. It was different, and it stirred something inside Scarlett. She wanted to ask; she had so many questions. But her questions were always met with anger or indifference. Scarlett didn't know if the question was too personal. She kept her eyes down and kept walking.

They waded uphill until the sun started peeking out from the clouds. And when it did, Scarlett realized by its position that it would be dark soon. Her night and day seemed so mixed up. They still hadn't reached the rest of the group.

"How far do you think they walked?" Kendrick asked. Scarlett could tell from his voice that he was reaching the end of what he could do. Everyone turned to Derrico for his answer. He shook his head.

"I don't know. It seems like we're almost to the top of the hill, but I don't see a sign of them up there. Do all of you want to rest? I can go ahead and see if I spot them or get a hint as to where they went."

Mara immediately shook her head. "No, we should stay together. We will find them, but you're the only one in this group who can hunt. And if you leave us and we can't find you . . ."

Scarlett suddenly realized how desperate their situation was. They didn't have food. They didn't know where their group was. Where would they even sleep that night? The whole world was a giant river.

"Okay, good point," Derrico looked around. "Not that there are any animals waiting to be hunted here. Maybe I should try fishing. Have any of you seen fish in this water?"

Scarlett shook her head as did Kendrick. "Okay, I'll keep an eye open."

Just as it was starting to get dark, Derrico suggested they find a place to rest. "I know we haven't gone far and we could keep going, but I would feel better waiting until the morning." The wind whipped his words away, and he pointed at it with his eyebrows. "This is why. Next time we see something above water where we can set up our covers, we will stop there." Scarlett pointed out a structure that was half-submerged in the water.

"Could that work?" she shouted ahead to the males. Derrico turned back just enough to nod, and everyone headed there. Scarlett's stomach rumbled. She didn't like feeling hungry. She sucked her cheeks in and moved about in the water, securing the tent so that she and Kendrick would have a patch where they could lay above the water. As Scarlett crawled under the covering and sat on the structure, she wondered what it could have been.

"This looks almost like a house," she said to Kendrick. He was taking his shoes and socks off and rolling up the wet edges of his pants.

"It probably was," Kendrick said. Scarlett reached for Esperanza before remembering that she was sleeping with Mara so that it would be easier for her to feed her during the night.

"What do you mean it probably was? We are far from any City. Who could have been living here?"

Kendrick shrugged. "Maybe it's from before there were Cities, when everyone was free." Scarlett remembered exactly what she had heard in History class. The Government had only been around in its current format for, was it twenty-five years now? "Whatever it is, I'm grateful for it," Kendrick added.

"Yes, I agree," Scarlett said. Her stomach rumbled loudly, and Scarlett laughed just a little. "Sorry."

"If your stomach is going to be making noises like that all night, I don't know if I can sleep," Kendrick joked.

Scarlett shrugged. "It's wondering where its evening meal is."

Kendrick placed his shoes and socks to the side and stretched his leg out several times before bringing it back in. "Are you worried about finding the group?" he asked.

Scarlett wished he hadn't asked that question. Of course she was! "Yeah, but Derrico and Mara, they know the forest well. I mean, maybe it takes a day or two, but they should be able to find them, right? And the group would look for us, too, huh?"

Kendrick shrugged, but Scarlett didn't see the small movement of his shoulders.

"What if they left us behind on purpose, because I . . ."

"Because you what?"

"Because I went into the City, even when I wasn't supposed to. They were going to banish me, but then they changed their minds."

"But they wouldn't leave Derrico and Mara and their baby," Kendrick pointed out. Scarlett's mind turned toward them. She remembered the kiss from earlier, and she felt like Kendrick would answer her straightforwardly.

"How come Derrico kissed Mara like she was a baby?"

There was a pause, then Kendrick laughed. He laughed hard enough that Derrico from his tent asked them to keep it quiet. "We don't want the babies to wake up, and Mara is exhausted."

"Sorry, sorry," Kendrick called back. Scarlett frowned at him.

"Stop laughing," she said in a whisper.

"Oh, Scarlett," Kendrick said, his voice also a whisper. He motioned for her to come closer to where he was sprawled on the structure. Scarlett leaned on her side, facing him and supporting herself on one elbow.

"I'm going to tell you something, but I don't want you to get freaked out. Promise?"

Scarlett already felt some nervousness lapping at her. "Um, okay."

"You know how when you're growing up in the training center, you're not allowed to touch?"

"Yes . . ."

"And we Citizens, us regular people, we can?" Scarlett nodded again. "And you know how guards like you never have children? Well, it's because touching is what . . . er, makes those children."

Scarlett's mouth fell open, and she sat straight up. "But . . . what? I don't . . ."

She could feel Kendrick shaking, but keeping his laughter quiet. "Why is it funny? You can't be telling the truth. Because, one male in the compound in City 6, he said that touching wasn't prohibited anymore."

Kendrick turned his head. "Interesting. I'm not sure if he was telling you the truth or not."

"But then . . ." Scarlett looked at her stomach fearfully, trying to recall each time she had touched a male. "But remember when you touched my neck? And then there was that time when . . ." Kendrick opened his mouth to say something, but then closed it as Scarlett continued. "I touched Rhys's hair, and he touched mine. And sometimes . . . I've touched his hand or . . ."

"Anything else?" Kendrick asked.

Scarlett's mind scrambled, trying to think of each time she had broken that sacred rule, wondering if she would have to pay the consequences with an enlarged stomach.

"No, I don't think so. I don't remember. It's not that I was trying to break the rule. It just seemed natural." Scarlett's eyes widened as panic crept in. "And I touched your leg just today and . . ."

"Okay," Kendrick said, reaching out and touching Scarlett's back. She squealed and pushed herself away from him until she was on the other end of the tent. Kendrick was laughing then, and he didn't seem able to stop himself despite Derrico's angry shushing from the other tent.

Kendrick finally stopped as Scarlett stared at him from the corner. "Scarlett," he said, his voice still shaking a little as a smile curled at his lips. "Not that kind of touching."

Her eyebrows scrunched down to the middle of her face, her heart racing. She continuously tried to think of other times she had broken the rule. "Scarlett," Kendrick said. "Come here. I don't want Derrico to break through the tent wall because we are being too loud."

Scarlett staunchly shook her head. Kendrick half-crawled over until he was sitting in the middle of the tent, and she could easily hear his whisper.

"It's not that kind of touching," Kendrick said. "Look, I can't explain it exactly, but you can touch someone's hair or their arm or leg or stomach or . . . well, basically anything. It's just that," Kendrick looked toward the tent wall as Scarlett stared him down. "Well, when you touch a little bit, it makes you want to touch more, and there's a certain kind of touch that can make you have a baby. So, they probably just tell you not to touch at all, because they don't want you to accidentally go too far and then, yeah, someone is pregnant."

Scarlett took a few deep breaths. "What kind of touch?"

"Uh, maybe, I'm not the best person to explain this to you," Kendrick said. He swallowed hard. "Maybe you can ask Mara. She has a baby."

"But I'm asking you," Scarlett pushed. "So tell me. I have to know. I don't want that. I can't do that. I was there when the female brought Esperanza into this world. It was messy and gross, and I can't have that happen to me. I have to avoid it."

Kendrick licked his lips slowly, and Scarlett found herself wondering what it would be like to kiss them. She asked. "Is it kissing? The touch of the lips? That's what makes a child?"

Kendrick shook his head. "No, that's not it." He scratched the back of his head, digging his fingers into his hair. "Scarlett, do you trust me?"

Scarlett swallowed, evaluating his question. "Yes."

"Okay, I wouldn't do anything that would hurt you. Just ask Mara. I don't feel like I can, um, really explain it well." Scarlett didn't like his answer.

"So you promise me that when you touched my neck and I touched your knee, that won't do anything?"

Kendrick nodded fervently. "I promise, Scarlett." He smiled. "Besides, you already have Esperanza to care for. You don't need another one."

Scarlett didn't think his attempt at humor was funny, but she relaxed from her position at the side of the tent and lay down, her stomach on the structure. She crossed her arms and laid her head on them, her eyes facing Kendrick.

"How come no one ever told me this?" she asked. Kendrick lay on his back, looking up at the top of the tent.

"I don't know. I think in the training center, they only gave you the information they wanted you to have, not the information you really needed."

"So, I could reach out and touch you right now, and I wouldn't get pregnant?" Scarlett asked.

"Yes, you could," Kendrick said. "Want to try?"

Scarlett smiled just a little. She moved her hand to his neck, trying to copy the move he had pulled on her back in the City. She tried to remember how he had threaded his fingers through her hair. Kendrick turned to his side and kissed her hand, and Scarlett smiled just a little.

"So, hold on a second," she asked. "You can kiss my hand, and that won't . . . you know?"

Kendrick shook his head. "No, it won't."

Scarlett reached out to feel his hair again. "Wow! Your hair feels just like mine. Rhys's hair was rougher. I mean, it's curly too, and . . ." She noticed that Kendrick looked almost angry. "Sorry, I didn't mean to . . ." She drew her hand away.

"No, it's okay," Kendrick said. "It's just that . . . I don't know. Never mind. We should go to sleep. We are going to be walking a lot tomorrow." Scarlett nodded and tucked her hands between her knees to keep her hands warm. Time to sleep.

CHAPTER 21

The next morning, Scarlett cracked her neck uncomfortably. Her back was aching just above her hips as well. She crawled out from under the tent without looking back at Kendrick. She saw that Derrico was already out. He had scaled a tree and was some five meters up. Scarlett wanted to yell up and ask what he was doing, but she didn't want to scare him into falling either. He appeared to be cutting something from the tree.

Mara came out from her tent and handed Esperanza to Scarlett right away. She took the baby and set about placing her in the childpack. The water was still rushing by, covering her feet, but it wasn't nearly as hurried as it had been the day before.

"She was quite fussy last night," Mara said. "I think even though I'm the one who gives her the milk, she knows you're her real mam."

Scarlett smiled and patted the soft tendrils of brown hair on Esperanza's head. "Don't go making trouble now," Scarlett said. Her stomach rumbled loudly, and she frowned. She didn't want to go any longer without food.

Derrico approached them, his pack in his hands. "Here, it's not the best meal, but it will keep your stomach satisfied and give us energy to catch up with everyone else." He handed them what looked like part of a tree. Scarlett raised her eyebrows and looked at it, confused, as a wet,

133

natural smell hit her nostrils. Everyone else was popping it into their mouths and chewing. Scarlett tentatively bit off a small piece. A flavor that tasted just like it smelled burst into her mouth. She pressed her lips closed to prevent spitting it out. But Kendrick was already laughing at her.

Scarlett tried to frown, but that proved impossible with the mass of bark in her mouth. She swallowed instead, shuddering. "Um, you can have mine," she said, dumping the rest of hers into Mara's hand. She took a few steps away from the group as she pretended to be focused on the child in front of her. She was angry. Why was Kendrick always laughing at her? She almost missed Malak's way of treating her when she proved to not know yet another thing. He would begin giving her all of the information she was missing. Kendrick just laughed as though it was funny that he knew more than her in a lot of areas.

Kendrick came over, and she felt him standing just behind her. She knew it was him, because who else would stand so silently watching her?

"Sorry," he said. "I don't want to make you feel bad."

Scarlett just shrugged and finished folding the tent covering. She stuffed it in the pack and flung the pack over her shoulder. She didn't know what he wanted her to say, and even if she did, she wasn't about to go around saying things just to please him.

Scarlett started up the neverending hill, but Derrico pointed more to the left. "We're going to walk at an angle," he said. "I'm hoping we can catch up more quickly if we move that way. We were heading toward the Government City. Going up this hill is only taking us farther away. I *think* once the storm finished, they would have gone back down toward the City." Derrico looked at each one of them. "That's what I think, but I'm open to a better plan." Everyone was silent as they continued to stare at him. "Okay, then." Derrico extended an arm in the direction he planned to go. "Let's march."

They started going across the hill instead of up it. Scarlett looked all around her. The water had gone down but only a little. "How long will it take the water to go down all the way?"

Derrico looked at Mara for confirmation. "Should be a couple of days. I would suggest we just stay where we are; it really wasn't a bad spot to camp. But I think it's best if we catch up to our group. The longer we are away from them, the more difficult it will be."

Scarlett had to ask. "Has the group ever been separated by a storm like this and some people . . . not made it back?"

Derrico shook his head, which encouraged Scarlett before she realized he was shaking his head in sadness, not in a negative answer. "It has happened. It doesn't have to be a storm that causes it either. In the past five years, we have lost three individuals. One was a child. She was five years old at the time. No one could find her. We sent out groups of people searching for her. We finally found her body, ravaged by a wild animal."

Scarlett hugged Esperanza so hard that the baby squawked in protest.

Mara seemed to understand her feeling. "I know. That is why I keep Moses close all the time. We since established a rule that you always be with someone if you are leaving the main camp, but then, children don't always follow rules." Her eyes fell from Scarlett to Kendrick. "No matter how old they are."

"The other two?" Kendrick prompted Derrico.

"The other two were older and weaker. We were packing up camp to move on as we always do after a short time, and they refused to come with us. They said that they would stay right there. They could live off the land without us as well as with us. So, there they stayed. We circled back around to that spot a few months later, but no one was there. No one to this day knows what happened to them."

Scarlett's stomach clenched as she remembered an old male, older than any individual she had ever seen before approaching her on the Mound. "What did he look like?" she asked, clearing her throat.

Derrico didn't answer right away, and Scarlett couldn't see his face as he was in front. But the look that Mara gave her was strange enough. "He was older," Derrico said. "I can't describe him very well. His hair was gray. He had a beard." The male Scarlett had seen also had a beard, but then again, so did all of the older males in this group.

"Was he wearing . . ." but she realized that her question was irrelevant. Everyone wore the same skins in this group. She wanted to transfer the picture from her mind to Derrico's to ask if it could be the same male. If she knew who he was, it might make her understand better what had happened between her and Rhys.

"Why are you asking?" Mara wondered.

Scarlett pressed her lips together, closing her arms around Esperanza as she had become accustomed to doing. "I met a male before I left the training center. He was old and smelly and . . . old. I just, wondered if it could be the same individual."

Now Derrico was interested. He stopped, his boots sucking further into the mud, and scrutinized Scarlett. "You met an older male. All older males, and females for that matter, are killed once they reach a certain age and level of uselessness, according to the rules of the City." Scarlett's mouth dropped open a little as she turned to Kendrick for confirmation. He nodded, his face grim. "So, he could not be a Citizen, and my understanding is that all guards are young like you."

"He wasn't a Citizen," Scarlett responded. "I know that for the same reasons. He wasn't from the training center. I don't know who he was, but your explanation just there, he being someone from your group, that could make sense. The thing is that he told me I would kill my best friend, and I think I did."

"No, no!" Kendrick interjected. "You didn't kill that male. I saw him alive. You saw him alive. You didn't kill him."

Scarlett wondered why Kendrick was so insistent. Her mind was muddled. She had certainly shot Rhys, which still felt unreal. But she knew it had happened. It didn't make sense unless that elderly male had some sort of power over her. Maybe he saw something in Rhys, a strength to support the Government, and he saw that Scarlett questioned the Government more easily. Was he capable of making her do something? The idea was appealing, so she didn't have to take the blame for what she did. Scarlett shrugged and kept walking forward, passing

Derrico who was still looking at her strangely, like he had a few questions of his own.

The four walked most of the day. Scarlett's legs felt more tired than normal as the mud sucking at them and the water pushing against them made them feel like jelly. But then, she saw something that made her almost collapse with relief. There, in front of them, was a person, a human, a male. The male waved to them and motioned them over. Scarlett picked up the pace just a little, only checking once to make sure Kendrick was keeping up. They had finally caught up with the rest of the Fringe!

CHAPTER 22

The rain had stopped at last. When Rhys emerged from the tent, it felt almost strange not to be assaulted by bullets of water. Rhys took a long sip of the fresh water they had collected using their bottles. It tasted fresh. Malak emerged from the tent next and grabbed his bottle from its place as well. They watched the water rush over their feet.

"Guess it's time to move on," Malak said.

Rhys nodded, his eyes searching the distance in the direction they had been heading. He didn't expect to see anyone or any other hints of where they had gone, but he felt like a clock inside him was ticking, ticking, ticking waiting to complete his mission. He couldn't rest until he did.

Irin stepped out of the tent. He sipped from his bottle of water. "Get up!" he shouted back inside the tent. A frantic scrambling was heard as those inside put on their mud-caked boots and got out of the tent. Irin had everyone moving away from their little camp in less than five minutes. "We're moving, and we're not stopping until we find them," Irin announced. Rhys's strides were long as he walked just a couple of meters away from Irin. His eyes continuously searched the horizon for anything that might give them a clue. After an hour walking up the hill, Rhys began to question if they should continue going in the same direction. Should they try a different route? Either way, he knew with un-shattering confidence that they would find them soon.

A few hours later, they came upon a structure that looked like a dilapidated house. The roof was made from metal which was partially rusted. The rest was a mess of rotten wood.

Rhys pointed to the structure. "They were here. Look at the way the mud is squished on the roof of the building. If they slept here last night and started walking about the same time we did, then they can't be far away."

Irin conceded and continued marching them in the same direction. Rhys found no other signs of Scarlett. If she had left something behind, some little clue, the unforgiving rush of the water would have wiped it away.

Rhys spotted something, a lump on a tree. He almost missed it, but his peripheral vision called to him. Rhys turned toward it without breaking stride. He examined it for a minute before daring to touch it. "Sir," Rhys said, motioning for Irin to come over. "Was this done by animal or human?"

Irin studied the mass of tree pulp, wiped onto the tree in a bulbous formation. It was still wet and smelled fresh. "My supposition," Irin said, turning to Rhys, "is that this was human. I don't see any one of these nearby trees missing bark, so a human got it from another tree, chewed on it for a while, decided they didn't want it, and left it here. Good eyes."

Irin walked around the tree, then approached it from several different angles. "We should change our direction more westward instead of northward. If they wiped their hand on the tree as they were walking by, then that would mean . . . they were going in that direction." Irin pointed ahead of them.

The group turned accordingly and continued marching forward.

"How will we know when we are getting close?" Devon asked. "I mean, I want to be ready."

"You won't be going in," Irin responded, not breaking stride.

"What? I won't be . . ." Devon broke off his answer as though he realized how disrespectful it was. "What's the, uh, plan, Sir?"

"The plan is for Rhys to go in alone. He will meet Scarlett, and pretend to have left the City for her. He'll scout out the camp and bring the information straight back to us." Rhys nodded in recognition of his duty. "Only then will we move in, unless we need backup, in which case, we will wait. You will remain quiet."

Devon nodded. Rhys could tell he wasn't happy with his role, but Rhys didn't care. He was on a mission, and he would succeed.

CHAPTER 23

Scarlett had left Esperanza with Laya. Laya had been so happy to see them again, especially alive, that she had happily taken the baby. Scarlett's head was still spinning from everything that Derrico had told her about the old male who had left the camp. And after having been around Kendrick non-stop for several days, she wanted some distance to consider what the future might hold for her. Scarlett was just walking out of sight of the camp- despite the fact that the elders had told her to always remain in sight- when Ariel ran up to her and threw her arms around Scarlett, squeezing the breath right out of her.

"I'm so glad you're okay. I thought you were going to be lost forever! Aren't you hungry? They're serving the meal now, and I bet you didn't get *anything* to eat."

Scarlett shook her head. "They fed us right when we walked into camp, so I'm actually quite full."

"Where are you going?"

Scarlett took a deep breath. "I just want some time to clear my head." She would usually exercise when she felt like this, but she couldn't just pick up a dead tree and do five reps. "I'll be back soon."

"No!" Ariel protested. "I don't want you to get lost. You're always supposed to be with someone. Remember?"

"Fine, you can come with me," Scarlett said, "but you have to be very quiet." Ariel nodded solemnly. She looked back at where they were serving plates of food, then followed Scarlett until they were beyond the edge of the camp. Scarlett could still hear everyone up there talking and laughing, still in high spirits despite the disaster.

She found a tree that had low-hanging branches and slopped through the pools of water to reach them. "You're going to climb the tree?" Ariel asked.

Scarlett nodded. "I don't want to get my bottom wet."

Ariel giggled. "Yeah, me neither. I've never been good at climbing though."

"Well, come on, I'll teach you. It's not hard." Scarlett wasn't planning on going very high. She placed her foot on the lowest branch and reached for a higher one, lifting herself just under a meter off the ground. She grabbed another branch and pulled herself up. This branch was wide enough to sit on comfortably, so Scarlett plopped down and waited for Ariel to copy her maneuvers. Ariel splashed around in the water for a few minutes, finally getting up the nerve to try. She reached her hands up, but her arms were just too short to reach the branch Scarlett had grabbed.

"Try that smaller one, to your left," Scarlett shouted down. Ariel tried it. The branch groaned a little but held. Soon, Ariel was sitting on the wide branch next to Scarlett. She hugged the trunk and looked at Scarlett a bit fearfully.

"One time I climbed a tree when I was five years old. I fell down and broke my arm."

Scarlett grimaced. "Well, maybe I shouldn't have brought you up here," she said.

Ariel shook her head. "It's okay."

"Sh!" Scarlett hushed, her eyes focused on a lone figure slopping through the slow-moving river. The figure was dressed completely in blue. Scarlett froze and stared at the figure, her eyes straining to make out the details. Familiar brown curls covered his head, and Scarlett knew. She *knew* it was Rhys. She gave a little squeal before falling off the tree branch. Her squeal of excitement turned into a groan of pain. The water softened her fall, but the splash stung. She took a deep breath.

"Are you okay?" Ariel shouted down even though she wasn't higher than a meter and a half.

Scarlett didn't answer her. She just rushed as much as she could through the water to the blue figure. Ariel called back from the tree.

"I don't think I can get down by myself. Can you help me?" Scarlett didn't turn around. She kept wading forward. Then, Rhys was there in front of her, only a few meters away.

"Rhys!" she said, not believing what her eyes were showing her. "I knew it! I knew you were alive, and I knew you would come. How did you find us? How did you survive the storm? Ohmygov, I bet you're hungry. Come on!"

Rhys smiled at her. His smile looked different, but Scarlett could understand the different emotions he must be feeling. Who knew what stories the Whites had been feeding him about her?

"Did you see my message? Is that how you knew?" Rhys nodded. Scarlett reached down to touch his hand then retracted her own. Better not to test the limits. "Come on. They've got food for everyone. It's not hot, because it's hard to make a fire right now, but you know, food is food." She pointed in the direction of the camp.

"Wait," Rhys finally spoke. "I don't want to go up there."

"Why not?"

Scarlett heard Ariel asking questions from her perch in the tree, but she didn't want to interrupt Rhys to answer them.

Rhys shrugged then pointed down at his uniform. "I'm a Blue. I'm from the City. I don't think they'll . . ."

"They will! They're so nice," Scarlett responded. "They accepted me and Kendrick and . . ."

"Kendrick is here? The male with the injured leg?" Rhys asked.

Scarlett nodded. "I was going back to get you to come with us, and I kind of ran into him, and he wanted to come, so here we are." Scarlett took a deep breath. "So, anyway, are you okay? How did you find us?"

"Want to sit and talk?" Rhys asked. Scarlett looked around. The only dry places to sit were in the trees, and Scarlett was soaked already from her little fall.

She didn't care. She just wanted to hear all about how he had gotten out of the City and if anyone would be looking for him. She looked back at the tree where Ariel was still clinging to the trunk. "Oh, maybe I should help her." Rhys caught sight of Ariel's dark brown hair surrounding her fawn-colored clothing.

"Who is that?"

Scarlett studied his alarmed face. "It's Ariel. She's a sweet little female. You'll see. Did you want to talk in private?"

Rhys nodded.

"Okay, well, let me at least get her down from the tree. Then, you and I can talk."

"But if you get her down, won't she just tell everyone here that I've come?"

Scarlett shrugged. "I don't know. Why does it matter?"

Rhys copied her shrug. "I, just, well, you say it'll be okay, but I'm worried that they won't want me here. I think it's better if no one knows. I just want to talk to you."

"Well, I can't leave her up there. I'll make her promise not to tell." Rhys shifted back and forth in the calf-deep water, which Scarlett took as an approval of her plan. She ran back to Ariel, not caring that she was splashing muddy water up her back. She half-climbed the tree, and Ariel reached for her. Even though she was nine years old, she was small. Scarlett was able to support her weight and set her on the ground with a small splash.

"Who's that?" Ariel immediately asked.

Scarlett looked Ariel right in the eyes. "Ariel, this is a male from the City I used to live in. I need to talk to him."

"About what?"

"About how he got here. And . . . we don't want anyone to know he's here yet, okay? I didn't want to leave you stuck in the tree, so I helped you. Now, you need to help me. You have to be quiet and not say any-thing about him. Promise?"

Ariel nodded solemnly. "I won't tell. But I won't get in trouble, right?"

"No way. We'll tell everyone about him, but we have to wait until the right time, like a surprise, you know?"

"Ooh! Okay, I won't tell." Ariel turned toward the group. "But you have to stay safe. You can't go wandering away again, okay?"

Scarlett smiled and patted Ariel's shoulder. "Of course. Go on now. We'll come soon." Ariel scurried to the Fringe, bending down to scoop something out of the water on her way. Scarlett motioned Rhys over, and they settled onto the larger tree branch.

"So?" Scarlett asked expectantly. She was glad to see Rhys's smile appear more normal once they were alone.

"So . . . how did you get here?" Rhys asked.

"No, no, I asked you first. You tell me, then I'll answer anything you want."

"Oh, yeah, okay. Well, I saw your note, and I thought you were dead." Rhys pressed his hands together as though he had caught a firefly and didn't want to let it escape. "So, of course, I had to come after you."

"But we must have walked twenty, thirty kilometers, I don't know. And the rain! How did you make it? We got lucky finding places to sleep, but you wouldn't have even had a covering."

Rhys pointed to the small pack of supplies on his back. "I got these before I left. I didn't know if you would be hurt, so I have this." Rhys pulled out some basic medicine as well as some bandages.

"Oh, that's excellent! I'm sure someone will need to use these. In fact, Kendrick might be able to use it for his knee. I was worried with it getting so wet." Scarlett reached for it, but Rhys pulled it back.

"What?"

"I don't want them to use it. It's for you. No one else. Are you hurt anywhere?"

"No," Scarlett examined her knee that she had hit when falling out of the tree a few minutes before. "I'm fine. But why wouldn't you want to give it to someone if they really need it?"

"Because, maybe you don't need it right now, but you might need it in a week or in a month. It's better to save it." Rhys stashed them in his bag again. Scarlett studied him. He wasn't acting like normal, but maybe it was just because he hadn't met these people yet. Scarlett had been skeptical at first too.

"Okay, well, once you meet everybody, it will be fine."

"Yeah, yeah," Rhys brushed it off like he wasn't worried at all. Scarlett tried to see into his brown eyes, but he seemed distracted by the flowing water beneath them. "So, how has it been for you? I mean, does everyone seem nice?"

"Yes," Scarlett nodded enthusiastically. She thought of some of the elders she didn't like as much and paused her nod. "Yes, they are. You saw the small female, and . . ." Scarlett suddenly remembered what she had heard. "Rhys, remember that male on the Mound who predicted the future?"

Rhys nodded slowly, looking at her as though he wasn't exactly sure if he remembered.

"So, I found out that there was a male that lived here with the Fringe." Rhys leaned in and watched Scarlett intently. "And he and a female decided not to move on with the Fringe when they packed up camp to leave. The Fringe moves around every couple of weeks, at least that's what they've told me. So, I guess this time, they decided not to go with them. I don't know why. But maybe the male could have been him. I don't know a lot about him, except that he was old. I need to ask Derrico for more details."

"Derrico?"

"Yeah, he's Mara's husband." Scarlett saw Rhys about to ask who Mara was. "She's a female who takes care of Esperanza. Esperanza is . . . Rhys, you just have to come meet everyone. Look, I don't even know everyone yet. But that's okay. The ones I do know are nice, and you'll have a place to stay here."

Rhys swung his legs back and forth. "How many people live here?"

"I don't know," Scarlett thought for a minute. "Why? You've never been the shy type."

"I don't know," Rhys shrugged. The way he was avoiding eye contact made Scarlett wonder if he was hiding something.

"Come on, Rhys. Tell me the truth." She spoke sternly. "Why are you acting so strange?"

"I'm not acting strange," Rhys responded. "This is me. You know, the new revived me, after you shot me."

Scarlett's body went rigid as though his words were bullets striking her. "I didn't do . . . I didn't *mean* to do that. It was a complete accident. Rhys, they told me you were dead! They sentenced me to be executed, because I killed you. So if I didn't kill you, then why did they want me to die?"

Rhys looked at Scarlett and shrugged. "I was told that my heart actually stopped once. So I kind of died?"

Scarlett's eyebrows rose then she shook her head. "No way. They lied to me. They said you had already been buried, so whether your heart stopped for a few seconds or not, you weren't buried. And if they lied to me, then maybe they lied to you, too. Maybe . . ."

Rhys wasn't saying anything, but Scarlett could tell he wasn't sure he believed her. "Tell me," she said. "Tell me what you're thinking."

"I just wonder if someone could have followed me from the City," he said. Scarlett immediately scanned the forest, but she didn't see anything other than dead leaves floating on the water which always rushed downward, downward. Scarlett wondered when they would ever see dry ground again.

"Why? Why do you think that?"

Rhys shrugged. "Maybe I'm just being paranoid, but I felt like someone was watching me when I escaped."

"How did you escape?"

"I cut through the side of the fence near the forest."

"With what?"

"I lost the knife in the storm. It somehow floated out of my pack while I was sleeping. My guess is the water has taken it kilometers away from here now."

"Okay, so you felt like someone was watching you. Maybe they know you came after me, because they know I escaped from their cell. I kept thinking someone would come find me or catch me when I entered the City, but they didn't. I think maybe they don't care as long as we aren't ruining the life they have going in the City. Can you believe we're going to see another City? We're going to the Government City. I can't wait to see it . . ."

Rhys held up a hand. "I'm not trying to be rude, but I have to ask. Is there any sort of security system? I don't know, some guarantee that someone from the City won't sneak up on us while we're sleeping?"

Scarlett nodded. "Yes, there are watchers. They stand a bit away from the camp and keep watch. No one would come sneaking up on us. Trust me, I tried to sneak past them once, and it didn't work."

"What sort of weapons do they have?"

"What? Why?"

"I mean, no offense, but I'm not going to feel very safe if they have a stick to protect us and the Whites come in with guns."

Scarlett shrugged. "You can ask them. I don't think they have guns though, but that doesn't bother me. I don't think the Whites or whoever would be expecting them. They're good at camouflaging."

Rhys didn't seem to have any more questions, so they sat in silence for a few minutes. The sky started to move from a clouded duskiness to full on darkness.

"We should go to the camp now," Scarlett urged. Rhys didn't say anything, so Scarlett started climbing down the tree, assuming he would follow her. Her feet splashed into the water again, and she was surprised at the change in temperature. It seemed a lot colder than it had before. "Aren't you coming?" she called back up to him. He hadn't moved.

"Maybe I should just sleep here," Rhys said. "I'm comfortable enough. We can do the whole 'meet the group' thing in the morning."

"No," Scarlett shook her head staunchly. "I don't know why you're being weird, but we're definitely not waiting until tomorrow. Come on!" She didn't have any patience for weird Rhys. She was tired, and she wanted him to meet Esperanza. She wanted to tell him about Phan and how she was right about the baby.

CHAPTER 24

Scarlett marched into the camp dragging Rhys after her. She didn't understand why he was so reluctant. He had been acting strangely, and Scarlett had been trying to ignore it. But sleeping in a tree without meeting anyone? That was too strange to let pass.

Some of the group had already found places to set up their coverings. Some were sleeping in the crooks of trees. Others had set up a tent on some crumbly cement pillars. Scarlett squinted in the fading light. She couldn't see Laya, which was who she wanted to find, or Kendrick, whom she wouldn't mind finding. Rhys's suit drew some attention though as soon as they got to the edge of the group. A few children gathered around them, Ariel not included, and started asking questions.

"Where'd you get those strange clothes?"

"Your pack looks funny."

"I never saw you before."

Scarlett tried to shoo them away, but they quickly brought the attention of the adults to their circle of questions. Scarlett smiled awkwardly as Laya came over, Esperanza in her arms. She fixed Scarlett with a steady look, her eyes briefly surveying Rhys. Rhys leaned close to Scarlett's ear.

"See, this is why I didn't want to come into camp yet."

But, he was there, and they couldn't change that.

Laya grabbed Scarlett's arm. Her grip was tight, and Scarlett tripped through the water after Laya. Rhys automatically followed. She led them to a tent that was set up on a platform of tree branches. Laya motioned for them to go inside.

Scarlett crawled in, the branches moving under her weight. To her surprise, she didn't see any elders looking at her with scrutinizing looks. The tent was empty. Rhys came in and sat by her side. Laya sat in the doorway, Esperanza on her lap.

"Scarlett, would you care to explain how this guard from the City entered our camp?"

Scarlett could tell that Laya wasn't nearly as understanding as she had been when Scarlett first entered the camp. "I left him a note in the City," Scarlett said. "He found it, and he came to find me."

"And who else?" Laya asked Rhys.

He shook his head. "No one else."

Laya cocked her head at him. Scarlett hurried to smooth everything over. "He already told me all about it. He stole this pack, and it had enough stuff to get him this far. We had to take tracking classes at the training center, so he got . . ."

"Thank you, Scarlett, but I would like to ask *him* a few questions." Laya fixed her eyes on Rhys. "First, what's your name?"

"Rhys," Rhys smiled. "Nice to meet you."

"I'm Laya," Laya responded. She brushed the loose gray wisps from her face and back toward her horsetail. "Tell me, Rhys, why did you leave the City?"

"I needed to find Scarlett," Rhys responded. Scarlett smiled just a little, but remained quiet. She wondered why Laya was just questioning Rhys instead of all of the elders doing it like they had before.

"Why?" Laya seemed to not like Rhys, and Scarlett didn't understand why.

"Because . . . because . . ." Rhys faltered for a moment. "I had to know that it was her. I thought she was dead, so . . . when I saw the message, I knew I was going to wonder about her forever unless I went after her."

"You can't return to the Cities now. Ever."

"I know," Rhys nodded. "I don't want what they have to offer."

Scarlett's eyebrows went up, and something bloomed in her, some sort of happiness. She felt like Rhys being there finally made her complete. She didn't have to be looking over her shoulder anymore, wondering what if.

"Why not?" Laya pressed.

Rhys shrugged. He didn't give an answer, but looked at Scarlett. Scarlett smiled at him. "Laya, you were so welcoming to me when I came, after understanding that I had escaped from the City. I want to show him the camp and how we live and Esperanza," Scarlett pointed to the sleeping child.

"How about you two sleep here for the night?" Laya suggested. "Do you have something to sleep on?" she asked Rhys.

Rhys took his pack off his shoulder. "Yes, in here."

"Okay, let's talk in the morning."

"But what about our evening meal?" Scarlett protested.

"Oh, yes!" Laya looked behind her, outside of the tent. "I'll bring it to you shortly. Wait here, will you?" She handed Esperanza to Scarlett, and they heard her hop off the platform and slosh away.

"She doesn't seem very friendly. Is everyone like her?"

Scarlett shook her head. "No, and she's not normally like that. I guess there have been too many new faces around here. First Esperanza, then a few days later me, then I bring both Kendrick and you. They aren't used to so many people leaving the City. Why would you? You wouldn't want to leave the City to die alone in the forest."

"Unless you find this group," Rhys said.

"Right, but what are the chances of that unless you know where you're going? I don't think I would have found this group if one of their watchers hadn't found me wandering around lost. In fact, I . . ." Scarlett didn't want to admit that she had been about to turn Phan in. "I had no idea where I was going," she tried to finish smoothly. But when she looked at Rhys, he was focused on Esperanza.

"Where did the small female come from?" Rhys asked. He looked like he was trying to remember something that was just stored too far for him to be able to grab.

Scarlett smiled down at Esperanza's pouty lower lip as she snoozed. "This is Esperanza. But you might recognize her as the child I helped deliver, with Malak, of course."

Rhys's eyes widened. "What? She's from the City? You must tell me how you did it. You escaped your cell, grabbed a child who was hidden in the compound, and made it out here?"

Scarlett shook her head. "No, I didn't take Esperanza. Phan was actually in charge of that."

"Phan?" Rhys shook his head. "I don't believe you. Phan executed a plan *against* the Government?"

"I know!" Scarlett joined in his disbelief. "I never would have thought so either. He started to tell me some things before, you know, I shot you and we were separated and everything. He . . ." Laya leaned into the tent and placed two cold turkey legs in front of them. The meat was a few days old and needed to be eaten soon.

"There's no making fires, so you'll have to eat it cold. You both okay sleeping in here?" They nodded. "I'll come back and get Esperanza for her feeding soon."

They were alone again. Rhys nodded toward Scarlett to continue, but she was looking at the turkey leg. She worked at it with her teeth, focusing on it intensely.

"Isn't it strange to know the Cities are behind us forever?" Scarlett finally asked.

Rhys shrugged. "I guess."

"It's scary, but exciting at the same time. I wish . . . I wish I could bring Esperanza's real mother here, so she could know her. But I know she was executed." Scarlett seemed to perk up. "Though they lied about you being dead, so I guess anything is a possibility."

Rhys shook his head. "No, I saw her executed."

Scarlett felt guilt seep through her. She focused her attention on the meat and didn't say anything else as she tried to comprehend what had happened that day. A smile teased her lips as she imagined Kendrick and Rhys meeting, except this time, they wouldn't be enemies. They would be working together for the same goal. Once Scarlett finished eating, she felt sleepy.

"I'm going to find Laya," she said. "I'll be right back. I'm so tired."

"Okay, see you soon," Rhys said. "Oh, is there a designated bathroom area? You know?"

"Down current," Scarlett said. "On that side of the camp."

Scarlett started to climb off the platform, bracing herself for the water, when she noticed one of the watchers a few tents over looking directly at her. It looked like the same one who had been her introduction to the camp. Scarlett smiled awkwardly then scanned the darkening camp for Laya or Mara. Even Derrico could help point her in the right direction. Esperanza woke and started fussing.

"Hold on," Scarlett said. "You've got to learn a little patience, female."

Scarlett continued walking between tents. Now, she saw the same watcher again, focusing on her. Somehow, he had gotten in front of her.

"Where are you going?" he asked, slopping through the water to get closer.

"I'm trying to find Laya or Mara. Have you seen them?"

The watcher shook his head. "No. I'll take the child to Mara, however. You can go back to the tent."

"Why do you want me to go back to the tent?" Scarlett asked, clutching Esperanza a little closer. The watcher reached for the child, but Scarlett shook her head. "I'll take her myself. I'm not trying to cause any trouble, and I won't be leaving the camp." Scarlett rolled her eyes. If the elders didn't trust her, then why should she trust them? Scarlett spotted Derrico and hurried over to him, feeling the watcher's eyes on her back.

"Hi, where is Mara?"

"She's in that tent over there. I'm sure Esperanza must be hungry again, huh? Moses is finally starting to sleep through the night, but I don't think Esperanza is nearly ready." Scarlett smiled and deposited the baby in his arms.

Relieved of her burden, she squished her way back to the tent and took off her boots. She rubbed her feet with her dry shirt sleeve, drying them and getting the feeling back in them. While she waited for Rhys to return from the bathroom, she lay down on the mat. She stared up at the top of the tent, wondering where Kendrick was sleeping. She had meant to look for him, too, but exhaustion was kicking in. She was ready for a long sleep.

Scarlett turned her eyes to the entrance, waiting for Rhys to pop through, but her eyes shut for the final time before he returned. Exhaustion slowly took over.

Rhys trekked through the water, resisting the urge to run. His timepiece told him he would be late for their meeting, but he couldn't have just left Scarlett at any time. He had to keep her from becoming suspicious.

Rhys was having trouble seeing the trees in the dark, but he couldn't take out his torch. He had no idea where the watchers were located, or if they were even out that night. Rhys remembered the mark he had left a quarter hour before seeing Scarlett for the first time. Now, he couldn't find it. Would Scarlett start to look for him when he didn't come back right away?

Rhys saw something move between two trees. He hurried toward the movement. Marse and Irin were hidden behind the copse.

"I'm here," Rhys took a couple of deep breaths. "I'm not sure how much time we have. Scarlett might come looking for me soon."

"You took enough time already," Irin said. "We were beginning to wonder if the . . . if you had decided not to come back."

Rhys frowned and shook his head as Irin handed him a drink of water and his nightly pill. Rhys swallowed the pill quickly. Irin started to ask him a question about his head and if he felt anything strange, but Rhys cut him off, surprised at his own boldness.

"I think there's about a hundred people in this camp. Some are called watchers, and they stay outside the camp at night to see if any threat is coming. I don't know if anyone is out tonight or how many watchers they have. They don't have any guns, but some pretty nasty knives.

Some in the camp are children and older males and females, so they wouldn't count in a fight."

"How many are under six or seven years old?" Irin asked.

Rhys tried to make his best guess. "I would say at least ten. There seem to be a lot of children. It was hard to get Scarlett to answer my questions. Phan! She said that Phan helped the baby escape."

"The baby. What baby?"

"There was a baby behind the kitchen. Remember . . ." Rhys pieced the events together as best he could. As soon as he tried to grasp at them, they were gone. "I can't remember. Oh, why is it so hard?" He wanted to curse or stomp his foot. He settled for balling his hands into fists instead, his nails biting into his palms.

"We'll figure it out," Irin said. He placed a hand on Rhys's shoulder. "Remain calm. Emotion will only make it harder to recall. Let's go back to what you said about Phan. What did Scarlett say about him? Don't try to remember anything else."

"She said that Phan helped the baby escape. That he organized it. I was going to ask her more, but then the food arrived."

"Food arrived? People in the camp saw you?"

Rhys nodded. "It couldn't be avoided. Scarlett practically dragged me into the camp. I couldn't just turn around and march into the forest again. I'm sorry." Rhys hung his head.

Irin shook his head. "You did well. How are they surviving with the storm?"

"They've built some platforms. There are some concrete blocks from what looks like another old-timey house. Everyone is up. They have covers. They sleep in family groups just like the Citizens do."

"Excellent. Did you speak with any of them directly?"

"Yes, one female asked me a lot of questions."

"A young female?"

"No, an older female. She seemed to be in charge, not in charge, but at least someone with seniority. She wanted us to stay in the tent, but you can see that I got out. I don't know if they'll start to search for me if I don't get back soon."

Irin studied him. "They're expecting you back, because they think you left the City for good."

"Yes," Rhys confirmed.

Irin sighed and looked at his timepiece, causing Rhys to check his as well. "You go back," Irin said. "Learn more if you can. I will call for backup. We won't be able to take them with the group we have right now. Is there any chance you can get Scarlett alone, away from the camp?"

Rhys gave a shrug-nod. "Maybe. I will try. I could grab her and bring her out, but if I don't wait for the right moment, she might protest. I don't know how others would react as she seems to know a few in the camp. Oh, and the injured male is in the camp. I haven't seen him, but Scarlett confirmed that she helped him leave the City."

"We need to take him alive," Irin said. "We will use him as an example to the other Citizens. Rhys, go back in. Try to get Scarlett away from the camp. She is our main target. We will keep someone here at all times. If they are this far from the camp, I think we would be able to knock them out without making any noise. If you can get the injured male to come with her, excellent. But, he's not the most important. I will connect with the City, and we should have back-up by tomorrow night." Then, Irin smiled. The look was so unfamiliar that Rhys wondered if he might have eaten too many of those canned beans.

"Keep it up."

Rhys nodded to Marse and saluted Irin, with three fingers over his heart. Then, he turned and jogged back toward the camp, his shoes kicking drops of muddy water on the back of his Blue suit.

CHAPTER 25

When Scarlett awoke the next morning, she smiled upon seeing Rhys asleep between her and the tent flap. He was stretched out straight as a board, sleeping on his back. Scarlett sat up and stretched slowly, giving herself time to crack each of the bones in her neck. Rhys woke up at the popping noise, his eyes flicking open and staring at her. Scarlett gave a little wave before cracking each of her fingers, too.

"You took so long last night," she said. "I wasn't sure if you got lost or what."

Rhys sat up and yawned. "Nope, just needed a little while. What do you eat for the morning meal?"

"You are obsessed with food," Scarlett shook her head, scooting to the edge of the platform and putting on her still-damp boots. She shuddered, sticking her feet into them.

When Scarlett pulled the tent flap back, she saw that the water had gone down a lot during the night. Now, she barely made a splash as she jumped off the platform onto the ground. The mud sucked at her boots, and it didn't appear that any grass had been left in place. Scarlett squished over to the tent where she knew Mara was sleeping. She pulled back the flap to see if Mara was ready for her to take Esperanza.

What she saw stirred something in her stomach, and she wasn't quite sure what to call it. Derrico and Mara were curled up together, Moses

158

and Esperanza each on a small rug, rolled so that they could not escape. Derrico's hand was on Mara's arm, and they were both sound asleep. Scarlett quickly let the flap drop, her cheeks reddening. She scanned the few individuals moving between the tents.

As she wandered among them, everyone greeted her with a cheery "good morning." Scarlett saw Kendrick leaning against a tree on the edge of camp. She hurried over to him, coming up from behind with a little "boo." Kendrick jumped, grunted, and landed on his good leg. "Oh, hey," he said. "Didn't see you last night. Is everything okay? You kind of disappeared."

"Yes," Scarlett couldn't contain the smile spreading across her face. "Sorry about that. You'll never guess what happened last night."

Kendrick smiled. "Esperanza took her first step?"

"What? No! She's way too young for that."

"I know, but I have no idea why you would be so happy unless it has something to do with her. You always smile at her the most."

"Really?" Scarlett tried to think about that. When did she feel happiest? Well, no matter what her answer yesterday might have been, she knew that it had changed with Rhys's arrival.

Scarlett heard some splashing behind her and saw Rhys approaching them. Kendrick's face fell immediately. "What is he doing here?" Kendrick asked.

"That's what I was trying to tell you," Scarlett said, smiling at Rhys. "Rhys came last night. He found us all the way from the City."

Kendrick made a grunting, harrumphing noise as Rhys reached them.

"Good morning," Rhys said, yawning again.

Kendrick stared at him and his Blue suit. "What are you doing here?"

Rhys finished his extraordinarily long yawn. "I'm here because Scarlett left me a message telling me how to find her. And she's my best friend. I couldn't just *not* come."

Kendrick continued to stare at him. Scarlett glanced back and forth between the two. "So, this is Kendrick. Kendrick, this is Rhys. Now you two can officially meet. It's weird, huh? It used to be guard and Citizen, and now, we're all the same." The two males continued to eye each other.

"How were you able to find us?" Kendrick asked. "I mean, we walked pretty far and through a storm. That storm was no joke." Kendrick looked down at the few centimeters of water still surrounding their shoes.

Rhys shrugged and shook his head as if he couldn't believe his own brilliance. "I managed. We received a lot of training in the training center. That's what it's for, after all."

Kendrick stared at Rhys's uniform. "When are you going to get rid of that thing?"

Rhys looked back at the camp. "What else am I going to wear? It's not like I brought a change of clothes with me."

"I'm sure they could find you something more camouflaged. That Blue would be easy for someone to spot from far off." Kendrick gazed into the forest as though someone might be watching them from among the trees. "Unless you want to be spotted."

"What do you mean?" Scarlett cut in.

Kendrick remained quiet, letting Scarlett figure out what he meant on her own. Scarlett looked at the ground, not sure what to say, now that two of the most important people in her life were together. "So, are you ready for the morning meal? They're probably about to serve it."

"Sure," Rhys agreed. "I'm always ready to eat." Everyone turned back to face the camp, and Scarlett slowed her pace so that Kendrick could easily keep up.

"How long are you staying?" Kendrick asked casually as though they were discussing the possibility of a windy day.

"What?" Rhys asked. "Isn't the point of this group that we can stay here forever?"

"Sure, sure," Kendrick said. "You can, I'm just wondering if that's your plan."

"Where else would I go?"

"Kendrick," Scarlett said. "Why are you being so rude? Just say what you want to say. I feel like you don't like Rhys, but I don't know why.

He's not a guard anymore. Just because he has the uniform, that doesn't mean anything."

Kendrick stopped and folded his arms. Rhys and Scarlett looked at him. Scarlett saw anger in his eyes. Had he met Rhys another time, other than when Rhys had come into the alley and found them touching? Had Rhys done something to Kendrick that Scarlett didn't know about?

"Did you come alone?" Kendrick asked Rhys. Rhys stared him in the eye, matching his posture with his legs spread and his arms crossed.

"I came alone, and what kind of question is that? What are you implying?"

"I'm implying that you're not trustworthy. Scarlett? She showed sympathy from the beginning. You? You're the one who turned in a little kid who was lifting rotten fruit just to show you could."

Rhys scoffed, but Kendrick wasn't done.

"You have always been quick to turn people in, report to the Government, and I don't know the whole story, but you did something to make Scarlett point her gun at you and . . ."

Rhys didn't have the patience for that. "Kendrick," he spat the name. "I suggest you shut up if you don't know what you're talking about. You've never been a guard, and you will *never* have the honor of wearing this color." Rhys pulled at his suit. "You think you know so much, but what you know is nothing in comparison with those of us who spent our lives training."

Kendrick stepped up to Rhys. They were about the same height, but Kendrick's body was bulkier. He took a deep breath, staring into Rhys's eyes. "The *honor* of wearing your Blue uniform. Someone speaking like that doesn't sound like they've given up their allegiance to the Government. Sounds like you're still working for them, and if you are and you're here, then that can only mean you're trying to cause trouble. What's your goal? Kill Scarlett while she's sleeping? Attack . . ."

"No! Kendrick! Don't say that! Rhys would never do that. I shot him by accident, and he knows that."

Kendrick shrugged, unusually calm. "Fine, Scarlett. I'm done with this." Kendrick turned and walked to where they were dividing the food for breakfast. Scarlett stayed beside Rhys. She looked up into his brown eyes, searching for something to negate what he had said. Did he still think of his Blue uniform as an honor? Scarlett swallowed. She knew that moving into the camp and becoming part of the Fringe was a process. All of their training didn't disappear overnight.

Scarlett grabbed Rhys's hand. He seemed surprised at her touch, looking fixedly at where their light and dark skin interlocked. "I can leave," he said suddenly, pulling his hand out of hers. "It's fine. Whatever. I don't have to be here. I'm not trying to make trouble."

Rhys took a step back from her, farther toward the forest.

Scarlett immediately shook her head. "No, why would you do that? Where would you go?"

"I would find a place to go. Don't worry about me." Rhys's eyes suddenly lit up. "You could come with me. Why don't we? You and me. We don't need them to cook for us. We could go wherever we wanted. We could sneak into the Cities if we wanted or stay away from them completely. Scarlett, why not?"

She always smiled when she looked at him. She couldn't help it, and he had this little-male energy about him. She let out a breath of air as if with it, she could let go of all her worries. Leave, go away, really have no one telling them what to do . . . it could work. Except, Esperanza was here. Kendrick was here. Ariel was here. Mara and Derrico were here. And even though she had only known them a week, she already felt close to them. Why leave with Rhys when they could both stay here?

"It takes some time to adjust," she said. "But I think you would love it here. There are so many people, people I haven't even met yet. But I know that you would fit in here."

Scarlett felt something hard in her stomach when Rhys's face fell. "I don't understand how you can care more about them than you do about me. You've known me five years, and you've only known them a few days. But, it's your decision." Rhys took another step backward.

"You shouldn't go either," Scarlett said, stepping forward to match his step backward. "Why? You want to live and die alone? People . . . I've found that people are what make the difference in a life filled with love and happiness and just a life where you follow orders. These people I've met, they . . . I can't explain it. But I don't want to go."

"You can make your own decision," Rhys said. "But you can't make mine."

Scarlett frowned. She didn't like the way Rhys kept looking at the forest like it had his back when she was the one who had always stood by him. "Fine, you're right. But I think you should at least try it for one day. I mean, you have to give them a chance. Ignore Kendrick. Get to know some other people. Derrico, you would like him. Come on, let's go meet him now."

Rhys hesitated. "Fine, one day. But after that, I'm gone."

"No, that's not how it works. After one day, you reevaluate."

Rhys pursed his lips in that frustratingly noncommittal way he had. Even if he did seem strange or different, at least there were still some things that were familiar about him. He hadn't changed completely. Scarlett realized that in all of their talking the evening before, she had not asked him a lot about when he was shot. And if he hated her at all.

Scarlett led Rhys over to the ring of people receiving their morning meal. She took the meal and frowned at it. She recognized the tree mushrooms they had had before. She had been cautious of them at first; now, she didn't mind their strange taste so much. But the other part of the meal appeared to be meat. The bones were so small that she wasn't sure what type of animal they could have come from.

Rhys's bright uniform immediately drew attention. Ariel sidled over, already stuffing her mouth with the food. "So, I guess I don't have to keep him a secret anymore?"

Scarlett shook her head. "Nope, he's here to stay, so you can tell anyone you want."

"But now there's no fun in telling, because everyone's already seen him."

"Well, you can tell them that you saw him first." Ariel finished cleaning the bone and threw it in the standing water at their feet.

"So, how come you left the City?" she asked.

Rhys nodded toward Scarlett. "Because she told me where she had gone. She couldn't stay in the City any longer, so if I wanted to stay with my best friend, then I had to come out here."

"Why couldn't you stay in the City?" Ariel asked Scarlett. Scarlett hadn't exactly gone around telling this part of her story to everyone. The people here just automatically assumed that everyone must want to leave the City because it was a terrible place where no one would want to live, of course.

"The people supporting the Government accused me of betraying them," she finally answered. She hoped that Rhys would understand that the look in her eyes meant he shouldn't add anything to that story.

"Oh, did you ever go to the Government City?" Ariel asked, her eyes wide. "I never even saw a City, but I heard that the Government City has buildings that are three floors high! And that everyone there has water that comes out of the walls, and there's lights on the ceilings and everything."

"Well, that's the way it was in the training center where I grew up. I would assume the Government City would have those things as well."

"Whoa! You've seen that before? I can't believe you never told me this!" Ariel was hopping back and forth from one foot to the other.

Scarlett shrugged. "I guess I never thought about the fact that you had never seen it. For me, it was normal, and this is the new stuff," she pointed at the cold meat in her bowl. "What is this anyway?"

"It's quail," Ariel responded matter-of-factly. "You didn't recognize it?"

"I don't think I've ever had quail before," Scarlett squinted at it. She didn't think she was a picky eater, but it didn't look very appetizing. Rhys eyed the meat, but didn't say anything.

"It's so yummy!" Ariel twirled around, her empty bowl spinning with her. "I'll eat it." Then, without waiting for an invitation, she plucked the meat out of Scarlett's bowl and popped it into her mouth, sucking the last morsels off the bones. Derrico came over, holding Esperanza, and Scarlett took the child immediately, handing her now-emptied bowl over to Rhys.

"Welcome!" Derrico said, shaking hands with Rhys. Rhys tried to reach out and grab his hand, but the two bowls weren't balanced well. He moved his other hand to try to keep hold of the bowl, but it toppled into the water and started a slow float downhill. Ariel dove after it dramatically, making everyone laugh. It seemed to get rid of the tenseness in the air.

Rhys finally shook Derrico's waiting hand. "I hear that you and Scarlett worked together in the City."

Rhys nodded.

"I actually have a few questions about some things. I don't know if you would mind discussing them, just about how the City works and the guards and rounds and whatnot." Scarlett watched as Derrico pulled Rhys aside. She wondered why he hadn't asked her questions about who was on what shift and what weapons they had. They had been together non-stop for several days. But as Scarlett watched, Rhys grew increasingly more terse. He finally stopped answering with a complaint of a headache.

"We can talk more about this later," Rhys said. "I don't know if it's the change in diet or in routine, but my head is throbbing." Derrico nodded and stepped aside to let Rhys return to the tent he had shared with Scarlett the night before. Scarlett hurried after him, but Kendrick intercepted her.

"Hey," he said.

Scarlett glanced at the tent where Rhys had already climbed inside. "What?" she asked exasperated.

"I'm going to tell the elders unless you do it first."

"Tell them what?"

"That he's not here for you. He's here on behalf of the City. He's here to spy on us."

Scarlett rolled her eyes. "He . . ."

"No, I'm not finished," Kendrick said. "You saw the way he was all too happy to answer Derrico's questions until it started to get too personal. He didn't want to give away any information that might help *us* infiltrate the Cities. He's still looking out for them. You can't deny it, and if you do, then you're just being stupid."

"Don't say that," Scarlett gritted her teeth. "Look, Rhys and I, we both grew up in the training centers. It's hard to turn your back on everything you grew up respecting and wanting. It just takes time. And it would be easier if everyone was nice to him."

Kendrick shook his head. "He can't stay, and I wouldn't be surprised if he's feeding information to someone. Did you check for a radio? I bet that's what he's doing right now," Kendrick pointed at the tent. "You don't have to believe me, but for all of these people here . . ." he motioned to the individuals, young and old, who were finishing their breakfasts and organizing themselves for their daily duties. "It's only fair that they have some warning."

Scarlett thought about telling Kendrick that Rhys didn't even want to stay. Was Kendrick trying to make her choose between him or Rhys? But as Scarlett felt the tiny burden in her arms wiggle, she realized that she wasn't simply choosing between the two males.

She had the option between Rhys and everyone else. And no matter how long she had known Rhys, no matter that he had been her only familiar face in City 6, she simply couldn't give up everyone else for him. So if he went, he would have to go by himself. And at the same time, she couldn't let him go. He had left everything else behind for her. So, Scarlett knew there was only one correct outcome here. She would fight for that.

"You won't say anything," she said, stepping closer so that Kendrick could see how serious she was. "I will talk with Rhys. He-"

"Talking won't make things better," Kendrick said. "It will only give him more opportunities to stab us in the back. I'm not wrong. Trust me."

"This has nothing to do with trusting you. It has to do with, being, welcoming people," she sputtered, her words not even making sense to herself.

She hurried into the tent, part of her on edge wondering if she would see a radio. She perched on the edge of the platform, the sun warming half her body. "Rhys, can I see what you have in your pack?" Rhys pointed to the pack against the side of the tent as though she might mean some other invisible pack.

"Why?" he asked.

"I just want to see everything you brought," Scarlett felt deceitful as she added the last part. "I mean, if we're going to leave the camp, then I have to know what we have to rely on."

Rhys's eyebrows went up. "So, you're considering it?"

Scarlett shrugged, her eyes on the pack. "Let's just see."

Rhys pulled the pack around to sit in between them, and Scarlett awkwardly pinched the clip open with one hand, holding Esperanza in the other.

"Here, do you want to hold her?"

Rhys shook his head. "I think I might break her if I do that."

Scarlett settled the baby in her lap so that both hands were free for digging. She found a wet piece of plastic. She pulled it out, and it seemed to get bigger and bigger, dripping onto Esperanza's face. Rhys took it from her.

"Sorry, that was my savior during the rainstorms." The bag smelled funny, and Scarlett wrinkled her nose as she dove further into it. She found a few packages of food like they had eaten on their trip to City 6, and she found some bandages and medicine. Another piece of cloth like a mat for sleeping and some strange pieces of bark rested at the bottom. Not a lot.

"Where did you find these?" Scarlett asked, holding up the packaged food. Her mouth was watering at the thought of eating one. But at the same time, she knew she shouldn't waste them. She had just eaten, even if it hadn't been very much. If the hunters were successful that day, then she would be guaranteed more 'normal' meat.

"I found them when I was raiding everything else," Rhys answered.

"I know, but I mean, where? Was it in the tunnel where we found Esperanza? Or somewhere in the kitchen? Or some new place that I don't even know about?"

"Oh, yeah, down in the tunnel. I found a lot of supplies there, but I didn't want to take a heavy load."

Scarlett nodded. "Rhys, you know we can never go back to the City, right? Does that ever make you feel sad?"

"I haven't had time to think about it."

"Well, think about it now, because that's the way it is." Scarlett wasn't trying to sound harsh, but she wasn't about to play a game either. And whether she liked it or not, a little bit of the doubt Kendrick had planted in her head began taking hold.

Rhys sighed, a big puff of air that seemed to take everything out of him. "Scarlett, I'm not going to stay."

"But, Rhys, you said-"

"I'm not going to stay. That's my decision. You won't change my mind. This group is just like the City, except for the fact that they have fewer resources, fewer promises, and they are a heck of a lot less welcoming. I thought from your message, maybe I just assumed, but I thought it was worth it. And we would always have enough to eat, and we wouldn't have to worry about rules. You were wrong."

"But-"

"And I'd rather be out on my own than doing the same thing out here." Rhys shook his head. "The only decision you have to make is whether or not you're coming with me."

CHAPTER 26

Scarlett had pleaded and begged over the last twenty-four hours, trying anything she could to persuade Rhys to remain, but he was determined to leave. Scarlett didn't say anything as she watched him walk deeper into the forest, back toward the Cities. Esperanza seemed to feel Scarlett's sadness, because she started fussing.

"Are you ready to eat again already? It's only been an hour. Are you trying to fatten up like Moses?" Of course, Esperanza didn't answer, but her tiny presence comforted Scarlett. She wasn't alone, and she didn't have time to be sad. Esperanza had too many needs.

When Scarlett re-entered the camp, she looked around, trying to find someone to talk with who would understand. She didn't want to even look at Kendrick right then, because it was his fault that Rhys had left. Scarlett almost wanted to make him leave too, not that she had the power to do that.

Cradling Esperanza, Scarlett sat on the edge of the tent's platform and watched everyone moving around. A hunting party had already left the camp, though they said a lot of animals had been drowned and half-eaten or couldn't be found. But somehow, they were still managing to feed everyone.

"We're moving tomorrow," Ariel crowed as she skipped over. Skipping in ankle-deep water is quite a feat, but she still kept some pep in her step.

"Oh really? Time to keep going already?"

"Yeah, my mam said that the water is low enough that we can keep going. And she said we need to get there before the next full moon, not that anyone can see the moon because of all the clouds."

"Why before the next moon?"

Ariel shrugged. "I don't know. That's just what she said. Where's that City person?"

"City person? Oh, Rhys?" Scarlett bit her lower lip, feeling nervous. She didn't want Ariel telling everyone he had left. But at the same time, she couldn't pretend it hadn't happened. Everyone would find out sooner or later. "He's gone out into the forest to relieve himself."

"Oh," Ariel wasn't interested in talking about him anymore. "Can I braid your hair?"

Scarlett remained still as the young female combed through her hair with her fingers and put together another one of her creations. Scarlett sat as still as she could with Esperanza waving her arms.

Ariel laughed. "Esperanza is saying, 'Me too! Me too!' Your hair is too short," Ariel said, patting Esperanza's head.

As Scarlett sat down for the evening meal, everyone was excitedly talking about moving on the next day.

"I'm ready to get going," Verona said. "I don't have anything to do unless we are near a City."

"So, what is your profession exactly?" Scarlett asked.

"I patrol any communication and let the elders know if something needs to be reported." Verona eyed her. "Have you not been assigned a post yet?"

"No," Scarlett motioned to the baby in her lap. Esperanza was just looking up at her with wide eyes. "I guess taking care of her is kind of my profession."

Verona didn't look impressed. "You've been with us long enough; you should have been evaluated and assigned a place. I guess this storm got in the way of organizing everything."

"What are the different professions?"

"Hunter, cook, educator, watcher or guides, communications, tactile team, or creator."

Scarlett just nodded, even though she didn't know what some of those meant. Esperanza's eyes grew wider, and Scarlett smiled down at her, bending down to kiss the tip of her tiny nose.

The next morning, the camp was a bustle of activity. Time to move forward. Scarlett was responsible for packing the tent where she had slept, but she had no experience doing it. She tried to leave Esperanza on the platform as she pulled the sewn skins off the poles. They seemed determined to stay in position. The poles rattled, but they didn't move. Scarlett sighed and tried pulling from a different angle. Nothing.

Laya came over and watched for a minute. Everyone else had already packed up their tents. Scarlett couldn't believe how quickly they had gotten ready. Laya smiled. She pointed at where the skin was tied to the poles. "You might try addressing that first."

"Oh," Scarlett bent down and dug her broken fingernails into the knot. She finally undid all the knots, and the skin slid right off. Esperanza blinked at the sudden breeze as the skin came down around her. Scarlett then took the poles apart and folded them as she had seen done. When she looked up, Laya was still watching her.

"Where's Rhys?" she asked.

"He left," Scarlett said, feeling an urge to cry.

"When? Why?"

Scarlett rubbed her lips together, telling herself that she could speak without showing how she felt. "He left yesterday. He and Kendrick kind of got into it. I don't know. Kendrick told him he wasn't welcome here, and I think he was bothered because he left everything he knew to come out here and find me."

"So, if he did all of that to find you, why was he willing to walk away so easily?"

"I don't know," Scarlett shrugged. She busied herself with Esperanza, looking into the child's perfectly-formed face.

Esperanza waved her arms, and one of her hands hit Scarlett in the cheek. Scarlett grabbed the tiny hand and gave it a kiss, thinking back to the two-year-old female's hand in the City, the one that had been burned, then learning that the mother had burned it herself to keep the Government from taking her child. Was going to a training center really so bad? How could the mother even know if she had never been to one herself?

"I knew there was something strange about him," Laya was saying. "Did he say where he was going? What direction did you see him go?"

"Why?"

Laya shook her head. "Do you know?"

Scarlett made eye contact with Laya, her heart racing. Would they force Rhys to return? What if he left again? Would he be a prisoner as she had been? She couldn't wish that upon anyone. Scarlett pointed vaguely to one side of the camp. "I think he went that way."

Laya slogged across the camp to speak with someone while Scarlett neatened the tent pack and strapped Esperanza into her childpack. They had a long day of walking before them.

Ariel found Scarlett. "I'm sorry," she said, hefting her pack higher on her shoulders.

"Why? For what?"

"Your hair looks terrible today," Ariel said.

Scarlett reached up and patted the hair nest tentatively. She wasn't used to thinking about her appearance. She usually wore her hair in a horsetail every day. "That's okay. At least it's not in my face."

"So how come Rhys didn't want to stay with us anymore? Did he not like us? He wanted to live in the buildings with hot water and lights on the ceiling?"

Scarlett hated that she was having to explain this a second time in an hour. "He didn't feel like this was his home."

"Okay, but he won't get us in trouble?"

"In trouble? You're not in trouble."

"I mean, he won't tell the Government about us?" Ariel's eyes were wide.

"No way. Come on, we need to start walking." The water was just sitting a couple of centimeters above the ground. They sloshed through in silence, though Ariel was happy to chatter about many different things as they walked.

"Ariel," Scarlett suddenly asked, realizing that she had the perfect fountain of information in front of her. "What profession do you want to have when you are older?"

Ariel laughed. "I don't know. I want to be a mam, but I mean, a mam isn't a real profession. It's just sometimes. I wish my profession could be doing people's hair. Sometimes, people don't do anything with their hair, and I wish I could just make everyone beautiful."

"What profession should I have?" Scarlett asked.

"How should I know?"

"If you were me, what would you pick?"

"But I'm not you," Ariel smiled. "My mam says that you are the only person who can really know you. And you should never let other people make decisions for you. So, I can't make the decision for you."

Wow, for a child, she sure had a lot of wisdom.

"I know I don't want to be a hunter because that's gross. You have to take the guts out of animals." Ariel shuddered. "But maybe I could cook food. I kind of know a little about cooking already. I don't know. The cooks are super good, but sometimes, we make the same meals over and over again. And I only want something new."

"What's your favorite meal?" Scarlett asked, remembering the food she would eat at the training center.

"Meat! Sometimes, we can catch wild boars, and that meat is so yummy!"

The group didn't even stop for the midday meal, giving out some plants for everyone to chew on as they walked. Scarlett wondered why they were in such a hurry. She thought that life here would have no set schedule.

"Do you know how far the Government City is?" Scarlett asked.

"Oh, we aren't going to the City," Ariel responded.

Scarlett frowned. "I thought you said-"

"We're going close, but we can't see it or anything. If we can see the City, then they can see us. And if they can see us, then we're in big trouble."

"Do you ever feel scared?"

"Why?"

"Because you basically can't ever get close to the Cities, or you would be taken and probably punished for not staying there. Did your parents used to live in a City?"

Ariel nodded. "Yes, my parents were from City 3. But they left before I was born." Ariel giggled as she recounted the story like it was funny. "My mam knew she was pregnant, and so, she didn't want to lose me. She and my dad found a way to leave."

"How did they?"

"My dad said he found a White who was sympathetic to them. So, he helped them get out. They were hiding in a Jeep." Scarlett remembered how thoroughly they had searched the Jeep when she entered the City. Did they not search it as much when someone left? "How did you get out?"

"There was a hole in the fence. Someone told me about it and how to find you all. He's the reason Esperanza is here too. I wonder how many other people he has helped. Do you have a lot of people come from Cities?"

Ariel shrugged. "Not as much as now. You, Esperanza, Kendrick, and Rhys, well sort of Rhys. He doesn't count."

Scarlett pressed her lips together. Why did it hurt so much? She hoped he was okay.

CHAPTER 27

Phan stood before the Black. He had known this moment would come sooner or later. But he hadn't expected it right then. He wondered what had triggered the questioning. The Black had made all others leave the room, and he had offered Phan a seat, not something he did often, if at all. However, Phan was a high-ranking White. He was not equal with the Black, but he had done a lot to deserve respect.

"We have tracked down the group that has been hiding from us the last two decades." The Black rarely showed emotion, but his lips were curling upward slightly. "It's a pity you couldn't have been on the mission. Do you know why you were passed over?"

Phan shook his head. Listening allowed him to learn more.

"Rhys suggested you might not be a good match for the mission."

Phan wanted to change the direction of the conversation. He nodded. "As expected, Sir. I am not one to raise both hands, but I am an integral part of the security in Section 2. It seems as though everyone patrolling the section was taken on the mission."

"True," the Black nodded. "Any other reason you can think of that *Rhys* would suggest you shouldn't go?"

"No, Sir," Phan responded. He clasped his hands together casually on top of his lap. He wondered if the Black could feel how hard he was squeezing his hands together.

175

"Yes, truly strange. You are one of my most trusted guards. You have done much good throughout the City, and I have always felt confident leaving the new Blues in your hands."

"Thank you, Sir." Phan wondered if his anxiety had been unwarranted.

"Have there been any unusual reports in your section?"

"No, Sir."

"Would any of the guards have a reason to hold a grudge against you?"

There it was. The reason he had been called into the office. One of the guards must have found out something. The Black wanted to give him a chance to explain himself first. "Sir, with all due respect, I am a hard person. I require a lot from those working under me, and I don't accept weakness." Phan took a chance. "If you explain to me the reason I was called here, I can perhaps specifically help ease your mind."

The Black created a tent with his fingers, taking his time to carefully match each one. "Yes, I can explain the situation to you. You are aware that Scarlett was not in her cell for her scheduled execution. You are aware that she has not been discovered in the City, and that Rhys, Rhys of all guards, discovered something we thought was merely a child's markings. He told us what they meant and how to find Scarlett. All of this, you know."

"Yes, Sir."

"You do not know that Scarlett has been found."

Phan squeezed his hands harder.

"I see. You certainly didn't know that." Phan looked at the desk. Looking into the Black's eyes would signal a challenge; looking down at his own hands would indicate nervousness. Phan tried to exude deference and confidence at the same time.

"No, Sir."

"Rhys talked with Scarlett. She had a child with her, a baby, the one she helped deliver. Said baby was marked as dead after she was found. That report was signed by you. Do you remember signing this?"

The Black threw a file across the table, and Phan caught it. He didn't have to look at it to know what it said. It said that he had found no sign of life in the child, and the child had been discarded properly.

"Do you perhaps need help in defining 'without life'?" The Black asked.

"No, Sir," Phan responded.

"Scarlett also told Rhys that you were instrumental to her escape." There was silence for a full sixty seconds. "Perhaps now that you know the situation, you would care to explain."

Phan kept his eyes glued to the desk. They had Scarlett. They had the baby. He had no idea where they were being held unless everything was made up, and they hadn't found her. But no, the description was too accurate. The Black had talked to Scarlett, or someone had. It had probably been Rhys, the traitor. Not that it was his fault.

He went with the safest answer he could. "Sir, it appears as though something must be malfunctioning with Rhys. I know it is a new method, but I have spent extensive time talking with the doctor about the chip and how it works. Is it possible that he confused his mission? Perhaps, he thought he was not only supposed to capture and get revenge on Scarlett for what she did to him, but also to get revenge on anyone he disliked?"

The Black leaned back in his chair and seemed to be considering Phan's idea. His chair squeaked, long and loud, filling the empty space. "Are you suggesting that the doctor doesn't know what he's doing?" his voice didn't sound pleased with the idea.

"No, Sir," Phan responded. Overexplaining made him look like he was trying to be convincing. He couldn't risk the Black seeing right through his sham, his play for an hour more of freedom so that he could make his own escape. After a meeting like this, there was no way he would be trusted again. He wouldn't have the opportunity to help any more babies. He would be useless, at least useless as far as he saw his purpose.

"You have an interesting theory. Why would Rhys want revenge on you?"

Phan shrugged. "Sir, as I said before, I am harsh with everyone under me, especially new trainees. I do not remember all I say or do; however, it's quite possible he was offended by something I said or did."

"I'll call the doctor." Phan felt the Black's eyes on him as he pressed a button that summoned another White. The White looked at Phan curiously as he took his order to fetch the doctor. The Black and Phan sat in silence waiting for him. Phan was desperately trying to plan how he could escape. The doctor certainly couldn't prove or disprove what Phan had alleged without the specimen there. They could merely discuss theories, which meant that Phan couldn't be charged with anything officially.

The doctor entered the room and saluted, his three fingers over his heart. He repeated the pledge of the Government. The Black did not motion for him to sit.

"Doctor, you are in charge of the pilot program. So far, you have only activated the chips in three individuals, is that correct?"

"Yes, Sir."

"Can you name those three individuals?"

"Yes, Sir. Branely, Harding, and Rhys. He is the most recent activation."

Phan knew the program had been tested before, but he did not realize that two Blues already had the chip activated. He didn't know how many months of data they had. "Have you discovered any malfunctions?" the Black asked.

"No, Sir. As long as they continue to take the pills, the chips have worked as desired."

"Have you noticed any strange side effects? Such as unusual hostility toward others or . . ." The Black let his voice trail off, and the Doctor waited a good thirty seconds before daring to answer him.

"Sir, while there has been a side effect of extreme fatigue when it is almost time for the pill, there has been nothing else to make us suspect it is not working just as it should."

"Thank you, Doctor. You have served us well. You may return to your duties." The doctor left the room on his own, and Phan was left alone with the Black again. The Doctor had left little room for doubt.

"Phan," the Black said. On his lips, the name sounded almost like the name of a friend, the way you would greet someone you knew well. "You have done wrong. There is no malfunction. And," the Black paused. Phan wanted to jump in and protest that they had no way of knowing for *sure.* "We found evidence of a child living in one of the labs. Evidence for which none of our scientists can account. You were hiding the child."

What choice did Phan have? He thought he had cleaned the room thoroughly, but perhaps the baby supplies, typical supplies stored with others, had appeared different when someone had entered the supply room. Perhaps someone had seen her while she was there, but hadn't reported it right away. Phan knew he wouldn't live another day.

"Yes, Sir."

"Why did you hide her?"

Phan had already admitted guilt. He didn't need to expose the pain behind his actions as well. He hung his head and waited for what he knew the Black would say. "You will be executed in one hour," the Black said.

Phan was given an hour to contemplate the end of his life, an hour that was only fifty-six minutes by the time he reached the cell. He had no hope of being saved. Though he had some connections to others in the compound, he had no way to get word to them in time. And he decided it wouldn't be worth it to trade someone else's life for his own.

Phan couldn't sit still, so he paced the cell as he imagined each of the people he had helped since he had realized the truth about the Government, something he had promised himself to pass on to a suitable disciple. Now, he would not have the opportunity. He cursed himself for his shortsightedness. He wouldn't spend his last minutes thinking of what he should have done.

He thought of Marla, the only female he had ever truly loved. Phan's relationship with Marla, a mere Citizen, was the reason for the operation when trainees became Blues. Phan had fallen in love with a Citizen, and she had loved him as well. Marla had conceived a child, and once Phan knew that he would have a child, everything had changed. He still wanted to serve the Government, but more than that, he wanted the child to be known as his. He wanted to teach the child everything. The child had been delivered and taken away immediately.

Phan should have known that a child with his genes would most certainly pass the basic tests given to certify the readiness of an infant for the training center. But Phan had not thought of that. He had thought that the child was his, his and Marla's. He had been blessed with his position and been able to see her periodically, but it wasn't enough. He would never have the chance to say goodbye to her now. She wouldn't know that he had been killed.

"I was a fool," Phan whispered. "I should have known." It didn't matter how many years passed, Phan would never forget the hopelessness in Marla's eyes when he had told her that their child had been selected.

"Our female is to be highly honored," he had said, visiting her in her home as he often had. "She has the intellect with which only a select few are gifted. She will be raised in the training center and given the potential to become a White one day."

Marla had shaken her head, tears leaking down her face. "Our baby, our baby. My little female!" she had wailed. Phan had sat beside her on the bed where she slept, still in her parents' house, as she had not yet been matched.

"Don't be upset," Phan had said. "Perhaps you will see her again one day. She can come back here and serve in City 6. Won't you be proud?" Phan said these things, even though he felt a ripping pain in his own chest. He had hugged her and kissed her hair as she cried.

When he visited her the next day, he hadn't expected to find that Marla had committed suicide, leaving Phan alone in the world. Though he felt a deep sadness take hold in his life, he had decided that he would do whatever he could to keep families together. Though it wasn't always enough, he had tried to give them the opportunity at a better life.

"I saved seven babies," he said. "I reunited two. I saved eighteen females and males from sure execution. I protected many." Phan's time was up.

He was led up the stone steps one last time and out of the compound, four Whites surrounding him. These were Whites he had trusted and worked alongside for years. They took him to an open space where two walkways crossed and stripped him of his White uniform, a uniform he wasn't fit to wear anymore. Phan stared into the barrel of the gun, his heart racing with fear, fear of the other side, fear of death.

The trigger was pulled, and Phan fell forward to move no more.

CHAPTER 28

Scarlett was exhausted by the time they reached the best place to set up their new camp. She plopped her packs on the ground. It was still muddy and soggy in places, but for the most part, she could trust it wouldn't suck her bag down under. She stared at the tent like it was her worst enemy.

Esperanza started crying, but everyone else was too busy setting up their tents or cooking what the hunters had managed to scavenge along the way to notice. They were cooking for the first time in days, having found dry wood by climbing trees and breaking branches off. The fire was smoking too much, but Scarlett still liked the familiar smell.

"Okay, Esperanza, calm down. I'm going to figure out this tent, then we'll find Mara, your food source. I wonder when you'll be able to eat normal food." Scarlett squinted at Esperanza, but didn't spend a lot of time on it. This tent was harder than it looked.

Kendrick limped over. "Need some help?"

Scarlett shrugged, not looking him in the eyes. "I just helped three families set theirs up while they were working on the evening meal. I don't mind."

"How about instead of doing it for me, you teach me how to do it? That way, I can do it on my own in the future."

"Sure," Kendrick walked her through the motions. They just focused on the poles and the skins. When they were done, Scarlett had to admit that it wasn't too complicated. "So, where's Rhys?"

Scarlett scooped up Esperanza, addressing her complaints. "Okay, I'll get you to your evening meal. There, there." Esperanza lowered her volume just a tad, but still kept up her complaints so as not to be forgotten.

Kendrick followed her, determined to get an answer. "He left?" Kendrick sounded happy about it.

"Yes, he left!" Scarlett said, holding Esperanza close as she whirled around. "Thanks to you! Now leave me alone! He was my best friend."

Kendrick crossed his arms, but the smirk on his face spoke volumes.

"Stop smiling," Scarlett said.

"Look, you want me to not speak; now you want to control my face, too. I'm not someone who can be controlled, not like Rhys, who is letting the Government control his life. You wait and see. He went back and told his buddies exactly where you are. They're hunting you down, and maybe me too, though I don't put as much stock in my importance."

Scarlett ignored him, trying to find something to do besides be haunted by thoughts of Rhys. She found a group of individuals whom she didn't know. She had seen them around camp some, but they were usually on the outskirts. She thought they were watchers. She listened to their conversation, standing just behind and to the side of a male, pretending that she was busy with Esperanza.

"We'll meet our first contact tomorrow."

"We need to leave early. We can't make him wait like last time."

"We should reach the City before the sun comes up. We should ask the night watchers to wake us after four hours of dark to give us enough time to get there."

"Did the guides tell us how far it is from here?"

"We're less than two hours away at a good pace. Due southeast."

Scarlett stepped forward then until she was even with the circle of six people. "Excuse me, where are you going in the early morning?"

"We're going to the Government City. Our contact has arranged for us to get some important medical supplies. We haven't been able to contact him, but we have to trust he's still going to be there and waiting tomorrow morning."

"You'll be going into the City?" Scarlett asked, amazed.

"Just to the edge," one of the males looked at Scarlett closer. "You're the female from City 6, right? I have been so busy with our planning and strategies that I never got the chance to introduce myself. I'm Phillip."

He reached out his hand as though to shake Scarlett's. Scarlett looked at it for a moment, worrying about what Kendrick had told her. Despite her recent anger at him, she didn't think he would mislead her about touching. Scarlett leaned forward and took his hand. Phillip raised and lowered their clasped hands several times, then let her go. Scarlett smiled at the others in the circle.

"I would like to go with you," she said.

"You can't," one of the females said. She bore a strong resemblance to Verona in the clipped way she spoke. Scarlett stared at her closely. This female was young, around Scarlett's age. "What are you looking at?" the female snapped.

Scarlett forced a smile despite the other female's rudeness. "Nothing, just didn't remember seeing you around here before."

"Because I'm working, pulling my weight," the female said.

"Don't let Amy bother you," one of the males said.

"You can't come," Amy talked over the male. "You have to be trained, and you're still too new here."

"Okay, how do I train?"

One of the other males answered, an older one with bushy facial hair. "You have to get one of the hunters to teach you how to use the different weapons in our possession. That's the first step. After that, it's pretty much a matter of trust. And didn't you go back into the Cities when you weren't supposed to?"

Scarlett shrugged. "Yes, I did. I had to give my friend the opportunity to live outside the Cities like me. I'm sure you would have done the same."

"I bet she understands a lot about the Cities," one of the group said. "She could probably tell us about it, since our contacts never have time to talk." The looks turned from accusatory to thoughtful as they studied her.

"When we get back tomorrow, we'll talk to you," Phillip promised. "Right now, we need to get some rest before our journey." That seemed to break the group up, and they went in separate directions.

The next morning, Scarlett looked for them, but they were gone. She had Esperanza in the childpack, pressed against her skin. That seemed to be the child's favorite place. But as Scarlett walked around the camp, she was itching to be useful. She came across Derrico who was readying himself for a day of hunting.

"Would you teach me how to use your weapons?" Scarlett asked. "I want to be a part of the group that gets supplies from the Cities, and I was told I have to know how to use your weapons. What do you have?"

"Basic bow and arrow and a few different knives," Derrico said, pulling them from his belt and showing her.

Scarlett grabbed one of the knives. It was carved out of wood, but it was still sharp enough. She found a tree a few yards in front of them, took her time aiming, then threw the knife. It bounced off the trunk and hit the ground, but she had hit it. She reached for the knife with a metal blade, but Derrico stopped her.

"We shouldn't be doing that inside the boundaries of the camp. Someone could get hurt." Scarlett nodded, but kept the knife firmly in her grip. She had been training for years on how to use all types of weapons and how to dodge attacks. The last thing she needed was extra training. She would show Derrico that she was already prepared as far as weapons went.

Scarlett found someone to care for Esperanza, then she and Derrico trekked farther into the forest. One of the other hunters called out to Derrico. "I'll hunt with Scarlett today," Derrico called back. "She wants some training with the weapons. And who knows? Maybe she will be the next great hunter." Scarlett smiled. She wasn't sure she would be able to stomach actually cleaning the animal after it was killed, but she would give it a try.

"So, what experience do you have with these weapons?" Derrico asked as they continued walkling.

"I've used them all before, though the pistol was usually my weapon of choice. You don't happen to have one, do you?"

"No, they are hard to come by, and if we do happen to get one, there are only a few bullets in it. We don't want to use that on animals."

"What do you use it on?"

"In the event of an attack," Derrico explained. "We would be able to fight more evenly." Scarlett imagined where they must keep the guns. She hadn't seen one.

"Do the watchers carry them?" Scarlett asked.

"Sometimes. Not always. Okay, let's focus on you and your skills." Derrico pointed to a tree which had a few low hanging branches. The branches were still wet from the recent flood.

"I like to hunt from above. Let's climb up."

Scarlett's stomach turned over, but she headed toward the tree like the idea didn't bother her at all. *This* was how her experience on the Mound had prepared her. She licked her lips and looked up at the tree, strategizing about which branches she would use. "How high are we going?" She was stalling, and she knew it.

"That branch there provides an excellent resting place," Derrico said. "It's not too high, but it will get us out of the animals' main area of vision."

Scarlett nodded and reached for the first branch. She pulled herself up and clung to the trunk. The second branch she had selected for her climb was higher than she expected. Scarlett grabbed it, but needed to pull herself up. She tried, but her arm strength was not enough. She let herself drop back to the branch where she had been, slipped on it, and almost fell to the ground.

She didn't dare look at Derrico. If she had been a Green trying to pass a test right then, she could just imagine how the Blue watching her would mark up the screen.

"Try that one to your left," Derrico said instead.

Scarlett reached. This one was a quarter way around the tree but not as high. She succeeded in mounting the branch, stood, and found another one she could climb. Finally, Derrico, always a branch below her, told her to stop. He mounted the branch beside her and turned to face away from the camp.

"So, now we sit and wait?" Scarlett asked. Being a hunter was not nearly as exciting as she had imagined.

"We saw signs of deer yesterday, fresh tracks in the mud, and based on their direction, they've been circling through this area. We should be able to get one or two."

Scarlett's mouth started salivating at the thought of fresh deer meat. While she had never had deer at the training center, she had been told that a lot of the meat she ate in the compound at City 6 was deer. Scarlett wondered how they got their deer and who was hunting in the forest regularly for it.

"How long do you wait?" Scarlett asked, her voice a whisper so she wouldn't scare away potential prey.

"However long it takes. Why don't you take a few shots with the bow and arrow so you feel more comfortable with it before anything comes? Aim for that tree," Derrico pointed to one a good distance away, but nothing Scarlett couldn't do. The problem was that she was sitting. She had never shot anything while sitting.

"I'm just going to stand," Scarlett said, working her way to a standing position. Her stomach felt alive with nerves as she put the trunk safely behind her back and got a feel for the bow. She took the arrow Derrico handed her, aimed at the bottom of the tree he had indicated, and fired. The arrow stuck. Scarlett secretly rejoiced, but looked to Derrico to see his reaction. He was handing her another arrow. Scarlett aimed for a spot slightly to the left of the first arrow. That arrow stuck too.

"So you have some knowledge of the bow and arrow," Derrico said. "Have you ever used it on a person?"

Scarlett shook her head. "To be honest, I practiced with them some at the training center because I liked them. But, we weren't even given bows and arrows once we got to the City. Should I go get those?"

"No," Derrico said, "they were scented with blackberry juice from a patch we found a week or two ago. It should distract the deer if they come close enough so we can shoot them."

"Oh," Scarlett was surprised by the cleverness of his plan.

"I think the reason those who go to the City to meet our contact are hesitant to bring you along is your previous status."

"What previous status?"

"You were brought up as a guard for the Government. You didn't have a family as you were growing up. Many say you don't learn compassion or mercy that way. You learn only to follow what the Government says."

"Well, they're the Government, and you shouldn't question what they want." Scarlett saw Derrico's eyes pop open a little. She rushed to self-correct. "I mean, that's what we're taught. But I wouldn't be here if I hadn't questioned it and gotten myself in trouble."

"I heard you were arrested for shooting your best friend, the one who came to the camp before mysteriously disappearing. I don't want to speak for everyone, but there is some talk that you and he are working together to report our whereabouts to the Government. Someone said that they heard the two of you talking about who guards the camp at night. And that information, that isn't the type of information that you simply bring up in normal conversations."

Scarlett wondered who had been listening to them when they were talking inside the tent. She didn't remember everything she had talked about with Rhys, but that topic did sound familiar. "The Government wanted to kill me," she said. "The only way to remain alive was to leave. I'm certainly not helping them now."

"I'm not accusing you," Derrico said. Her voice had sounded so defensive. "I just think you should know what some people are thinking.

While we did have that older couple decide to stay behind, we aren't just a group of people that you walk away from. Where else would you go?"

Derrico shrugged as though the topic didn't matter to him. "Like I said, I think you should know. And if it's not your intention, then ask fewer questions. Don't be so suspicious. I think you're a nice female and that you had the unfortunate circumstance of being taken to the training center. However, some people may always see you as working for the Government."

"That's not fair," Scarlett protested. Derrico sat up straighter, putting a hand in her face to shush her. Scarlett noticed a small movement in the forest, so far away that she couldn't identify the animal. However, she remained still, handing the bow to Derrico as he slowly slotted an arrow into place.

The deer moved closer, slowly as though it were enjoying its day leisurely. Another deer bounded up beside it, this one younger and smaller. Scarlett realized that this was probably a mother and child pair. Her heart pounded, and she wanted to tell Derrico to let them go, that they didn't have to die to feed them. But she couldn't. She knew that the people in camp needed the meat.

Scarlett swallowed and watched as a perfectly placed arrow felled the bigger deer. The younger deer went over to its mother and sniffed cautiously. Scarlett screamed inside her head that it should run away. But Derrico took it down with another arrow. Scarlett watched as it twitched and finally became still.

"This is why we always hunt in pairs," Derrico said, quickly beginning his descent of the tree. "If we get lucky, we might have a big haul back to camp, and sometimes, we need help from more than two people." Derrico studied the deer then Scarlett. "How about you go back to camp and get a few big males to come back here and haul these in? I'll stay here to guard against predators looking for an easy meal."

Scarlett trekked into camp by herself. It was less than half an hour to walk. As she walked, she wondered if Derrico didn't see her as capable of hauling the deer or if it really took more than two people. However, once Scarlett came back with the required help, she saw what Derrico wanted to do. He was skinning the animals.

"Why are you doing that right here?"

"We can't use every part of the deer," Derrico explained as Scarlett covered her nose and mouth to keep the smell at bay. "The few parts we can't use, we prefer to leave here so that any animals interested in it don't wander into the camp."

Scarlett recognized the antlers as they were sawn off the head. They looked exactly like the spoons they used for their soup. Scarlett held both in her arms. They didn't weigh much. "Why don't you go ahead and take those to the creators?" Derrico suggested. "We'll bring these in soon."

Once more, Scarlett took the walk back to the camp on her own. She delivered the antlers as requested, then found Esperanza. Mara asked if she would watch Moses as well. No one had slept well the night before, and Mara wanted a nap.

Scarlett strapped Esperanza into the childpack and balanced Moses on her hip. He was getting chubbier by the day, while Esperanza seemed to stay thin.

Moses kicked his feet excitedly, moving his fists in time to his own beat. "What are you so excited about today?" Scarlett asked. Moses's eyes focused on her face, and she felt as though he were really listening to her. The two babies kept her busy for the next few hours as she kept an eye out for the group that had visited the Government City in the early morning hours.

She didn't see them until just before the evening meal. Scarlett rushed over, a hand on Esperanza to keep her in place.

"Hi, how did it go?" she asked Phillip, the one she felt most comfortable approaching.

Phillip smiled. "Well, we retrieved the supplies, and no one was alerted of our visit. Those are always our two main goals to make ourselves successful. How was your day?"

"Fine," Scarlett said. Kendrick was suddenly by her elbow. She turned her head away from him, pretending she didn't see him listening to their conversation. "I was wondering if I could go with you the next time you visit a City."

"Why do you want to go?" Kendrick asked.

Phillip nodded. He wanted to hear the answer to Kendrick's question as well.

Scarlett ran her hands through the fuzzy wisps on Esperanza's head. "It's the Government City. I've never been there, and I think I could be a real asset to your team. Like you said last night, Phillip, I have a lot of knowledge about City life. I would help any way I can. And Derrico took me hunting today. You can ask him how I did."

Phillip looked over at Amy, who rolled her eyes. She clearly didn't like Scarlett. "I think talking things through is the first step. Then, we can see if you would be a good fit for our next mission."

Esperanza gave a strange whimper at that moment, and Scarlett kissed her forehead, rubbing the baby's fingers against her cheek.

"Mothers generally don't come on missions," the female said. "What would happen to your child if you died? It can happen, you know."

But the female's threat of death meant nothing to Scarlett. "Her mother was already killed. And if I'm better at working with the Cities than being a mother, then shouldn't I do that instead? I'm sure Laya would be a great mother for her."

The female crossed her arms. "No, you shouldn't do anything that puts the rest of us in danger. We don't trust you, and taking you closer to the City would just give you another opportunity to communicate. Trust me, you're going to be out of the Fringe in a week, if not dead."

Scarlett's mouth dropped open just a little. The venom in the female's voice hurt. Scarlett didn't want them to see the wetness in her eyes, so she turned and left. They didn't want her? Fine, she didn't have to help. She didn't have to do anything for them at all.

CHAPTER 29

Scarlett heard footsteps behind her, but she didn't turn to see who was following her. She was angry at herself for thinking that this group of people would accept her. She had grown up in a training center. She was born to serve the Government. They didn't want her here. Scarlett looked back the way they had come.

How far away was Rhys? Was he too far for her to catch up with him? She toyed with the idea of leaving, but she felt Esperanza's tiny body in her arms. She knew that if she took Esperanza with her into the forest, it would be equivalent to a death sentence for the small child.

Kendrick caught up to them, matching her pace with a step, drag, step, drag. "Scarlett, I'm sorry," he said. She hadn't expected him to apologize. She hugged Esperanza and kept walking toward her tent, bypassing the welcoming smells of a warm dinner. "I wasn't trying to make Rhys leave. I was just teasing him, as we males do. Look, I know he's your friend, but I didn't trust him. Something in my gut said he wasn't safe."

Scarlett whirled on Kendrick. "Now you see me upset, and you think apologizing is going to fix it? It's not! What you did to Rhys is just what that female did to me. She made me feel like I don't belong here, and maybe she's right. Why should I help these people if they don't want me here?"

"Because that's not true. Many people *do* want you here- Laya, Ariel, Esperanza, even Mara and Derrico. They seem like friends, yes?"

Scarlett shrugged as Kendrick named every one of the people important to her. "Derrico said the same thing today," Scarlett's voice was small. "He said that some people were talking about me being a traitor." Scarlett plopped onto a log. She felt the dampness seep into her pants, but she didn't care. "I don't belong in the City, because they said I betrayed the Government when I shot Rhys, even though it was an accident. I don't belong here; people think I'm a traitor. But I've never done that. I've never betrayed anyone. Why does everyone mistrust me?"

Kendrick plopped gracelessly onto the log beside her. "Not everyone. *I* know you wouldn't hurt anyone. And I know when you shot Rhys, it was an accident."

"But that doesn't help me."

"A lot of people here trust you. They gave you the child to take care of. They wouldn't do that if they didn't trust you, right?"

Scarlett shrugged, a tiny movement of her shoulders. "Maybe they say they do, and they act like they do, but deep down, there's that doubt. Like the doubt I carried ever since entering the City about if everything I had learned about the Government and the Citizens was true."

"Well, you had a reason to doubt that, but it doesn't mean that every doubt someone ever feels is realistic. Keep being yourself; keep proving to them that you are here for them and to help. They'll begin to trust you eventually."

"I guess it's my own fault," Scarlett said. "I started sneaking away to the City when we were camped out by City 6. I *had* to, but I guess it looked suspicious." Kendrick nodded as she continued. "They almost threw me out for that. Maybe they were just looking for an excuse to get rid of me. Do you think I'm the first person from a training center to join their group?"

"Maybe," Kendrick said. "I don't know."

Alone. She was the only one. No one else knew what it felt like to have everyone you grew up with, the Government she had faithfully served for seventeen years, turn their backs on her. She was the only one who had left that community looking for another group to take her in, one that appeared to be more open and accepting, but wasn't. This group whispered rumors about her behind her back, but never spoke to her about it or told her how she could fix it.

Kendrick opened his arm to her, and Scarlett didn't hesitate. She laid her head on Kendrick's shoulder and felt his arm around her back and arm. He squeezed her gently, and that hug felt more comforting than anything had in days.

"I have to prove them wrong," Scarlett whispered. "I don't want to leave what we've found here."

"And you shouldn't," Kendrick agreed. "We will find our places, and in a few weeks, this will feel completely normal. We will live lives filled with walking in the forest, bathing in the river, taking care of a needy baby." Scarlett kept her head on his shoulder. She watched as the light in the forest turned from bright to a dusky orange.

"How do I prove them wrong?"

Scarlett felt Kendrick's hand moving up and down on her bare arm, and even though it wasn't cold outside, she felt her arm start to turn to chicken flesh, tiny bumps all over. She didn't want to move.

"You have to be there for them. Don't go off by yourself, and stay away from the communications tent. You don't need anyone saying that you are trying to know what's going on in the Cities or to communicate with them."

Kendrick's advice was sound. Scarlett had no reason to do any of those things, so if she did, it would look suspicious. She took a deep breath and pretended to fix Esperanza's blanket while she wiped under her eyes. She heard footsteps behind her, and they both turned. One of the females from the group that went on missions was approaching. She waved, moving her hand in a quick loop.

"Hi, Harold sent me to talk to you." She was looking directly at Scarlett. "You're welcome to listen if you like," she said to Kendrick. Scarlett straightened, scooting a little bit away from Kendrick as though she had been caught doing something bad. "I'm Dariah, by the way. I know you're Scarlett and Kenny, right?"

"Kendrick."

"Yes, so, Scarlett, Phillip wanted to know why you want to go to the Government City and why you would be a good addition to our team."

"Why doesn't he ask the questions himself?" Kendrick said.

Dariah shrugged. "Maybe he thought it would be better if a female talked to her, and *not* Amy. Verona's daughter can be a bit of a handful," Dariah said to Scarlett. "So, don't get your feelings hurt if she doesn't like you. She barely likes anyone, except Phillip of course. The fact that Phillip is considering having you in the group does nothing to make her less prickly."

"Oh, okay, so, I want to go to the Government City because I feel like missions like that, the dangerous ones, are where I really fit in. I've handled weapons since I was a Red. I feel comfortable with a mission and knowing I'm doing something useful. And I think my knowledge of the Cities could help everyone on the team."

"We don't actually go in the Cities," Dariah explained. "I mean, we have once, a while back, but it's a last resort."

Scarlett looked down at Esperanza. She couldn't explain the desire inside her to see the Government City.

"Sure, I just think that's where I would fit in best. I feel a need to be useful. In the Cities and in the training center, we had a set daily schedule. We were serving, learning, exercising, or something every hour of the day."

Dariah studied her carefully. "What do you know about the Government City?"

"Just, anything?"

Dariah nodded and leaned forward. Scarlett swallowed, trying to think back on her classes at the training center. "I've never been there before," Scarlett said. "So, you might know more about it than me. I know that all the Government officials live there. The Blacks are the only ones ever allowed there, except for a few Whites who serve them. I know that it's smaller than the other Cities, because it doesn't have any Citizens living in it. And I know that they are always communicating with the training center and the Cities. Once, we were able to talk with one of the Government officials in class. He introduced himself and told us about our duty serving the Government."

Scarlett smiled just a little, remembering how much she had looked forward to the day when she would see someone who really lived in the Government City. She had seen only his head, full of gray hair, and his face, wrinkled like shoe leather. Behind him, she had seen a wall, made of a different material than their training center walls. The wall had a pattern on it, some sort of blue swirls. Other than that, she had not seen more of his house on the screen.

"Not everything you know is true," Dariah said. "They have given you some of the basic facts, but I don't think you will understand how this Government works until you see the Government City. I think you should see it, if only to assure you that you made the right decision when you came to join us."

"The right decision?" Scarlett asked. Here was another person, someone besides Kendrick, saying that she belonged here. The idea of going to find Rhys was sounding less and less appealing.

"Sure, although from my understanding of your story, you didn't have an option. You kind of had to leave City 6, correct?"

"Yes, I did. I don't think I ever would have left if I hadn't been sentenced to death. I mean, why leave something that's working even though I have doubts?" Scarlett touched Esperanza's face gently. "I helped this child come out of her mother. And when she was found a few days later in a different house, I took her to the compound. I didn't know what happened to her until I accidentally stumbled upon her. Phan was helping her stay hidden until he could take her to this group, I suppose. I visited her often, because it didn't seem right that a child so small should be alone so much."

"Yet that is what happens in the training centers," Dariah cut in. "Babies are hooked up to machines which feed them and monitor their signs of life. Someone comes in to change their nappies, but they aren't given the same sort of love you are giving this child."

Scarlett wanted to refute what Dariah said, but the truth was that she had only visited the Tinies once. She had been responsible for the Tinies who could walk, and they were a handful. She didn't know what some-one Esperanza's age would live like. But it made sense in an awful way. It made sense why when Scarlett kissed Esperanza's head, she felt a twinge of jealousy. She wished Mrs. had loved on her the way that Scarlett saw Mara love on Moses.

"I don't think anyone tells me the complete truth," Scarlett finally said. "I grew up learning not to question the Government, to do as I am told. I was given information, information that I trusted, and now, I find it's not true. Everyone here gives me new information, but I have to question it. I think everyone has their own truth that they believe, and . . . maybe I have to find what I believe on my own. I don't think anyone can tell me."

"I will tell you this," Dariah said, brushing off the back of her pants. "We look out for one another, and we keep each other safe. We need everyone to do the same thing. If you don't think you can trust us or that you can look out for us, then we can't trust you either."

"I can! I can," Scarlett hurried to agree. "I want that. I want the trust."

Kendrick had remained quiet the whole time, but now he spoke. "Scarlett is one of the most trustworthy persons. She took a chance on me, even though I was a Citizen and she worked for the Government. She came to check on me after I was shot. Not many Blues would do that."

Dariah shrugged. "Well, love makes people do crazy things. But . . ."

"Love? No!" Kendrick said. "That has nothing to do with it. It's . . ."

"You don't love me?" Scarlett asked, feeling betrayed.

"No, I, you, we're friends."

"How can you say you're my friend if you don't love me?" Scarlett asked, rising. Kendrick stood as well.

"Because, you're, we're friends, but I don't . . . we're not . . ."

"Scarlett," Dariah said, cutting in. "Of course friends love each other, but it's a different kind of love. I just assumed since you're a guard, and he's a Citizen. It seemed natural that the only way you would have entered the camp together would be if there was some spark there. I didn't mean . . ."

"A spark? What do you mean? Like a fire? We didn't start any fires."

"No, she's talking about, like, love, or something. Some people say a spark, because when you feel love for somebody, it grows, and," Kendrick was still explaining awkwardly when Scarlett interrupted him.

"I just can't believe I would talk to you about everything and trust you, and you would say you don't love me."

"I'm going to let you two have this discussion on your own," Dariah said, walking away.

"Scarlett, I think maybe it means something else to you than it does me," Kendrick said. "We don't know each other that well, and love is more like for people who are getting married. And I'm not that far along yet."

"Married?"

Kendrick's mouth dropped open just a little, and he stopped his shuffling. "Yeah, married. Do you not know . . . ?"

"Don't make fun of me because I don't know some crazy City thing."

"I'm not making fun of you. That's just when two people, you know, leave their families and get their own house. They sign a paper and get the tattoo and everything. Well, here there's probably no tattoo. But, it's when you're sure that you want to be with that person for the rest of your life."

"That's married? You only love that one person?"

"Yeah, so you can see why, well, we're friends and everything, but," Kendrick started his shuffling again. "I'm not quite to that point. So . . ."

"Oh," Scarlett felt relief flood through her. "I guess it is different. I told my friends, Jaylin and Miya, back at the training center that I loved them all the time, and I know I love Esperanza, and Rhys, and you, and Mara, and chubby little Moses. Well, there are some people I would do anything for and people that I trust. I guess I thought it was different."

"Yeah, there's friends, and then, there's the marriage kind of love."

Scarlett felt calm again. She wanted to throw her arms around Kendrick and hug him, but she settled for squeezing Esperanza a little tighter. "Sorry, I didn't mean to get upset. Sometimes, I forget that things are very different between the ways that we grew up. We need to keep talking about it, so I can learn more about the Cities."

Kendrick nodded, his smile back in place.

"But first, I need to get on a mission to see the Government City."

CHAPTER 30

In the morning, Derrico found Scarlett walking Esperanza back and forth. Apparently, she had been crying all night long. Derrico and Scarlett yawned simultaneously.

"Dariah asked me to find you and bring you to the communications tent."

"Really? Why?"

"The team is having a meeting about their next trip to the Government City."

Scarlett definitely wanted to be a part of that, so she followed Derrico immediately. The walking seemed to soothe Esperanza somewhat, though she was still fussing in a low tone.

"Scarlett," Dariah said, before motioning for her to come in and sit at one of the stools around the communication table. Scarlett sat down, aware of all their eyes on her. "Scarlett and I had a talk yesterday." Scarlett nodded, making eye contact with the five other people in the tent.

Derrico still stood behind her. "Scarlett, I already talked to them about your skill during our hunting yesterday. They wondered if they could see it for themselves. I guess they don't trust me or something," he said with a tiny chuckle, but Scarlett wondered if it hurt him.

"First," an older male with bushy facial hair said, "We need to tell you a few details about what our missions are typically like. You need to decide if it is for you. I'm Harold, by the way, and the leader of this team, though Phillip likes to think he is sometimes," Everyone except Scarlett laughed. "Derrico, you can go about your business if you need to," Harold said. Derrico left the tent, and Harold turned to Scarlett.

"We have a few contacts in the Government City, fewer here than in other Cities. Their duty is to gather intelligence and materials that we can't provide for ourselves. They communicate when they want us to meet. Sometimes, we pre-arrange meetings months in advance. Other times, they use a code word on the radios to tell us how our meeting will go. This is why we have to always have someone-"

The radio crackled, and everyone silenced immediately, except for Esperanza who took that as a whining challenge.

She upped her crying and whining as Scarlett stood and bounced her back and forth. Everyone around the table gave her a dirty look, so she left the tent to try to calm the child. She desperately wanted to hear what was said, but Esperanza was making that impossible. She glanced back at the tent as Esperanza's whining continued.

"Sh! Esperanza! Now's not the time!" Scarlett said harshly, but Esperanza seemed to sense her frustration and broke into full-fledged crying. "Esperanza," Scarlett said, heaving a big breath. Esperanza cried, tiny tears running down her face as her fists beat the air.

"I can't deal with you right now," Scarlett said, "I need to have this meeting. I *need* to see the Government City." Scarlett jogged to find Mara or Laya or someone else who might be interested in holding the crying child. She couldn't seem to find anyone as she hunted around, not yet peering in tents but feeling that same level of desperation. Finally, she located Laya, but Laya was cooking the morning meal.

"I can't hold her right now," Laya said. "I'm busy. She's your responsibility. Please find something else to do with her." Scarlett bunched her lips into an angry knot, but continued searching for someone else who would understand how important it was that she join those in the communications tent. Finally, Scarlett found Mara who was bouncing a smiling Moses on her knee. She saw Esperanza crying and smiled sympathetically.

"Aw, she must be growing. I just fed her, but that's her hungry cry." Scarlett wondered how Mara could know what her cries meant when Scarlett didn't.

"I'll come back really soon," Scarlett said. "I have to go to the communications tent." She hurried in that direction. When she re-entered, the stares didn't appear nearly as welcoming as they had been before.

"You missed an important communication," Verona's daughter said.

"What did they say?"

Amy rolled her eyes like she couldn't believe Scarlett had asked that question. But what else was she supposed to do?

"We're going to meet them tonight at midnight," Phillip said.

"You can come with us," Harold told her. "We will be reaching the edge of the City and getting the information they have to share. Our contact got spooked during our last trip, so we didn't get any information. This contact may also have some extra supplies."

"Like what?" Scarlett wanted to know everything.

"Anything we can't make on our own, combs, cloth, other things, they pass along to us. We will be coming directly back. We will not be seen by anyone in the Government City, and if we are, it could be deadly for us."

"I understand," Scarlett answered solemnly. "I can do that. What time should I be ready to leave?"

"We will leave shortly after the evening meal, which means that you should try to get some rest during the day today."

"If that'll be possible with that baby," Amy's sarcastic comment touched Scarlett the wrong way.

"Do you have a problem with Esperanza? Because she has done nothing to hurt you! Neither have I. So, I would appreciate it if you would calm down," Scarlett said, taking a step forward without realizing it.

Amy stepped forward, too. "Yes, I have a problem with you. I trained for months before being allowed on a mission and in the communications tent. I don't think it's fair or safe that you be allowed in right now.

But I guess my opinion doesn't matter." The female stormed out of the tent.

Dariah came over and touched Scarlett's arm. "Don't worry about her. We do have a process, but having you join us was something new. Everyone is learning, and expectations are different for different people." Scarlett shrugged like it hadn't bothered her. But really, she didn't understand how someone could dislike her so much without even knowing her.

"It's fine; I'll meet everyone at the time you said," she told Harold, feeling deflated as she went to take care of Esperanza. All she could think about was the City and what she might or might not see. Scarlett napped when Esperanza slept that day, resulting in a couple of hours of sleep before the evening meal. Kendrick caught up with her as she was gulping down the hot soup.

"Where have you been all day?"

"Sleeping, or trying to, when Esperanza would let me," Scarlett gave the baby a grumpy look, but her big, gray eyes looked up at Scarlett with such innocence that she had to kiss her wrinkly forehead instead. "I'm going to the Government City tonight," Scarlett announced, trying to keep the squeal out of her voice. "I can't believe it."

"Be careful," Kendrick said. He glanced around, but no one else was listening. "I'm not trying to be superstitious or anything, but I have this weird feeling like you might get hurt or something."

Scarlett squinted at him. "Yeah, that is a weird feeling. It's not like I'm bringing Esperanza or something. I'm trained for this, and Derrico can testify that I am excellent at hitting my target." Scarlett smiled at the thought of having the weapons in her hand again. Her body hadn't been challenged to nearly the same level since she had left behind her daily exercising. The thought of having a mission and doing something useful was just what she needed.

"We're going to meet them at midnight, so I should be back before you wake up in the morning." Kendrick didn't say anything, but he took Scarlett's empty bowl and stood up to go wash them out. Scarlett stared after him, feeling a bit unsettled herself. But she didn't have time to reflect on how she was feeling, because Ariel bounced over just then.

"Can I braid your hair?" Scarlett imagined herself raiding the Government City, sneaking in and out with a fancy hair-do.

She shook her head. "Not tonight. I'm going with the team to the Government City."

"What?" Ariel covered her mouth in the perfect expression of surprise. Then, she clapped her hands together. "I'm so happy for you. This is just what you wanted."

Yes, it was, and Ariel's smile made Scarlett hug her. Finally, someone who seemed to understand her. "Yes, and I'll tell you all about it when I get back," Scarlett said. "We're not actually going inside the City, but that doesn't mean I won't see anything important."

"I want to know everything."

Scarlett reiterated her promise, then stood and stretched, taking several long lunges to stretch out her legs. Esperanza bounced with the movement, seeming to enjoy it. Ariel copied Scarlett's lunges and fell over sideways, laughing. "I can't do that," the young female said.

Scarlett laughed at Ariel and helped her up. "I just like to stretch my legs before walking."

"Can you imagine walking like this?" Ariel joked, taking several long, lungeing steps.

Scarlett laughed along with Ariel. She saw Phillip and Dariah moving toward the communications tent and took that as her cue to get moving. "I've got to get Esperanza settled with Mara, then I'm leaving."

Ariel waved goodbye to her and continued taking some long, lungeing steps. Scarlett found Mara exactly where she had said she would be and left Esperanza with her. "Esperanza," she said, "don't be making trouble for Mara now, or she might kick you out of the tent." Esperanza didn't look impressed with Scarlett's speech.

"I'll come get her once it's light out," Scarlett said. "I'll take Moses too, if you want."

"Won't you be awake all night on this mission?" Mara asked.

"Won't you be awake all night feeding them?" Scarlett asked back, smiling. "I don't mind. I'd love to do anything I can to help you." She also felt energized just at the prospect of what would happen that night. She felt excitement bouncing through her and wanted to skip just like Ariel always did. But she didn't. She kept her composure as she walked over to the communications tent.

Verona was filling them in on everything important she had heard over the past few hours. Dariah handed Scarlett two knives, one with a slightly longer, curved blade. Scarlett tucked them into her belt, then reached for them and pulled them out quickly to make sure she was comfortable with her ability to get to them when she needed them.

She bounced back and forth on the balls of her feet as Harold gave some last minute instructions. "We'll divide into two groups as always. First group will be Phillip, Amy, and myself. The second group will be Dariah, Scarlett, and Madrick. You three will watch our backs as we go to the edge. Remember to always stay within the edge of the forest." This reminder seemed to be directed at Scarlett. She nodded then listened carefully to Madrick's instructions, as he seemed to be the leader for their squad. She fingered the knife in her belt, hoping she wouldn't have to use it. She had no way of knowing that her little knife would be nothing in comparison with what awaited her.

CHAPTER 31

Two hours into the trek to the Government City, Scarlett still felt uncontrollable excitement coursing through her. She hoped she wouldn't be disappointed, like that one time at the training center when they had planned to celebrate everyone's birthday like they had learned about in history. Scarlett had thought about it for weeks, the balloons she had seen in the pictures, the cake that looked good enough to eat in one sitting, and the gift boxes the children had opened. But when the training center had held the communal "birthday party," it was nothing in comparison. All of that excitement for nothing.

Scarlett saw a tall building spire above the trees and knew they were close. Everyone remained silent as they got closer to the Government City, the gravity of their mission resting on their shoulders.

Then, they were at the edge of the forest. The trees stopped in an even line like guards awaiting an order to move forward. Scarlett, Madrick, and Dariah stopped with them. Harold scanned the Government City, waiting for some indication to move forward. The others seemed to fade away as Scarlett saw this place where the leaders resided.

The buildings in this City were taller than City 6. There had to be at least four floors in most of them. One building drew all of her attention. It had a massive dome on top that served no purpose Scarlett could see other than making it look more formidable. Perhaps there was a circular room inside, though the idea of one was so strange that Scarlett smiled just slightly.

She saw Amy, Phillip, and Harold move forward, but her attention remained focused on the grandeur within the concrete wall. If they hadn't had the slight advantage of being uphill from the Government City, she probably wouldn't have been able to see in at all. The barbed wire along the top faced outward instead of inward, making it clear that no one was allowed to enter. Scarlett wondered how this team was planning to make contact with anyone inside. The wall was easily double their height.

The other buildings reminded her strongly of every picture she had seen in History class. One had tall white columns in front, holding up a long roof and shading windows at least as tall as Scarlett. She could see a few lights burning inside some windows, even at this late hour.

"Are you listening?" Dariah asked.

"What?" Scarlett responded.

"I thought I saw someone in the street over there," Dariah said, pointing to a street far to their left. "Do you see anything?" Dariah passed the binoculars to Scarlett.

"No," Scarlett responded, looking through the lenses to get a better view of the Government City. Madrick had distanced himself from them without leaving the cover of the trees. Then, as Scarlett turned, she saw inside one of the windows. The light flicked on for a minute, and a male moved around inside. Scarlett couldn't see many details except that he was wearing light blue clothing and had facial hair. He moved to the wall opposite the window, and Scarlett's mouth dropped open just a little as he ran his hand over tens, no, hundreds of books.

He finally pulled one out and opened it. After a brief moment, he shook his head, shoved it back onto the shelf, and selected another one. "What is that?" Scarlett asked Dariah softly.

"What?" Dariah was still watching the street where she thought she had seen movement. "The, that window over there," Scarlett pointed to the lit window where the male had now tucked the book under his arm and was strolling toward the other side of the room. The light flicked off, and it was dark again.

"That's one of the Government officials," Dariah looked at Scarlett like she had expected Scarlett to know that.

"Yes, I guessed as much, but I mean, where is he? Is that whole building a library or is it just that room?"

"That's his house," Dariah explained. "So, I have to assume the other rooms are bedrooms or a kitchen or a bathroom, not libraries."

"That's his *personal* library?" Scarlett asked, her voice a bit too loud.

"Sh!" Dariah shushed her. But as Scarlett considered that information, that all those books belonged to just the one male, she felt anger growing in her. She wondered what they contained, not so much for herself, but for Malak. It didn't seem fair that they were limited to one bookcase, and this one male had a whole library full. Scarlett had been told that all of the old literature that did not live up to the Government's standards had been destroyed. That was why only a few books were left, along with a couple of new books that were Government-approved. Scarlett balled her hands into fists.

"That's not fair," she mumbled, the injustice of it striking her. Clearly, the Government officials had kept the books that were supposedly destroyed and were using them for their own amusement to read before bed. Scarlett thought of how strict it had been living in the training center. Sure, she had free hours, but even during her free hours, she was usually doing some training on her own or just talking to her friends. Even decks of cards were hard to come by. There were only a few floating around the training center.

"There!" Dariah pointed out, and now Scarlett saw the movement Dariah had mentioned. It was only one street away from where their three teammates were waiting directly outside the concrete wall. They had an uphill, five-minute run to the edge of the forest if they were spotted. Scarlett wondered if there were guards patrolling the perimeter. She also now realized that in reality she knew little to nothing about the Government or their City.

Scarlett watched as a stone in the concrete wall started moving. It popped out, and a small window appeared. A face peered through, and Harold leaned closer. Scarlett's stomach clenched. They obviously knew the individual, but she still felt like something might go wrong. She couldn't take her eyes away from them as several objects were passed through the window. Amy and Phillip hurried back to the group with the objects and divided them among backpacks as Harold stayed and continued to converse with the male. Finally, the block was shoved back into place, and Harold ran up the hill.

Everyone walked a good five minutes into the forest, catching their breath and putting some important distance between themselves and the Government City.

"I have some solemn news," Harold finally said. "Our contact in City 6, Phan, was executed."

"What?" Scarlett's step faltered.

"Apparently, he was discovered somehow. Our contact doesn't know how, but he said that it would be our last communication with him for at least six months. He wants to lay low for a while, and I understand. He has to think of himself."

"Why did they execute Phan?" Scarlett asked, even though she knew the answer. "Was it because of me? Did they know he helped me escape? How long ago was he executed?"

"I don't know how long ago, and babies were mentioned. Our contact mentioned that Phan had helped several babies leave the City, which was the stated reason for his execution. I don't know more than that, but it may mean we need to avoid all Cities for a while. We can't spook our contacts. I'll meet with the elders, and we can figure out what to do." While Harold spoke practically, Scarlett felt her anger growing. She finally burst out.

"It's not fair. We work hard! Everyone in the Cities works hard like Kendrick did, but they don't even have enough to eat or the chance to enjoy themselves. Why should all those people have thousands of books and big houses and who knows what else? Why don't we storm the City and take from them and give it to the other Cities? We have to-"

"No, Scarlett," Phillip said. "You can't let your anger control what you do. What's done in anger is never done well."

"Okay, so we don't do it right now," Scarlett responded. "I just mean that we have enough people in the camp. We shouldn't be living off their scraps, what they throw our way. We should be enjoying life, instead of fighting for it."

"While I agree with you," Dariah said. "Phillip speaks the truth. We shouldn't try to overtake the Government City or any other City. Doing something like that would result in a lot of death. I'm not willing to sacrifice someone else's life so that things can be more fair."

"But isn't that what this is about?" Scarlett asked. "They're controlling everyone, while they live in those luxurious houses. Meanwhile, Citizens are slaving away so they can have enough food to work again the next day. We have to do something to change it."

"Sometimes," Harold said, "we can't change the world. And we don't have to. Maybe we can just change one person or one person's point of view. Maybe we just make a difference in one other person's life, and that's okay. Because at least we were able to love that person and take care of them and change the way their life goes."

Scarlett thought about Esperanza, the tiny female who depended upon her. Scarlett imagined her growing up, getting taller, having longer hair, speaking, and coming to Scarlett for things because she knew that Scarlett loved her.

Scarlett pressed her lips together. She couldn't explain the amount of love she felt for this tiny human. She then thought about Ariel, who had taken a special liking to Scarlett. She was someone who made Scarlett feel important, and Scarlett hoped that she made Ariel feel the same way. She didn't have anything else to say, but her thoughts were busy as they continued walking at a steady pace back to the camp.

A piercing scream hit their ears. Scarlett looked wide-eyed at the others to see if they had heard the same thing. Everyone broke into a run, heading toward the camp as fast as they could.

CHAPTER 32

Smoke burned her nostrils. Scarlett already had her knife out, not sure what was happening, but trying to be ready. They broke through into the clearing to pure chaos. But what caught Scarlett's eye was the clean White uniform splattered with blood. Scarlett paused at the edge of the camp to catch her breath. There wasn't only one White. There had to be at least a dozen.

Shots fired directly by her. Many screamed and ducked, or perhaps fell from being hit. Scarlett's brain couldn't process everything that was happening, but she knew what she had to do. She ran up behind one of the Whites and jumped him, shoving the knife between his shoulder blades.

He immediately dropped the gun and stumbled forward. Scarlett scooped up the gun and pointed it at the male. He turned to face her, pulling a knife from his belt. Scarlett shook her head and pulled the trigger, aiming directly at his head. For the first time, she had killed someone. She couldn't breathe. She felt like the world was closing in around her as the male fell. She remembered seeing Rhys fall after she had shot him. Her hands held the gun loosely. It suddenly felt too heavy for her.

Another scream, this one was a child's, and Scarlett snapped back to the world around her. Some of the tents were on fire, and the White uniforms reflected the light, making it easy to spot them. Scarlett aimed at two more and shot. They fell. It was just like one of the simulation activities.

Scarlett whirled around, looking for someone else to shoot when she was tackled from behind. Something sharp pierced the back of her neck, and the pain was so intense that Scarlett wanted to crumple into a ball and stop feeling. The gun flew out of her hands and skittered a meter away. Scarlett gasped for breath, her lungs filling with smoke instead.

"Scarlett!" the male yelled in her face. Scarlett finally caught some smoke-filled air. She pushed Rhys off her.

"What are you doing here?" she asked. But his yell had brought two other Whites their way. Turning her back to him, she lunged for the gun and grabbed it. Now, she was laying on the ground with the gun pointed at Rhys, again. Her finger was on the trigger as Rhys stared at her. Scarlett heard a scream as one of the Whites was attacked from behind. Her head was throbbing, and her vision seemed to shake. She could feel blood pouring out of her neck. Her muscles screamed for attention.

Rhys held the knife up in his hand, staring at her. The look on his face was vacant. He knew who she was as evidenced by his shout, but she didn't know him. This was not Rhys. Rhys threw the knife at her, and Scarlett rolled to the side, the knife nipping her ear. Rhys pulled another knife from his belt and aimed again.

Trembling, Scarlett acted before she could think. She aimed the gun and fired, his forehead clearly in her sights. He fell to the ground and let out such an ear-piercing scream that Scarlett dropped the gun. His scream ground to a halt, and a Blue rushed over to grab him.

"No!" Scarlett shouted, grabbing his arms and pulling at him. The Blue dropped Rhys's legs and pulled his pistol from his belt. He aimed at Scarlett and just as he was about to fire, a figure in dark clothes pounced on him. Shots were fired. Screams echoed. Scarlett crawled over to Rhys. He was still breathing. She hadn't hit his head after all. Her bullet had buried itself somewhere in his upper chest. His breathing was ragged. Scarlett was crying.

"I'm sorry. I'm sorry," she repeated over and over. The fighting continued around her, but she couldn't move. Rhys's breathing crackled like a radio without signal.

"Move out!" a commanding voice shouted, and the shout was repeated by other Whites. Scarlett looked up to see six or seven retreating into the forest. Their uniforms no longer looked perfect as they retreated from the light. Several from the Fringe ran after them, having taken guns from some fallen guards. Scarlett heard shots fired.

The flames continued to crackle, and a few individuals began dousing the burning tents with buckets of water from the nearby stream. Scarlett could see the blood soaking Rhys's uniform. It dribbled down his arm and into the pine needles. Scarlett pressed her hand over the hole, her tears mixing with the blood. Tears fell off her face onto his Blue uniform.

"Rhys," she said. He gurgled something, but she didn't know what, if anything, he had been trying to say. He wiggled, writhing under her grip, but Scarlett pressed on the wound in a desperate and futile attempt to keep the blood from escaping. "It's okay," she said. "It's okay." But she knew it wasn't. Kendrick came over and sat on the ground by Rhys's head. Scarlett wanted to push him away as though anyone coming close to Rhys was a threat. But the fighting was done, at least for that moment.

"He's dying," Scarlett said. "He's dying! Stop him from dying!"

"I can't do anything," Kendrick said.

Scarlett pressed harder against Rhys's wound which seemed to hurt him more than help him, based on his jerked reaction. Rhys started coughing, his body convulsing as he coughed and coughed and coughed. He spit out a lump of bloody gunk, then collapsed again onto his side. Scarlett tried to roll him over, but his body was so heavy.

"Rhys," Scarlett said again, not sure what she was asking for, except knowing that this hurt too much. She closed her eyes and pressed her fists into her eyes just as she had cried when she was a Red. Rhys's blood smeared around her eyes, but she didn't care.

"Is he dead?" Scarlett asked.

Kendrick placed a hand under Rhys's nose then two fingers against his neck. "I think so," he said. But it wasn't the end. Scarlett touched Rhys's neck, desperately searching for a heartbeat. She thought she felt a flutter of something, but nothing. She stared at him, tears falling from her blood-stained eyes. He didn't move. He didn't react when Scarlett pressed against his wound. The blood was slowing and starting to coagulate.

"I'm going to help put out the fires," Kendrick said. "Are you okay?" Scarlett didn't respond, but she felt him leave. She was left alone with Rhys's body. She had shot him before. Supposedly, she had killed him, but later, he had been alive. Scarlett kept waiting for his body to move. For him to get up and smile at her and explain what had happened. But he didn't. He was motionless.

Laya came over to Scarlett, sat on the ground despite the blood, and hugged her. Scarlett cried into Laya's shoulder, letting more tears fall than she knew she had in her. "I think he's dead," she said.

"He's dead, honey," Laya said. She reached out to check just to make sure. "He's gone. I know it hurts." She patted Scarlett's back, and Scarlett just wanted to stay there. She didn't want to think about the fact that she would have to stand up. She would have to help with the fires. She would have to . . . Esperanza crossed her mind, and Scarlett hopped up.

"Where's Esperanza? Is she okay?"

"I don't know," Laya said. "We can look for her." Scarlett's heart was torn. She was scared that if she left Rhys's body alone for a moment that it would disappear, that he would come back to life and attack her with a knife again. Laya noticed her sleeve was red from hugging her. "You're bleeding! Let me get you something to cover the wound and keep it clean."

Scarlett waited as Laya found her something. She tied it around her neck with enough pressure to stop the bleeding. Reluctantly, she stood and left Rhys. Only one tent was still on fire, and a pair of males were occupied with bringing water back and forth to deal with it. Scarlett wasn't prepared for the charred bodies that would be revealed inside. Her stomach clenched, and she looked away.

Mara ran up, her face black with smoke. She was crying. Scarlett saw she carried something in her hands. "Do you have-" Mara shoved the bundle at Scarlett then hurried back the direction she had come. Scarlett pushed the blanket back. She saw Esperanza's familiar face and breathed a sigh of relief. She returned quickly to where she had left Rhys. He was still there.

Scarlett checked under his nose and on his neck with two fingers as Kendrick had done. No movement. But as Scarlett looked at Esperanza again, she realized that something was wrong. Her eyes seemed glazed over.

Suddenly, she gave a wracking cough. She coughed and coughed. Scarlett flipped her onto her stomach and patted her back, trying to be gentle. Esperanza coughed some more. Scarlett knew it had to be the smoke affecting her. Scarlett sat on the ground, where there was little to no smoke. Esperanza moved slowly as though she had been sedated and continued sporadically coughing. Scarlett held her loosely, her eyes constantly flipping back to Rhys.

"He's dead," Scarlett said the words out loud, hoping that if she said them out loud, then she would convince herself. But it did nothing except make the tears come down her face again. Scarlett felt light-headed, and she wanted to lay down. She felt like she might pass out. Scarlett lay on the ground, cradling Esperanza closely. She reached back and felt her bandage. It was wet all the way through.

Even though she fought it, she felt her world turning black.

Scarlett woke up in a very different world. The smoke was gone. The chaos and shouting had stopped. Esperanza was still tucked between her arm and her side. Scarlett squinted in the bright sunlight and tried to understand what was happening around her. Esperanza reacted to Scarlett's movements, and she waved her arms a little. "Are you feeling better?" Scarlett asked. Esperanza formed an 'o' with her mouth and coughed hard. "Guess not."

Scarlett turned her head and found Rhys's body still there. It hadn't moved. Of course it hadn't moved! He was dead. Scarlett tried to accept the fact, but it seemed impossible to comprehend. Scarlett stood and took a few steps farther into the camp, looking for a familiar face. The smell of burnt meat sickened Scarlett. She leaned over and vomited, nearly dropping Esperanza in the process.

"I'm sorry," Scarlett said, wiping her mouth. She went to the river to get some water. That was where she found Kendrick. He helped her take some of the purified drinking water as he took another big bucketful and started the purification process all over again. Scarlett drank slowly then used a bit of the water to clean the ash off Esperanza. Esperanza squinted and winced as the cold water touched her skin.

"I don't know what to do," Scarlett said. "I know people probably need help. Some are more hurt than me, but I'm not trained for this."

"You can help when you're ready," Kendrick said. "You need some time to recuperate first. Let me see your neck." He started to untie the bandage of sorts, but Scarlett pulled back.

"I don't want you to touch it."

"Why not?"

"It might get infected. I need a doctor to look at it."

"Sorry to say, but there aren't any doctors waiting on the edge of the forest to help us. Besides, I was a chopper long enough to know how to deal with these wounds." Scarlett finally permitted him to peel back the cloth. It was stuck to her neck with the dried blood, and Scarlett winced, wiggling away like an unruly child. Finally, the peeling was done, and her neck was exposed. Scarlett leaned forward slightly, and she felt her skin protest the movement.

"Ouch!" Scarlett reached up to touch it, but Kendrick smacked at her hand.

"If you don't want to get it infected, then don't touch it with your dirty hand."

Scarlett stayed still as Kendrick wet the cloth and washed it thoroughly with the clean water. When he squeezed it, water came off it in pink currents. Finally, the cloth was clean. "Don't move," Kendrick said. Scarlett felt him dab, first gently then a bit harder at the wound. She forced herself to stay still. It hurt, but she knew it had to be done.

"How does it look?" she asked.

"It's pretty deep. But you're lucky it's not a bullet wound. Then, I would have to dig out the bullet." Scarlett winced as the cold cloth touched her feverish muscle. Kendrick continued talking to distract her. "I think it needs stitches, but I'm not qualified enough to do that. I'm just going to wrap it up again."

"What happens if I don't get stitches?"

"It will take a lot longer to heal. You have to be careful if you start losing blood again, but it looks like it's already stopping up on its own. If you move your neck too much or too fast, it could trigger opening it again."

"I'll be careful. Maybe you can help someone else," Scarlett said. Kendrick studied her. "Yeah, I will. But I want to make sure you're okay first."

"You just checked."

"I mean, Rhys is gone. And I know that hurt."

"I shot him. I killed him . . . again."

"You had to," Kendrick said.

"Maybe he didn't know it was me. Maybe he thought it was someone else. I think . . ."

"Scarlett, you have to accept that Rhys brought everyone here to kill us. The Government doesn't want us living outside their walls. And I know they will come back soon enough. We have to get everyone feeling better again and get out of here."

"I'm just going to . . ." Scarlett stopped. She didn't want to admit that she was checking on Rhys to make sure he was really dead. She didn't want him to be dead, but she couldn't be surprised by him again. "See who needs help. Maybe I can send them to you, and you can help clean their wounds."

Kendrick shrugged. "Sure, my leg is hurting, so it's better if I just stay here."

Scarlett hurried back to where she had left Rhys. He was still there. While it was exactly what she was expecting, it was a relief. Scarlett took a deep breath, wrapped Esperanza so that she was protected from any of the lingering smoke, and started to circle the camp. She saw a young male, maybe five or six years old, not moving. He looked like he was sleeping. Scarlett bent over and touched him gently on the arm.

"Are you okay? Were you hit?" He didn't respond, so Scarlett rolled him onto his back. "You okay, buddy?" When she saw the wound on his stomach, she knew he was dead. His stomach had been slashed completely open, and Scarlett could see his organs peeking through the open skin. She blanched, but there was nothing left in her stomach. "Okay, okay, I'm okay," she said out loud, not speaking to anyone specifically. Who could hurt a child like this?

Scarlett cautiously approached two males in Blue suits. They had clearly come with Rhys, come to attack the camp. But were they still alive? Scarlett reached for the one knife she had left and held it in one hand, Esperanza in the other.

"Hello?" she called, standing half a meter away. One of the Blues moved, and Scarlett waved the knife at them. The male turned to face Scarlett, and she dropped the knife. There was no mistaking the familiarity of the face.

"Malak?" Scarlett said.

Malak opened and closed his mouth, like he was trying to say something.

"Are you okay? Where are you hurt?"

Malak didn't answer, but Scarlett scanned until she saw that there was a pretty serious cut on his right arm. It looked deep, like the cut on her neck.

"Okay, your arm is hurt. Anywhere else?" She didn't want to infringe upon his space, but she had to see what was going on.

Malak shook his head.

"I'm going to get you some help," Scarlett said.

Malak shook his head again.

"What do you mean 'no'? You don't want help?"

"No," Malak croaked out.

Scarlett bent down. Malak wouldn't hurt her. "Why? You need help. We don't have great medicine, not like in the City, but I'm sure we have something."

Malak's voice was low and raspy. "I'd rather die like this than die being tortured."

"Tortured? You wouldn't . . . no one here will hurt you." Malak shook his head. Scarlett tried to understand.

"Please kill me," he said.

Now it was Scarlett's turn to shake her head. "I won't do that. I'll help you get better. It's okay. Kendrick can help you. Can you walk?"

Malak shut his eyes again, signaling the end of the conversation. Scarlett frowned and marched away. She would help Malak. Because while Malak wasn't her number one friend, he had never betrayed her or lied to her or given her a reason to mistrust him. He could figure out what he was going to do later, but she wouldn't allow him to die.

Scarlett found Laya. "I want to help, and I need some medical supplies. What do we have?"

Laya shook her head. "What you picked up last night won't be enough to help everyone. We do have plenty of clean cloths, but only Onya is skilled enough to stitch people up. Do you need stitches?"

"Maybe, Kendrick says I do. My friend needs stitches."

"Kendrick."

"No, Malak," Scarlett said.

Laya frowned. "Who is that?"

"He is one of the Blues I worked with," Scarlett explained.

Laya's face hardened. "We will take care of our people first. Once they are treated, then I will send the healer to him."

"He could be one of us. It's not fair to decide who is more important and help them first."

"Yet it has to be done. And those who brought this upon us are not first in line to receive medical help." Scarlett stomped away, angry. She found Kendrick by the river where he was cleaning someone's knee. The skin was red and inflamed, and the person was crying uncontrollably. As the female looked up, she looked very familiar. But no, it wasn't her little friend; it was Ariel's mom.

"Are you okay?" Scarlett asked. Her knee made Scarlett's stomach turn, but the rest of her didn't look hurt, just black with smoke and ash.

The female shook her head. "My baby, my babies!" she cried. Scarlett clutched Esperanza. This female didn't sound right in the head.

"Esperanza is my baby," Scarlett said, even while thinking that she wasn't technically her child, but everyone viewed her as such.

"No, my Ariel is dead! My Stella is dead! They are both gone!" the female shouted through her tears. Scarlett froze.

"No, she's not," Scarlett said.

"They were roasted alive!" the female proclaimed in Scarlett's face. Scarlett took a step back.

"Where? Where are they?" Scarlett asked, as though she might be able to do something. The female pointed toward one of the charred shells of a tent. Inside were three blackened bodies. Scarlett forced herself to go closer. One of them was much smaller than the others. It was half-dragged out of the shell of the tent, but the burns were bad, so bad that her skin no longer resembled anything human. Scarlett knew exactly who it was. It was Stella: Ariel's little sister. The one beside her must be Ariel.

Scarlett swallowed. Rhys had done this. He had brought all of this pain and death to their group. But as Scarlett looked around and met with angry stares, she realized that they didn't blame Rhys. Many of them hadn't even met him. But Scarlett, she had been with them for a couple of weeks. She had worked for the Government. Did they think she had caused this?

CHAPTER 33

An older male stood in front of those who had gathered. All of the fires had been put out, and Onya had been working tirelessly for hours addressing wounds. Scarlett didn't have the stomach to assist her. Anytime she started digging bullets out of bleeding flesh, Scarlett felt like she would vomit again. Instead, she had gathered all of the weapons she could find among the dead and wounded bodies and brought them to Derrico so that he could account for what they had.

"We have finished assessing the situation," the male said, speaking slowly. He was shaking, and Scarlett wondered if he was nervous or just overly tired from the long day. "We have suffered sixteen deaths. And two children have not been found. We have to assume that they were taken when the guards fled." Scarlett's eyes went to Mara's empty arms. Was that what had happened to her chubby little Moses? Scarlett didn't know which was worse, having a child die or having them taken.

"We know they will come back. The Government won't accept defeat and as close as we are to the Government City, they could send troops from there. They know we are injured and will make easy prey." Was his speech supposed to animate them? Because right then, Scarlett didn't feel encouraged about their situation.

"A grave has been dug, and we will bury our dead now. If you would like to say a few words as we put them in the grave, you are welcome to

221

do so." The male waited as body after body was taken and lowered gently into the grave where the middle of their camp had once been. Each person's name and age were announced. Then, someone spoke about how that individual had meant so much to them. Many in the crowd were crying, but Scarlett noticed that Rhys was not placed in the grave. She stepped away, and he was still in the same spot, plenty of flies finding him a comfortable resting place. Scarlett shooed them away, but they landed back on his body as soon as she paused.

Scarlett marched back, about to demand they bury Rhys with the others, but dirt was already being shoveled over the bodies. It shouldn't matter. It was just a body; Rhys wasn't there anymore. But it still felt like she should do something to honor him.

The male cleared his throat and stood once again. "This is a sorrowful day, but as we believe, nothing happens without a reason. This great tragedy seems without reason now, but we must find the purpose for which we have experienced this." He paused. "We are going to divide into smaller groups to provide a harder target for the Government to track. Your groups will be assigned shortly, but we will be on the move tonight. We can't risk sleeping here another night. Please take apart your tent. If you no longer have a tent, let us know, and we will make sure your group has enough tents. I'm greatly sorry for all of you who have lost someone today."

A few clapped, and the group broke apart. Scarlett immediately went to Malak. He was still in the same position. His arm hadn't been addressed.

Scarlett bent down and shook him. She saw a flicker of movement under his eyelids. He was alive. "Malak," she said.

His eyes flew open, like when she had pretended to be asleep as a Red so she wouldn't get in trouble. He looked at her completely differently now. "It hurts so much," he said. "Make it stop." Scarlett saw the pain in his eyes, and she remembered how differently her neck had felt after she had received pain pills from Laya, but she was sure Laya wasn't about to give two to Malak, not after her earlier response. Suddenly, Scarlett remembered Rhys's pack. It probably still had the same things it had when he had arrived at camp.

"I'll be right back," Scarlett said. She scurried away and ripped the backpack off Rhys's body, glad now that he hadn't been tossed into the mass grave. His backpack had a package of pain pills, enough for a week. Scarlett got some purified water and hurried back to Malak. She sat on the ground and helped Malak sit up. He winced, and Scarlett saw that his wound was still bleeding. His bandage was soaked.

"Drink these," she said. He took the medicine and drank the whole cup of water.

"Thanks," Malak said, laying back down. He stared at Scarlett. "I thought you would be dead after this raid. I'm glad I didn't have to kill you."

Scarlett suddenly realized what a gold mine of information Malak could be. She settled to the ground next to him. "Do you want more water? The cooks haven't made anything today, but I don't think many people have a stomach for eating after everything that's happened."

Malak ignored her offer. "Are they going to kill me?" he asked. "I've noticed a lot of other people getting help, but they have avoided us."

"You mean the Blues and Whites? I think they're hoping if you're not already dead, then you'll just die without their help."

"I can leave now and go back to the City," Malak said. "If I can make it, they will heal me there."

"You're only two hours from the Government City," Scarlett pointed through the trees in the direction she had gone the night before.

"Really?"

"Yes." Scarlett didn't feel like they were two enemies talking. This was her friend, and she didn't want him to die. "Would you have killed me if you saw me in the battle?"

"Yes," Malak responded. He blinked his eyes several times. "I had to. You stole a baby from the City. You shot Rhys. We came out to the forest to bring you back to the City, alive if possible."

"Malak, I have to tell you something. The Government is lying to you."

Malak blinked his eyes several times, as though his blinks stored the information in his brain. "How so?"

"They don't want the best for the Citizens. They want the best for themselves. I didn't go inside the Government City- that would be too dangerous- but I saw the outside of it. Malak, one male, one of the officials, had a whole roomful of books, just for himself. And he flipped through them casually to pick which one he would read that night. I've never seen that many books before, and they were just for him."

Malak perked up at the mention of books.

"I wish I could have seen inside everything, but don't you think it isn't fair how they make the Citizens work hard, every day, and the Citizens barely have enough to eat? Meanwhile, they are enjoying luxurious houses. I didn't see a single open window, which means they probably have the cold air."

"But you don't know that for a fact," Malak said.

"No, but probably. Malak, you didn't *see* the Government City. If you had seen it, then you would understand."

"Why are you telling me this?"

"Because I know that you like the truth, and the truth is that we're serving a Government that we know nothing about. We are trusting people we have never met. We are trusting people who are keeping all the good things for themselves, not sharing equally with the Citizens like they preach."

Malak studied her, then his attention turned to his arm. He reached out and probed the open skin, wincing. "That pain medication is strong. Is it something you have here in the camp? Is it made from natural resources?"

"I got it from Rhys's pack," Scarlett admitted. "He brought some supplies with him into camp when he visited me. And, I guess he never got rid of his pack when you all came to . . . you know."

"Strange," Malak commented. "We were told to leave everything except one knife and our pistols behind." Scarlett thought about what that might mean.

Suddenly, making Malak understand how backwards everything was meant more to her than figuring out what had happened with Rhys. "We were told not to ask questions, not to doubt what we were told. If they had nothing to hide, why would they tell us that?"

"I don't remember being told not to ask questions," Malak said, continuing to probe the flesh.

"Stop. You're going to infect it with your dirty fingers. I'm going to find some medicine for it, but first, I want to-"

"You want to make sure I'm not going to kill you."

"That's not what I was going to say."

"I won't," Malak promised. "And I'm not one to tell a lie. I have completed my mission. I would have retreated with everyone else, but I was physically unable to do so. I will not lie, but I can walk away from here with a clear conscience without killing you."

"They could kill you for not killing me," Scarlett said, trying to make him realize how dangerous they were. "They killed Phan."

"They killed Phan for helping you and the baby escape. Is that her?" Malak asked, pointing to the sleeping bundle in Scarlett's arms.

Scarlett nodded. "Yes, he helped us both escape. And she has a name. It's Esperanza." Scarlett pulled back the blanket, and Malak took a good look at her.

"She's much bigger than that first night." He reached out to touch her, then pulled his hand back as if afraid to soil something so perfect.

"How did they know Phan helped us? Because I told Rhys?"

"Yes, Rhys talked with Irin, and then he was called in to talk with the Black. It's my understanding that he was responsible for reporting what Phan did."

"But why would he report that?" Scarlett suddenly remembered another lie. "They told me that Rhys was dead. They told me that I was responsible for killing him, and that's why I was going to be executed. But if I didn't kill him, then why did the Black say that?"

"I don't know," Malak appeared bothered by this. "You didn't kill him. He did go into surgery, though."

"So, they said I did. Why would they tell me that? I asked to see his body, and they said he was already buried." Scarlett pointed in the direction of Rhys's immobile body. "He still hasn't been buried. They lied to me! Why did they want to execute me if I hadn't done anything wrong?"

"Please don't take offense, but it was my understanding you did shoot him. He has a scar now from where you shot him. I'm pretty sure that shooting a fellow guard is worthy of an execution."

"But it was an accident!" Scarlett protested. "I told them that. I didn't mean to do it. And even if I did, why would they want me to think he was dead?"

"I can't propose to understand the working of someone else's mind," Malak said. "He was changed after you shot him."

"He had a scar."

"More than that," Malak said. "I overheard a conversation I wasn't supposed to hear. You know that I am quiet with information when I don't think it should be shared, but I think you need to know this." Malak paused, and Scarlett leaned forward eagerly.

"I believe that Rhys was part of a pilot program that involved controlling the part of his brain responsible for processing emotion- the amygdala. With this part of his brain shut down or at least moderated, he would only do what he was told to do." Scarlett could see that Malak was excited by the science behind it. "Why do humans make a lot of their decisions? Emotions. They feel angry, so they punch the wall. They feel nervous, so they bite their nails. They feel betrayed, so they act vengefully. But, if you feel none of those emotions, how would you choose what you do?"

"I guess, you would do what you think is right . . .emotions wouldn't sway you."

"Yes, and Irin was giving Rhys some sort of pill at night. I don't know if it was a continuous dosage of the hormone or what. That's all I know about it. But Rhys, the real Rhys, wasn't in there anymore."

"Wow," Scarlett breathed out. So, she hadn't really killed Rhys. She had killed a robot. She took a few deep breaths then refocused her attention on Malak. "Let me get you some more water to drink or see if there is something I can bring over here to help your arm."

"Don't," Malak said. "It's better if my arm is still injured when I reach the City." He sat up and pressed a hand to his forehead. "You said the Government City was that way?"

Scarlett nodded, pointing in the correct direction. "Yes, about two hours. So, you're actually going then?"

Malak nodded. "I have no choice. I have been chosen to serve the Government, and I stand a much better chance of being reunited with them if I go that way than if I try to find the way back to City 6."

"Okay," Scarlett said. Malak stood and examined his arm again. He was much stronger than he had been an hour ago.

"I should go while I have the energy. Don't tell them," Malak said, glancing at the camp. "I don't want them to send people out to kill me."

"They wouldn't-"

"Don't."

"Fine, I won't." Scarlett watched Malak walk away, but watching him walk away didn't compare to the pain she had felt seeing Rhys do it.

CHAPTER 34

Scarlett was called to join her assigned group. She had been conversing with Malak while they were assigned, so she didn't know where she should be. However, she assumed that Kendrick motioning her over was a sign she should follow.

As she watched the people milling around, her eyes continued searching, searching for someone. The pain hit her hard when she was a few steps away from her group. She stopped and swayed slightly as she realized that Ariel would never grab her hand and pull her on walks through the forest. She would never skip around or braid Scarlett's hair again. Scarlett struggled to find her breath.

"Breathe," she told herself, forcing her feet to take her the rest of the way to the group.

She was standing with Mara, Derrico, Verona, and Amy. Amy hated Scarlett's guts, but the annoyance was so small in comparison with the pain she was trying to suppress. The elder was going around to make sure each group had all of its members and a radio. Amy spoke up as soon as he reached their group.

"Can we pick our own groups? I don't think this is a good mix." She motioned to the whole group, but gave Scarlett a nasty look.

"Each group has to have someone skilled in each area so that the group is fully able to function on its own. We have a hunter, a creator, a communications engineer, and someone trained in combat. If we were to take you away and put you in a different group, then this group would be left defenseless."

"I think we would be fine without Amy," Scarlett said. "I've probably been training longer than she has when it comes to using a knife."

The elder peered closely at Scarlett. "Yes, but would you protect the others if the situation came down to choosing between hurting a White or one of us?"

"Yes, I would," Scarlett looked around at the others in her group even though she hesitated when she saw Amy. "These people have been here for me when the City wanted to kill me. Despite what people may be saying, I am here for everyone."

The elder didn't seem moved by her speech. He turned to Amy instead. "It's best if we keep groups as they are. If we begin to rearrange groups, then we will never get started. Besides, I don't think we would find a volunteer for this group." Scarlett took that as another dig at her and possibly Kendrick as well. She knew then that she couldn't tell anyone about her conversation with Malak. They would take it the wrong way.

"Fine," Amy huffed. "If you never hear from us again, you'll know why." The elder continued to the next group without comment. Scarlett stared at Amy.

"Mygov, you're-"

"Oh, it's your Government, now is it? You can't even swear without thinking of them."

Scarlett almost repeated herself, pressing her lips together. She did have something Amy needed to hear. "You sure are lucky that you were born out here, with the Fringe. Because I didn't get to pick where I was born. I didn't get to pick to be sent to the training center. I didn't get to pick to be sent to City 6. I didn't choose any of it. If you want to blame someone for my existence, blame the Government." Kendrick placed a hand on Scarlett's arm. Maybe it was meant to calm her, but it just made her angrier like someone else was trying to control her.

She wrenched her arm out of his grasp. "None of us chose the life we were given, so don't hate someone for what they are. Hate them for what they do!" Esperanza felt the anger in Scarlett and started to wail. Mara reached for her instinctively, and while Scarlett might have shied away, feeling like Mara's motion was somehow saying Scarlett was inadequate, she felt sorry for Mara and Derrico who had such sad looks on their faces. Mara cradled Esperanza gently, and Scarlett looked at Amy again.

"See, *this*, this sense of taking care of each other, *this* is what your group is supposed to be about. The City doesn't even pretend to have that, but you do. So act like it."

Amy frowned and opened her mouth, but Verona stepped forward. "Scarlett is right, Amy. Maybe you should think about what she said. The hate in the Government can't be put on her shoulders. So keep your mouth closed, and appreciate what you have. Judge Scarlett for what she does from here on out, but not what has happened in the past." Amy turned her steely eyes on her mother, but didn't say anything. Scarlett's eyes widened at Verona's unexpected defense of her.

Verona took charge and spoke to the whole group. "We've been told to stay far away from the Cities. We're going to head east, then north. We'll pass a lot of the same territory we were in before, but we have to hope the flooding is still down in that area."

"Isn't that where the Whites and Blues were going?" Derrico asked. "Would it be smart to follow them?"

Verona nodded, taking in his point. "They've been traveling at least twelve hours. I wouldn't think they would camp out, but that's why we'll be taking the turn north. There are no Cities to the north. In fact, we haven't charted that area much at all." Verona rubbed the button on the radio. "We're heading into the unknown. The point is to remain within talking distance of one group, but far enough away from the other groups that we wouldn't all be attacked at once."

Scarlett glanced over her shoulder toward the Government City. She couldn't see it, but she imagined Malak reaching the City, entering it, and telling his story. He didn't have any information that he wouldn't have had if he hadn't talked to Scarlett, so she couldn't blame herself for any more deaths, though Phan's weighed heavy on her shoulders.

Her calculating mind was suddenly overwhelmed with pain. Ariel and Rhys were both gone. She sat on the ground hard and pulled her knees up to her chest, sinking into the pain, wishing she could go back and change everything. If only she hadn't left the clues for Rhys to follow them . . .

"What's the group that we will stay close to?" Kendrick asked, looking around as the groups huddled. Verona pointed to another group nearby. Laya and Ignatius were in the group, along with Dariah and two people who must be Dariah's parents. Another male was in the group as well. Somehow, it was comforting to Scarlett knowing that Laya would only be a radio call away.

Everyone was given a few extra supplies, leftovers from their evening meal, as well as a share of the medical supplies that had not yet been used. They took their time eating their share of food and packing up their belongings. Some were injured and moving slowly. The smoke still hung around everyone, making moving quickly difficult.

"Did no one ever look at your neck?" Laya asked when she came over to deposit the three pain pills designated for their group.

"No," Scarlett said. The pain was a dull throb, but she had gotten used to it.

"Before we split up, we should have someone check and make sure you don't need stitches." Scarlett looked over at the group where Onya was and thought that her group was the luckiest. If someone got hurt, they would know exactly what to do, or at least have one person who knew. If someone in her group got hurt, they would just have to hope they didn't die. There were benefits to splitting up but some negatives as well.

Ignatius patted Scarlett hard on the shoulder, making her wince. "It's been a pleasure gettin' to know you. You're a good one."

Scarlett nodded, not sure how to respond to him, itching to touch her wound, but knowing she shouldn't.

Scarlett waited patiently as many of the groups started moving out of the camp, but her group, Laya's group, and Onya's group stayed behind while she peeled off the bloody bandage.

"What happened to you?" Onya asked once the cool air was dancing on the wound.

"Someone stabbed me with a knife," Scarlett said.

"Hmm," Onya's 'hmm' didn't sound very encouraging. "And you haven't touched it?"

"Just to put the bandage on. Is something wrong?" Kendrick sidled around to get a look as well. She saw his limbs instantly straighten. "What?! Tell me!"

Onya frowned. "It's just got some pus, and it looks like it has been trapped in there because of the cloth. You need to let it air for a little while, so the pus can come out."

"Does that mean it's infected?" Scarlett asked.

"No, well, it could become infected if you don't let the pus out. Laya, do we still have any of the water we brewed?"

Laya nodded toward a container. Onya washed the cloth in the river water then soaked it in the warm water and placed it on the wound. Onya pressed the cloth on tightly, but that wasn't what made Scarlett's back arch. She could feel something running down her neck. Onya dabbed at it.

"Okay, that's good," Onya said. Everyone was behind Scarlett, looking at her neck. She was the only one who couldn't see what was going on, and she hated the feeling of being the center of attention.

"Let's leave that there for a few minutes," Onya said.

Scarlett looked around. "I don't want to hold everyone up. You should probably get going."

"It's okay," Onya said. "I won't see you for a fortnight or two, so it's best to address it now. I know you can't see your neck, but you need to be changing the bandage every hour or two, max. You need to give it time to air out before putting a clean bandage on. We don't have anything to address it other than that, though Verona does have some pain pills for your group. I wouldn't suggest using them right away as we aren't guaranteed to get more City-made medicine for a while." Scarlett thought about the package of pills she had gotten from Rhys's pack. She still had them at the bottom of her pack. She wasn't sure why, but she hadn't wanted to tell people about them. She felt selfish, but not badly enough that she would change her mind and share them.

"Okay, does it need stitches?"

"I think it should be fine," Onya said, touching the edge of the wound again. Her fingers felt like ice on the overheated skin. "It's already started to heal, but you don't want it to close when there's still pus inside." Scarlett nodded, trying to remember all of the instructions. Onya took off the warm compress and rinsed it once again. "Give it some air for half an hour, then you can put this on again."

She stepped back and joined her group. Scarlett looked to Kendrick, and he smiled, encouraging her that she would be alright. Onya's group took off at a jog into the forest to catch up with their partners. Only Scarlett's and Laya's group were left, and Scarlett felt a sudden wave of emotion. She hugged Laya, and Laya hugged her back. All signs of battle had been fiercely scrubbed from her clothes, and Laya looked the firm, but welcoming female that she always did.

"I'll miss you," Scarlett said.

"We'll remain in contact," Laya said. "Remember that-"

A crashing in the trees caused them all to turn toward the noise. Even though it was beginning to get dark, Scarlett saw something Blue. She froze for a moment. They were back already. She looked toward where Mara was holding Esperanza, and she saw the fear in Mara's eyes as she clutched Esperanza even closer.

A few meters away, Scarlett saw a snatch of Blue. Scarlett grabbed her knife and held it up. Derrico strung his bow and arrow. The male stepped out of the forest, and Scarlett saw it was Malak. She dropped her arm that had held the knife ready, but Derrico shot the arrow. Malak dodged, and the arrow stuck in the tree right where he had been standing.

"Wait! Please!" he begged.

Scarlett looked behind him into the forest, but it was silent.

Derrico already had another arrow ready and trained on Malak. Malak held his hands up to show he wasn't carrying anything. "I'm not here to hurt you," Malak said.

Dariah scoffed, lifting her arm to throw the knife.

"Don't hurt him!" Scarlett said, leaping away from her group and toward Malak. "Don't hurt him!" She had no idea why he had returned, but she could see that the wound on his arm had not been treated. Had he gotten lost? Had the Government City not believed his story? Even if they hadn't believed him, they wouldn't have just let him go unless they were following him. Scarlett peered into the forest.

"It's just me," Malak said.

"Who are you?" Kendrick asked, crossing his arms. "The next Rhys? Come in here, gather intel, then take it back to your little friends?"

"Take me as your prisoner," Malak suggested. "I don't want to go back and serve the Government." Scarlett's mouth dropped open at this proclamation. Malak? Turning his back on the Government? Of course, she had hoped he might do that during their talk earlier that day, but she hadn't given it much thought. Malak was so careful about always following the rules and never questioning authority.

"We don't take prisoners," Laya said. She reached for the radio, then decided against it. Derrico and Dariah still had their weapons pointed at Malak. Scarlett went over and stood next to Malak, hoping they wouldn't think it was easier to just kill her rather than continue dealing with the trouble she seemed to bring to them.

"I talked to Malak today," Scarlett said. "I told him about the Government City. I told him how they lied to me, and I'm glad that he's back here. I told him you would all welcome him."

"He's going with your group," Dariah's father said, pointing to the group where Kendrick and Scarlett were. "We don't want that kind of risk with us. I don't trust them. They're-"

His wife placed her hand on his arm. "I think it would be a good idea to keep all of the City-born together." She looked worried. "I feel sorry for you," she said to Malak, especially when she saw the open wound on his arm. "But you must understand that we can't trust you after everything that just happened."

Malak nodded and lowered his head. "That's why I'm willing to come as your prisoner. You never let me out of your sight. You never let me have a weapon. I understand that trust must be built. But in exchange, I have information to offer about the Government."

Scarlett's eyes lit up as she saw his angle. "Malak was the best student at the training center. He was always studying and learning more, and he was trusted with more intel than anyone else."

Verona studied him accusingly. Clearly, the rift between the Government and the Fringe was not one that could be easily overcome.

"Please give him an opportunity," Scarlett begged.

"Fine," Verona huffed. She made eye contact with Mara and Derrico, "as long as it's okay with you."

"We have nothing else to lose," Mara choked out. Her eyes filled with tears.

"Come on, then," Verona said. She turned to Laya, who was in charge of the radio for their team. "Don't talk about your location or anything vital unless I give you the okay." Laya nodded. She pulled Scarlett to her once more.

"Be safe, Scarlett. Please take care of your team." Why was Laya asking her to take care of her team? Clearly, Verona was the leader here.

CHAPTER 35

Verona led them into the forest, and Malak fell in line with Scarlett. Amy made a big show of walking behind Malak, so she could see if he tried to leave. Kendrick walked on Scarlett's other side. They set off in silence, but Scarlett was worried about Malak's arm and why he was back.

"Why did you come back?" she asked.

Kendrick leaned in to hear the answer as well. "I went to the Government City, to turn myself in and explain how I got separated from my party, but, Scarlett, you were right. I didn't enter the City. I just looked at it from the outside.

"I saw all of them, cruising around in cars instead of walking. I watched one male exit a house, get into his car, and go the distance it would have taken us ten minutes to walk. He then got out of his car and entered the building. We were told that Jeeps are used very rarely because the fumes are dangerous for the environment. If that is true, why would they use a vehicle to travel such a short distance?"

Scarlett started to add to what Malak was saying, but he wasn't done.

"I have learned all of the history before the Government began. I know *why* and *what* and *how*. I know what it says the Government life is like. It says that those in the Government live just like Citizens. However, the Citizens also work to support the Government, because the members of the Government are too busy keeping order to chop their own wood, sew their own clothes, etc." Malak shook his head. Scarlett had never seen him so fired up. "The life of ease I saw, that was nothing like what we were told. And you are right. I love the truth too much to work for such liars."

Everyone seemed to have been listening, because Malak talked louder and louder the more fired up he became. Derrico turned around and patted Malak on the shoulder.

"Malak, that is exactly why we are living this way. The Government doesn't take care of the Citizens. They take care of themselves and take and take from the Citizens. We said that we would no longer put up with that level of injustice. We left."

"Did all of you live in the Cities at some point?" Malak said, distracted from his anger by the possibility of gathering information.

Derrico nodded. "Yes, all of us lived in Cities at one point, except the younger generations. Amy has grown up here," he nodded toward her. She didn't seem impressed by Malak's speech and was gazing off into the forest.

"However, many of us parents left on our own. Verona, may I tell them your story?" Verona shrugged, so Derrico continued. "Verona and her husband, Harry, left the City together, City 5. They thought they were out, but then Harry tripped and fell. Verona got behind the cover of some bushes as shots flew around her. She couldn't go back for him, because she was holding baby Amy at the time. Harry didn't make it. Unfortunately, that is the ending most escapes have. Many of the Cities are patrolled specifically to prevent people from leaving."

Scarlett remembered being one of those patrolling. She had never shot anyone, not before Rhys. There was something in her that had told her human life was valuable. Scarlett looked up at the clouds in the sky. They seemed to glow a freakish blue, reflecting the light of the moon. Mara had reluctantly handed Esperanza back to Scarlett, and she settled her in her childpack. She looked at Mara's empty arms and felt guilty. She wanted to bring up Moses, ask if someone would attempt to find him, but she didn't want to cause any more pain.

Malak had plenty of questions to fill the walking time anyway. "Have any other Blues such as Scarlett or I defected?"

"No, normally, if guards see the refuge we provide, they dedicate their lives to helping us, providing materials, or helping Citizens escape. It is a risky process. We mainly focus on the babies. Some families in the City know they will have to give up their child to grow up in the training center, so they prefer to have a White help that child come live with us instead."

"I could certainly help with that," Malak said. "I'm not one to shy away from danger, and I believe it is the right thing to do."

Verona shook her head. "We won't have contact with any of the Cities for at least a couple of months. Phan was killed because of our contact, so we must let things cool for a while." Everyone digested this news. Scarlett thought of a baby being born and not having the opportunity to escape because Verona was "letting things cool off." She pressed her lips together. She had already caused enough waves, no need to complain about this as well.

"Malak, let me see your arm," Scarlett said. Malak held out his arm, and they paused as she peeled off the bandage. "Let's let it air for a bit," she said. "That's what they told me to do with my neck. I don't need you passing out."

Kendrick offered to clean the rag with some of their water.

"Don't use too much!" Amy scolded. "We aren't walking beside the river, so we have to find a new water source. And if you use all our water on him, then we'll die just so his arm won't get infected. That makes a lot of sense." Her hostility was grating on Scarlett.

"What can you tell us about the Government's plans?" Derrico asked Malak. "Or about your City specifically?"

"I know that they are going to go back to that same campsite again," Malak said. "Our instructions were to eradicate your whole group, so your contacts wouldn't have anyone with whom to communicate. However, that's always harder than it sounds. The plan was to attack while you were sleeping, to find the guards, kill them, then attack the sleeping tents with gasoline and fire. We didn't expect one of the guards to warn half the camp before we arrived, or for another group of fighters to be hidden outside the camp." Malak licked his lips. "I'm sincerely sorry for any loss you might have experienced."

"They took our baby," Mara said, holding on to Malak's hurt arm. He grit his teeth and pulled his arm out of her grip.

"They took him?" Malak asked.

Mara nodded. "I grabbed them both, Esperanza and our Moses. But someone came up and ripped him out of my arms. I fought, but I couldn't with Esperanza in my arms. I tried to chase after them, but whoever it was went running into the forest. I couldn't keep up." She was crying. Malak nodded awkwardly as her tears fell.

"There was talk of taking back the babies taken from the Cities. They wanted to see how they would do coming back to live there after having had several months or a year away. Sort of an experiment to see how much those first few months affect a child's life."

"Moses is not an experiment!" Mara shouted. Derrico wrapped his arms around her as she cried. Malak scratched his neck, then his face, then his stomach, clearly uncomfortable with such a show of emotion.

Mara sobbed as they continued to move forward, her crying the only sound echoing in the forest. Scarlett imagined Esperanza ripped from her arms. Even the thought made her shudder. Scarlett's body felt exhausted. She hadn't slept at all the night before, and other than passing out for some time that morning, she hadn't had the chance to rest. The wound on her neck was throbbing, and she had to resist the urge to touch it.

Finally, Verona decided that they were a good distance from their original spot. She determined that they could rest. "I'll take the first watch." She looked around at the others. "Amy, I'll wake you in four hours, and you can take the second watch." Amy nodded.

"I don't mind taking a shift," Derrico said.

"You can tomorrow night," Verona said. "We shouldn't stop here for long anyway." Everyone took out the leftovers they had been given and started eating. Scarlett started to pull out the poles and skin to put up the tent, but Kendrick reached for them instead.

"You eat. I'll take care of putting up the tent."

Scarlett ate the remnants of their meal. Derrico offered to go out hunting for something, but Mara was against him leaving the camp. Everyone said they could wait until the next day for a hot meal. Tired, everyone climbed into their tents. Scarlett handed Esperanza over to Mara for the night, and Mara grasped her eagerly.

"Are you hungry?" Mara asked Esperanza, stroking her cheek.

"Sleep well," Scarlett said, rubbing her baby's fingers one last time. She turned and entered the tent where Kendrick and Malak were already laying down. Scarlett rolled out her mat and lay down, staring up at the top of the tent, the tiny hole that showed her a patch of sky. She rolled over, trying to turn so that her neck didn't throb as much. Her body felt exhausted; even the thought of rolling over seemed like too much. But her brain was moving, chugging, turning.

Ariel, Rhys, Ariel, Rhys. Her mind kept replaying moments she had spent with each of them, and she tried to shut it all out so she could just escape the pain.

She looked over at Kendrick and Malak. She couldn't see Malak well, but Kendrick's mouth was half-open, his eyes closed, the picture of a sleeping baby. Scarlett forced her eyes closed. But she just couldn't sleep. She didn't know how long she laid like that, pretending that she was asleep in the hope that she soon would be. She heard the flap of the tent open, and she stiffened, not sure who would be peering in. Unless someone was trying to get out.

Scarlett waited until the flap fell back in place, then she opened her eyes. Kendrick and Malak were still fast asleep. They hadn't moved. So, if neither one of them had been leaving, then someone had to have been looking inside. Scarlett sat up. She didn't like this feeling of being watched.

She listened to some footsteps getting farther away from the tent, then the radio crackled. "Laya, over, Laya." It was clearly Verona's voice. Scarlett hugged her knees to her chest as she shamelessly listened for Laya's response.

"Verona, I'm here. Can you hear me clearly?"

"Yes, we've stopped for the night, and everyone is asleep. We'll pick up walking in another six hours or so. Is everything well with your group?"

"Yes, everyone is safe and sound. Dariah will be taking a turn watching in an hour, so I can rest. So if you call then, she'll have the radio."

"Okay, Laya. Thanks." The radio crackled for a moment then went silent. "I don't know if I can trust Scarlett," Verona said, lowering her voice a little. Scarlett heard her loud and clear, though. Her heart started pounding out of her chest. Would Verona and Amy attack Scarlett? Were they that desperate to be rid of her? What about Malak and Kendrick? Scarlett couldn't help feeling alone.

"Scarlett is a good girl," Laya responded. "She might not always have the best judgment, but you can trust her. She would *not* turn any of you in."

Scarlett's heart warmed with Laya's words. At least someone believed in her.

"I know why you put her with our group." Really? Because Scarlett had no idea why Verona and Amy were paired with them. "I just need someone to know that I will be checking in every day. If we don't check in, then something has happened to us."

"Verona, we have split apart for this very reason, to protect everyone from the Government attacking us again. Those in your group will not hurt you."

"Then why did you not put any older individuals with us? Everyone here is fit and able to protect themselves."

The radio crackled, and Laya's reply wasn't clear, at least to Scarlett. Verona seemed to understand her well enough, though. "No, I know. I have to trust the process. I simply wanted to voice my concerns." Once again, there was silence.

"Tomorrow, you can announce the plan for the next year," Laya said. "We will protect our own first and foremost. And Scarlett, Kendrick, and Malak are our own now. I would happily have Scarlett guarding my back any day." Scarlett hugged her knees closer, but Verona seemed done talking. The radio crackled, then was silent.

CHAPTER 36

Kendrick woke Scarlett by brushing the hair from her face. She was surprised that she had fallen asleep. It had seemed like she might not ever sleep after the conversation last night. Kendrick was looking at her with this strange smile on his face.

"You're tired today, huh?" Scarlett thought about telling him what she had overheard, but with so few people around, she didn't want someone eavesdropping on how she had eavesdropped. Their conversation wouldn't be lost in the noise of the morning.

"I couldn't sleep," Scarlett said, looking over to where Malak should have been. "Malak!" she sat up immediately, and felt a sharp pain in her neck. Kendrick put up a hand to stop her.

"He's helping Mara make some breakfast."

Scarlett's eyebrows went up. She had no idea that Malak knew anything about cooking. "I just thought maybe he left."

Kendrick leaned forward so that their faces were only a few centimeters apart. "You don't trust him?"

"I do," Scarlett said, but after hearing so much against him, it was hard not to let it get in her head and start to bother her, too.

"You don't think he reached the Government City, and they said, 'You missed the perfect chance to spy. Get back in there'? It's possible."

"No," Scarlett shook her head. She tried to formulate an answer, but she was distracted by Kendrick's face so close to her own. His skin was a deep tanned color, and his hair was almost black, straight and long, falling across his forehead, covering the tops of his ears. He had stubble growing on his chin. Scarlett reached out and touched it, surprised by how sharp it was. Kendrick leaned back, like her touch had stung him.

"Sorry," Scarlett said. "Did that hurt you?"

"No, I just . . . didn't expect you to touch my beard." Kendrick ran his own hand across the short hair, which made a grinding sound.

"It's sharp," Scarlett giggled. Rhys hadn't had any facial hair. His face had been smooth. She felt sad at the thought of him. "I need to get Esperanza," Scarlett suddenly said, "and we should pack the tent up. We will be moving forward soon." She hurried out of the tent and found Esperanza in Mara's arms.

"How did she sleep last night?" Scarlett asked.

"She did fine," Mara responded, not taking Scarlett's hint that she was ready to take the child.

"Good, good to hear. Well, I'll go ahead and get her strapped into the childpack for the day, so you can help Derrico get your tent packed up or whatever else you might need to do." Mara handed Esperanza over to Scarlett. Esperanza studied Scarlett for a few minutes before breaking into a smile.

"Yes, my sweet little female. Are you ready for another long day? I hope so, because we don't want that fussing." Derrico approached Scarlett as Kendrick came up with their tent and stuffed it into the pack on Scarlett's back. She waited patiently as he moved it around.

"Good morning, Scarlett. I'm going to walk a ways away from the group today to try to get in some hunting so that we can have meat for the evening meal. Would you mind checking on Mara, talking to her or encouraging her during the day? I don't want to leave her, but I need to be responsible for my duties as well."

"Sure, of course, I will," Scarlett promised.

"Derrico," Kendrick said. "Do you think I could learn a bit about hunting? I know I've got my bum leg here, but I'd like to learn what I can, earn my keep around here." Derrico studied him for a minute.

"We can try it out," he said. "We won't be climbing any trees today, just walking along. I'll teach you how to use a bow and arrow. Ever used one before?"

Kendrick shook his head. "No, they don't trust us with weapons in the City."

"Well, it's not too hard, though it takes a while to get used to the resistance when you're aiming."

"I'll give it a try," Kendrick excitedly reached for the weapon.

"Good luck," Scarlett said as the two males took off into the forest. Their party seemed very small with only five adults and one tiny human.

"Derrico!" Mara called when she saw that her husband was leaving. Scarlett watched as she spoke a few hurried words with him, asking him to take a radio so he could call for help if he needed it. But they only had one radio. Who would he be calling if he took it? Laya? Her group would be too far away to do anything in time. Derrico whistled a three-note tone, and Mara wiped tears from her eyes. She leaned forward and kissed him on the mouth. Derrico kissed both of her cheeks then her forehead, and then he and Kendrick took off.

Scarlett wondered what it would be like to kiss Kendrick like that. Would she feel something different than she felt when she kissed Esperanza's tiny forehead?

"How are you doing today?" Scarlett asked Mara, trying to make conversation.

She nodded, her arms swinging freely as she walked, instead of on the childpack with Moses as they had been before. Scarlett noticed she didn't have the childpack anymore, but she didn't want to ask what had happened to it. That might sound insensitive.

"I wonder what animals Derrico and Kendrick will find today," Scarlett said. Her conversation sounded forced even to her own ears. "How long did it take Derrico to become such an excellent hunter?"

"Derrico has always had a penchant for hunting. Derrico and I are a strange couple as we are one of the few that met in the Fringe. Many who come to the Fringe are either families or babies," Mara's face broke when she said that word. She took a deep breath. "We both came at about your age, before the Selection Ceremony. I was from City 2, and Derrico was from City 6. And it was love at first sight."

"What do you mean love at first sight?" Scarlett questioned.

"It means that when we saw each other, we knew that we were meant to be together, to be husband and wife. A few years later, one of the elders married us, and we had Moses. In the City, I had always told my parents that I would never have a child. I didn't want the child taken to the training center. I couldn't imagine purposely choosing to bring someone into my life only to have them taken away."

"Why did you leave City 2?"

"When you turn eighteen, you get married. And if you don't have a match, then the Government chooses a spouse for you. I didn't want that. I didn't even know about this group. I found my own way out, then wandered in the forest for at least a week. When the Fringe happened to stumble upon me, I was almost dead. I believe providence brought us together. If not, I would have been nothing but a corpse in another week without food." Mara pressed her lips together as she recalled the memory.

"So many people in the Fringe say that they hate City life, but . . . has anyone ever said that they wished they hadn't come here?"

"Not everyone agrees with the elders and their decisions, but that is why we choose our elders. If we believe that one or more elders are not making good decisions, then we change elders. I think you can never have things be 100% the way you want them to be, but you have to learn to be 100% happy even when things are only going 80% your way."

Scarlett looked at Mara's empty arms. "And now?" she asked gently. "Do you feel like you can be happy again?"

Mara hung her head. "I think there will always be a hole in my heart. I want to think that I will find Moses, that somehow, one of our contacts will hear what happens, and we can swoop in and rescue him. But

I have to settle within myself that it's not likely." She bit her lower lip, and Scarlett wished she hadn't asked the question. They were silent for a long time, as Scarlett's brain constantly turned back to Ariel and Rhys.

Scarlett wasn't keeping track of how long they had walked, but her legs were calling for a break when Kendrick and Derrico rejoined them. Scarlett watched the joy on Mara's face as she hugged Derrico, while he held two rabbits out to the side so that their dead bodies wouldn't touch her. Kendrick's face spoke volumes.

"Are you okay?" Scarlett asked as he dragged his leg stiffly toward them.

"Let's have a break, cook these rabbits, then get moving away from the smoke of the fire," Derrico suggested. Everyone agreed, and Derrico began skinning the rabbits as Mara and Amy gathered wood for the fire.

Kendrick sat down heavily on the ground, not even looking around for something on which to sit. Scarlett squatted next to him. "Can I see your leg?" She touched the bottom of his pant leg.

"There's nothing to see," he said.

"I want to make sure it's not infected. Is it hurting . . . a lot?"

Kendrick shrugged, but Scarlett already knew the answer. He had acted this same way the first night she had brought him to the camp. That felt like it was so long ago. With this group, Scarlett didn't know how often they would stop. It wasn't fair to go so fast that Kendrick hurt himself.

Derrico came over once he had handed the skinned rabbits off to Mara. "Kendrick did great! He got real comfortable with the bow and arrow."

"Derrico is the one who shot both of those rabbits, though," Kendrick clarified. Scarlett felt proud of him.

"Still, it took me daily training for years to shoot like I do. Shooting anything is not easy. And anyway, when they attacked us the other night, you didn't need any weapons to save me from that male who was coming after Rhys's body and me."

"Rhys is dead?" Derrico asked.

Scarlett nodded. Esperanza was fussing, so Scarlett stood and started pacing back and forth in front of Kendrick. The baby calmed immediately.

"Sorry for you," Derrico said. Scarlett accepted his condolences without a word, and Derrico returned to where his wife was cooking the rabbit over a small fire. The smell made Scarlett's stomach grumble. The radio crackled, and Laya made contact to see if the smoke in the distance was from them or if they should be worrying about someone else in the forest.

When everyone had eaten their share of rabbit meat, Verona announced that they needed to put a good five to six kilometers between them and the fire. Everyone stood and stretched. Scarlett's back was starting to ache from carrying Esperanza, even though she couldn't weigh more than six or seven kilos.

Kendrick remained on the ground for a moment then rolled to his side, using his hands to push himself off the ground. He wavered a bit once on his feet, and Scarlett reached out to steady him.

"We can take it slow," Scarlett said, her patience for him much higher than on that first night when she had been worried about the guards catching her sneaking back.

Kendrick nodded, and as Verona started forward, Scarlett and Kendrick followed them at a distance that grew steadily. "Hey, keep in this direction, okay?" Scarlett called up. "We'll be along as we can."

Verona gave her instructions on where they were going, and the larger group drew ahead. Scarlett tried not to let Kendrick see that she was watching him. She saw the way he dragged his leg stiffly, the way he winced as though he had no desire to take one more step.

"Why do you keep waiting for me?" Kendrick asked. His question didn't make sense at first.

"I'm not waiting for you. We're walking."

"I mean, you're walking here with me, instead of with the group. Why?"

"You shouldn't have to walk by yourself. And I kind of feel guilty for Phan shooting you. I know I didn't do it, but I keep replaying that moment in my mind, when the male jumped Phan as he was reaching for his gun. If I had acted faster, if I had shot the male who was attacking him, then Phan wouldn't have tried to fire his gun at all."

"It's not your fault," Kendrick said. "That whole situation should never have happened. But we can't go back in time. I won't get my leg back. I'm stuck like this forever."

"But it doesn't seem to stop you from a lot," Scarlett admitted. "Maybe it hurts you more than you admit, but look at you. You hunted this morning with Derrico. You helped clean our wounds by the river. You attacked the male who was after me."

Kendrick didn't say anything.

"Thanks, Kendrick," Scarlett said. She kind of smiled then. "Just think, if your leg had never been shot, then I probably wouldn't have talked to you in the streets that day to see if you were okay. And if I hadn't done that, then I definitely wouldn't have tried to bring you with me when I left the City, and even if I had, you probably wouldn't have left."

"Of course I would have," Kendrick responded.

"Why? You would have still had your profession. We wouldn't have had a reason to communicate, so I wouldn't have told you I was leaving. Then, you wouldn't have been there to save me two nights ago."

The cascade of accumulating events was overwhelming. She could have been dead if Kendrick had not been shot that day while she was working with Phan.

"I would have left, because I like you. You give me a reason to keep going and keep trying, even when it feels like other people don't care." Kendrick was being open, and Scarlett had to admit that she had felt the same way.

"Sometimes, I feel alone too, like why am I here always trying to do the right thing but always doing the wrong thing instead?"

"You don't always do the wrong thing."

"It feels like I do."

Kendrick's hand brushed Scarlett's as they walked beside each other. She looked down at his hand, its fingers giving no indication to the injury on his leg. She reached down and grabbed his hand as she had seen Derrico and Mara do many times before. His hand felt rough, covered with callouses. His fingers immediately clasped hers, and they walked, their entwined arms swinging between them. It was a strange feeling, moving in time with someone else.

Scarlett pulled her hand from his a few moments later. "Why do people walk like this? It's not very comfortable." Kendrick laughed, a short chuckle that quickly turned into a full out belly laugh so hard that he couldn't continue walking. He had to lean over to catch his breath. "That wasn't funny," Scarlett said, feeling partly offended.

"It was . . . you . . . and the City . . ."

"I have no idea what you're trying to say."

Kendrick finally caught his breath, but he still had a dopey grin on his face.

"Want to try to explain your little joke to the rest of us?" Scarlett motioned to the trees around them, which only made Kendrick break into a smile again.

"You're a special person," Kendrick said. He looked in the direction they had been going. They couldn't see their group anymore, but that didn't worry Scarlett.

"Thanks," Scarlett felt warm from the compliment. "You are, too. You persevere."

"I want to tell you something, but don't freak out, okay?"

Scarlett looked at him skeptically. What could he possibly have to tell her that would make her freak out? Was he going to leave the group, try that noble, 'leave me behind; I'll catch up later' thing again?

"You know how Laya and her husband, and Mara and Derrico, how they have something special that made them want to be with each other?"

"Okay . . ."

"I feel that special thing with you, like no matter what other people were doing or no matter what they said, I would still want to face each challenge with you."

"Because I'm a good fighter?" Scarlett asked.

Kendrick placed his hands on his hips, and they stopped walking. "No, not like that. Just because you make me laugh. You make me feel . . . wanted. Not like how I felt with my parents. I'm sure they were glad when they saw I wasn't coming back, just because they didn't have another mouth to feed. But you, I felt like if I wasn't coming back, you would care. You might try to find me."

"Of course I would!" Scarlett said, her eyebrows knitting in the center. "You're my friend, my, well, my closest friend at this point."

Kendrick reached out and touched Scarlett's arm, and she felt a tingle move upward, into her neck. She looked up at him and smiled. She didn't know why she felt that way, but she liked it.

Kendrick started to say something else then closed his mouth, his jaw moving like a baby bird squawking for food. "I think we should get moving, unless your leg needs a longer rest," Scarlett said. "I don't know how far they're planning to walk today."

"No," Kendrick said shortly. "I don't need a longer rest. Just know, Scarlett, that I know the Government has betrayed you before, but I'm not that kind of person. I am here for you if you ever need anything." Scarlett smiled, knowing by the seriousness on his face that Kendrick was being completely honest. And despite what Mara had said earlier, Scarlett felt 100% happy in that moment.

CHAPTER 37

By the time Kendrick and Scarlett caught up with the group, Esperanza was screaming for something to eat. Scarlett happily handed her over to Mara. Derrico wasn't there, but Verona had already put up a tent and was asleep in it.

"Shut the baby up, would you?" Amy said. "My mother is trying to sleep."

"Sorry, maybe I'll just cover her mouth, so she can't breathe. Will that be to your liking?" Scarlett shot back. She had had enough of Amy. Amy rolled her eyes and stomped over to Mara as though she was going to do something, but Esperanza was already drinking milk. The silence seemed big after the crying. Scarlett pulled the tent from her bag and started to set it up, but Kendrick offered to do it.

"No, it's okay," Scarlett said. "I can do it. You can rest."

"I'd prefer to help," Kendrick said. So even though Scarlett didn't think it was the best idea, Kendrick stood and put together the poles, lengthening them until they were tall enough. Then, he tied them together and set the frame upright. The covering took two people and was laid over it shortly. Scarlett went around tying the covering to the poles.

"Where's Derrico?" Kendrick asked.

"He was scavenging for some berries or some edible vegetation."

"We need to find a water supply before tomorrow evening," Malak announced. "Unless we have more water than these two giant bottles." Scarlett waved her bottle, but only a small amount sloshed around at the bottom. Panic set in. How long would it take them to die without water?

"We're going to get to another branch of the same river soon. My mom knows where she's going." No one responded to Amy, who clutched the radio as if it were a sign of her importance. Scarlett glanced over to where Esperanza had fallen asleep in Mara's arms. Scarlett started to walk over to take Esperanza so Mara could rest, but she stopped herself. The picture was so sweet. Scarlett backed up and sat on the ground next to Malak.

"How is your arm?"

"It's fine," he said. "I've been washing the bandage in small amounts of water and letting the wound air. It looks as though it is healing on its own." An angry bump of flesh was on his arm, as though the skin was healing but wouldn't let him forget how he had mistreated it. "How's your neck?"

Scarlett reached up to touch it, but stopped herself. She didn't want to cause an infection. "It's getting better." Kendrick came over.

"Can I touch your arm?" Kendrick asked Malak.

Malak looked at him like he was completely crazy.

"I mean, to check the temperature. It could be blood poisoning if it's too hot."

"Oh, you are trained in medicine?" Malak asked.

"No," Kendrick admitted. "But the doctor in City 6 could never do anything to help us, so we had to come up with our own remedies. I've got something that will help you with it." Kendrick pulled some flowers out of his pocket.

"Where'd you get those from?" Scarlett asked.

"I sat beside a bush of echinacea while we were resting and thought they might come in handy for your neck. It looks like we'll need them for Malak's arm instead."

"Wow," Malak asked multiple questions about the flowers and their use. Kendrick easily filled him in with what he knew, though he didn't understand the why behind how it worked. The males talked, and Scarlett decided to work on arranging the food Derrico had retrieved. Mara watched from her perch with Esperanza. When Scarlett looked over, she saw tears on Mara's face.

"Uh, Derrico, I think Mara might need you," Scarlett said, trying to whisper quietly. Derrico went over to his wife, and Scarlett arranged her first meal ever. She wasn't cooking anything, so it wasn't that amazing of a feat. However, she was still impressed with herself. She took a bowl to each person, even Amy, and they all began to eat. Amy guarded Verona's bowl for when she woke up.

"What time are we leaving in the morning?" Scarlett asked the group.

Everyone shrugged. Their leader was asleep, so Derrico took charge. "I guess she'll wake us when it's time to get moving, but I think we're planning on spending the full night here. Amy, you're taking the first shift, I'm second, and Verona is third?"

Amy nodded. Scarlett was glad she didn't have to stay up all night, but as she crawled into the tent, she realized that was probably because they didn't trust her.

The next morning, Verona was wide awake. Apparently, she had gone out gathering during the early morning hours and had found that they were less than fifteen minutes from a stream the whole time. She had refreshingly cool water for everyone. Scarlett drank thirstily.

"I talked with Laya," Verona announced once everyone was awake and gathered around. "She and I are in agreement that while we have an important mission in the Cities, our first goal is to take care of ourselves. One of the other groups heard that our contact in the Government City was executed. No one knows how he was found out."

Verona sighed. "We think it's best if we all remain far away from the Cities. We were thinking a month, but now we have decided that we must wait a year before attempting to make contact again. Too many lives have been lost, and we can't try to help any more young babies if we can't give them a safe place to go."

Everyone took in her news, then Mara burst into tears. Derrico wrapped his arms around her and stroked her hair. Mara was holding Esperanza, and Scarlett was afraid the child might be crushed between the two of them. Scarlett suddenly realized that if they wouldn't be returning to the Cities, whatever that meant as far as medicine and supplies, it most definitely meant that they wouldn't have a chance of rescuing Moses.

Scarlett felt badly for Mara, but what could she do to comfort her? She had no words or touches that could make up for sweet Moses. "What about their son?" Scarlett spoke up to Verona as Verona watched brazenly.

Verona frowned at Scarlett. "We have all had to make sacrifices." Scarlett almost accused Verona of not making any sacrifices before she remembered how she had lost her husband when first leaving the City. Still, Scarlett was recovering from losing Rhys. Losing Esperanza would be something completely different. The idea of an innocent life, not given the chance to grow up and make her own choices bothered her. She remembered Ariel and felt the tears welling up in her eyes. It wasn't fair. She stood up.

"I think that's the right decision for you," Scarlett said. "But I don't think it's the right decision for me."

Everyone looked at her, waiting for an explanation. Scarlett looked around at the faces, some of which made her heart feel calm. As for the others, while she might not like them, she certainly knew they would have her back if they were attacked again.

"I was given a second chance at life. And it's only fair that I use it to help others. Maybe I can find Moses," Scarlett said. "Maybe I can't. I don't know. But I want to try." Scarlett looked at the group, and her throat clenched when she saw Esperanza snuggled up to Mara.

"Mara, I can't take Esperanza with me. Will you take care of her?" Mara was wiping her cheeks and nodding.

"Of course I will. I love her as much as I do Moses." Mara's chin trembled. "Thank you. Thank-" She buried her face in Derrico's chest as Scarlett heard her start to cry again.

Kendrick stood beside Scarlett, rocking for a moment before finding his balance. "I'll go with her. I can help her. Besides, she's the whole reason I came out here. What's the point of living in the forest and being free, if I'm not with the person I'm closest to?"

Malak looked at them then stood as well, his thin frame towering next to them. "It's not too late," he said. "I could still make it back to the City and claim I'd been wandering several days." He made eye contact with Verona and did something Scarlett would never have thought of doing. "I would like your input on this. Yes, it is risky to us, but would it endanger the Fringe at all?"

Verona reluctantly shook her head. "No, we wouldn't be close to the Cities, but you need to think through what you are doing. None of you knows how to hunt or how to live off the land like we do. You are proposing rescuing babies, I suppose. But how can you take care of them? You don't have the resources."

"We'll think through a plan," Kendrick said. "Besides, if we give even one baby a chance to grow up in freedom, then I will say we have been successful."

"I plan to save more than one child's life," Malak said. And for the first time since Scarlett had met him, he showed emotion. The corners of his mouth turned down. His lower lip trembled just the slightest. "I want to give whole families a chance to escape, give those children the chance to see their mother and father like Amy has with Verona."

"When will you leave?" Verona asked.

Scarlett looked at the two males, one still in his Blue uniform and the other in his rags from the City. "Why wait? We should start today."

Everyone agreed, and as Scarlett started to say her goodbyes, she was suddenly filled with sadness. She reached for Esperanza, and Mara handed her over, more willingly than she had the day before. Scarlett cuddled the baby and kissed both her cheeks and forehead.

"You, my dear, are very lucky. You get to grow up here, with Mara, and she will love you. I know it." Esperanza waved one of her arms. "Bye to you too," Scarlett said, cradling the baby just a little longer.

Laurel Solorzano has enjoyed writing since she was in middle school, exchanging manuscripts for years with her best friend. After traveling the globe for a time, Laurel set her goal to become a published author. As she works teaching English and Spanish, she writes stories in her free time. Laurel currently lives in Raleigh, North Carolina with her husband, Yader.

www.ingramcontent.com/pod-product-compliance
Lightning Source LLC
Chambersburg PA
CBHW070633100726
47907CB00007B/1975